SKY, THE STARS,

Skyler McMasters never thought she'd find the courage to follow her stars. But her phone-in radio astrology broadcasts are a big hit, and the consequences of her predictions spark romances from Maryland to Texas!

After heeding Sky's advice, Allison heads off to Wyoming to recapture a lost love, and C.J. helps her best friend, Michael, out of a jam by marrying him—for six months only! Even Skyler gets into the romance game, by disregarding all her instincts to fall in love with a man determined to ruin her!

Three original stories about women who

WISH
UPON A
STAR

by three of your favorite Harlequin authors,
**Kelsey Roberts,
Judy Christenberry &
Margaret St. George**

As our gift to you at the New Year,
a bonus *astrological love guide* follows these
stories to help you chart your own course
for romance in 1999!

KELSEY ROBERTS'S
first novel, *Legal Tender,* was published by Harlequin
Intrigue in 1993. Since then, she has produced nineteen
novels and garnered numerous award nominations for her
talents in writing romantic suspense. Before turning to
writing as a full-time career, Kelsey worked as a paralegal, a
profession that has provided wonderful inside knowledge
and technical expertise for the types of stories she loves to
write. She makes her home outside Annapolis, Maryland,
with her college professor husband and teenaged son.

JUDY CHRISTENBERRY
began writing Regency novels in 1982, and produced ten of
them before turning her talents to contemporary romance.
She has now written twenty contemporary novels, in
addition to "The Perfect Match," her first novella. A former
high school French teacher, she now devotes herself full-
time to her successful writing career, and has served as a
president of her local chapter of Romance Writers of
America. The mother of two grown daughters, she lives in
Plano, Texas, and writes her Western-tinged stories from
personal experience.

MARGARET ST. GEORGE
is the talented author of over thirty novels, in categories
ranging from historical to mystery to romantic romp. In
addition to her very popular Harlequin American Romance
novels, she has contributed to several special limited
Harlequin series, such as WEDDINGS BY DEWILDE and
DELTA JUSTICE, and has also written a number of novellas
for anthology collections, of which "The Arrangement" is
the most recent. Maggie brings a wealth of life experience
to her writing, having served as a flight attendant for
United Airlines, as well as the national president of
Romance Writers of America. She has received numerous
awards for her work, and lives in her home state of
Colorado with her husband, George.

KELSEY ROBERTS
JUDY CHRISTENBERRY
MARGARET ST. GEORGE

WISH UPON A STAR

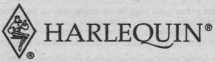

HARLEQUIN®

TORONTO • NEW YORK • LONDON
AMSTERDAM • PARIS • SYDNEY • HAMBURG
STOCKHOLM • ATHENS • TOKYO • MILAN • MADRID
PRAGUE • WARSAW • BUDAPEST • AUCKLAND

Special thanks and acknowledgment to Susan Kelly for her contribution to this work.

ISBN 0-373-83373-3

WISH UPON A STAR

Copyright © 1999 by Harlequin Books S.A.

The publisher acknowledges the copyright holders of the individual works as follows:

SKY'S THE LIMIT Copyright © 1999 by Rhonda Hardling Pollero.

THE PERFECT MATCH Copyright © 1999 by Judy Christenberry.

THE ARRANGEMENT Copyright © 1999 by Margaret St. George.

CONTENTS

Sky's the Limit

by Kelsey Roberts

PROLOGUE

"BUT ONE OF MY EMPLOYEES wants me to wait, to give him an opportunity to raise the cash."

Skyler McMasters used the seven-second tape delay to thumb through the astrology guide she had purchased that afternoon. Moving closer to the microphone, she said, "Jonathan, since your Mercury is in Aries, you have to make fast decisions." She ignored the amused roll of Kyle's green eyes. Kyle was on the opposite side of a glass partition that separated her broadcast booth from his engineering equipment. It was a good thing, since he made no secret of his feelings about her new show. Skyler couldn't really blame him. She wasn't exactly thrilled with the turn her career had taken.

"You're right, Sky. This is an opportunity I just can't pass up."

"The stars agree," Skyler told him. "I think this sale will not only bring you financial gain, but also personal satisfaction. Taurus is an Earth sign, Jonathan. Which means—" she paused to find the list of zodiac traits she had prepared earlier in the day "—you are practical and uninhibited."

"Thank you, Sky." Jonathan's voice conveyed a sense of relief.

Maybe I'm not so bad at this, after all, she thought. "I'm glad the stars could help guide you in your decision." Again Kyle rolled his eyes, and again, she ignored it. "Let me know how it works out."

"I will," he promised.

"I'm Sky McMasters," she said, lifting the headphones away from her ears. Grimacing slightly, she launched into the marketing slogan that was a requirement of her employment. "If you want the stars, call the Sky."

Kyle slipped a cart in, starting a loop of commercials. "Way to go, 'the Sky,'" Kyle teased.

She cast him a sidelong glance, then pressed the button that allowed them to speak back and forth during breaks. "We can switch places.... You could be Kyle in the Cosmos."

He laughed. "Benton doesn't pay me enough."

Skyler wasn't being paid enough, either, though after twelve months and seventeen days of unemployment, she couldn't afford not to take this job.

She looked down at the control board in her booth and felt her shoulders slump forward. Red lights from the jammed phone lines flashed demandingly. "Doesn't anyone sleep anymore?" she grumbled to her engineer.

"Get ready," Kyle warned as he replaced his headphones. "Round two of 'Astrology for Insomniacs' is about to begin. Grab your cheat sheets Skyler, because—" Kyle paused to open his microphone "—Mildred from Salisbury is on line one."

"Hi, Mildred," Skyler said with the enthusiasm required of her job as an on-air personality. "What can the stars and I do for you?"

"This is a privilege, Miss McMasters. I used to listen to you when you did political commentary in D.C."

"Thank you, Mildred," Skyler said. "The stars and planets are all lined up to give you advice. Which area of your life would you like to evaluate?"

A long cackle came over the phone line. "I don't want any silly horoscope readings. I just want to know how you could go from interviewing the movers and shakers in Washington to selling terrestrial snake oil in the middle of the night."

CHAPTER ONE

"BEFORE I WISH YOU all a happy and safe New Year, I need to let you in on a secret. I'm searching for the perfect man," Skyler said. "According to the stars, this is my year for personal fulfillment."

Kyle, sporting stubble he apparently hoped would evolve into a beard, pretended to gag himself with one finger.

"So, listen up, guys, because WSHR, Shore Radio, is having a contest. I'm going to describe what the stars have in store for me. If you fit the bill, come on down to Bayview Mall in Ocean City, Maryland, this Saturday. I'll be doing astrological charts from noon until two. If your destiny matches mine, WSHR will send us on a romantic dinner cruise Saturday night."

Kyle played a sound clip of thunderous applause, then spoke into the microphone. "Gentlemen, what we're offering here at WSHR is your shot at sharing the stars with our Sky."

She smiled at him with a mixture of humiliation, relief and gratitude. Kyle was a great guy and a dear friend, but he did have an impulsive sense of humor. It wasn't unheard of for him to play snoring sounds into her headphones when a caller got long-winded. Luckily, Kyle was a professional, and his antics were usually restricted to the booth. Unfortunately for her, Skyler's reactions to his comedic touches occasionally slipped out over the airwaves. A similar accidental slip of the tongue had cost her her job as a respected interviewer in Washington. But thankfully, the occasional honest opinion was expected of her at WSHR.

"My ideal man has to be driven, self-sufficient, confident, but sensitive. He's got to enjoy life to the fullest and have a sense of fun. So, if this sounds like you or someone you know, listen up while Kyle gives you the details. Happy New Year."

Skyler turned off her microphone and removed her headphones. She didn't want to listen to the rules and regulations of Benton's latest brainchild.

Grabbing her purse from beneath her chair, Skyler made a mad dash for the door. It was a wasted effort. Gil Benton was waiting in the hall.

Benton was her producer and a major shareholder in the station. He was also a major pain in the butt.

"Great show, Sky," he said as he draped a beefy arm over her shoulders. "I liked the way you handled that woman. Will the alignment of Mars in late April really have an impact on her garden?"

"That, or the fact that late April is the right time to plant impatiens in Maryland."

Benton sighed. "I need to talk to you for a minute." His barrel-shaped chest puffed out with self-importance. "I am good, Sky. I knew you could pull this astrology stuff off when I took a chance and hired you."

"I'm not pulling anything off," Skyler said defensively. "At least, not anymore. I've learned astrology inside and out in the last year."

After steering her into his cluttered office, Benton offered Skyler a seat. That wasn't good. Being invited into Benton's stale, coffee-scented sanctuary usually meant yet another concession on her part.

He half sat, half fell into a well-worn chair. His office decor was early waterfowl. Ducks and geese in all shapes, sizes and poses stared back at her from shelving that lined three walls. Interspersed among the tribute to taxidermy were several framed mementos: Benton's college diploma, an award from the local Rotary Club, a caricature that accented Benton's thick eyebrows, and the *USA Today* article that mentioned Skyler's show.

"We've been picked up in seven new markets," he said.

Skyler nodded. "That's great."

"More revenue means more money for all of us. We're bumping your salary twenty percent when your contract comes up for renewal."

"Thanks."

The initial enthusiasm drained from Benton's face. "C'mon, Sky. Geez, do you know how many people would love to be in your shoes?"

"I do."

A red stain began seeping up over his too-tight collar. "No. You still think you belong at the White House."

Skyler met his eyes. "We both know that will never happen."

"Then try being grateful for what you have here. Every time the rating books come out, our numbers are up. We're drawing big-time regional sponsors and you're a celebrity."

"Kyle and I work hard to do a good show," Skyler said simply.

"I wouldn't mind if you did another *good*

show like the Kemper thing. Your advice that he sell his software company to the conglomerate Computer Servers made the guy a cool billion plus.''

"We both know that was a fluke," Skyler said.

Benton grinned. "But we're the only ones who know that." He laughed. "Your advice to Kemper is what made this show. It's what has taken us from a graveyard-shift call-in to an evening drive-time syndicated success. If you pull another rabbit out of your astrology Cliff Notes, we can probably go national."

"That would be great."

"Stop acting like I kicked your dog. I didn't con you into this, Sky. You knew exactly what you were doing when you signed on."

She was growing irritated by his oft-repeated litany of why she should be thrilled at all times. "Sorry, Gil, but if I seem less than enthusiastic, maybe it's because you decided to raffle me off like some door prize. You know I didn't want to do this 'Skyler's Ideal Man' contest."

"You'll get used to it," he said.

"I doubt it. I'll just be glad when it's over."

"That's what I wanted to talk to you about."

Her gut knotted as her sixth sense warned her

she wasn't going to like whatever he was going to say.

"The brass thinks this would be a great way to introduce you to folks in the new markets."

"Excuse me?"

Gil loosened his tie, then came around the desk and leaned against the edge. "It's exciting, Sky. We'll do remotes from seven different cities."

"Remotes? For what?"

"The contest."

"The contest is over this Saturday," she reminded him. "Maybe you think having dinner with a total stranger who may be a serial killer on a boat in the frigid waters of the Atlantic is exciting, but I don't."

"We decided to expand the contest to each of the new markets. It'll be just like here, only you'll have to play up the fact that you *still* haven't found Mr. Right. Now, we've got you booked to do readings in various shopping centers, then dinner with the lucky winners."

Skyler raked her hand through her hair. "You can't be serious. I'm not risking my safety for the sake of market share."

"No risks," Benton insisted. "We provide the limo, crowded restaurants. You'll never have to be alone with any of the contestants."

He grinned slowly. "Unless you find someone who rings your bell."

"I'd rather wring your neck," she shot back furiously. "I'm not comfortable with this. I've been cooperative, Gil. I don't complain when you send me out to do appearances, but this is something completely different."

"This isn't an option, Sky. Your contract specifically states that you'll make yourself available for promotion of the station, the show and yourself."

She stood, clutching the straps of her purse. "Promotion, yes. Prostitution, no."

"No one's asking you to do anything other than have a few dinners. Hell, Sky, you live to eat. We're going to some great cities. Chicago, New Orleans, Miami. First-class accommodations—you'll have fun."

"Do I have a choice?"

"No."

She let out a slow breath. "I want a clothing allowance."

"For what?"

"Clothing. I'll also need an extra few days in Miami."

"For what?"

"A tan. I'll also need a per diem."

"For what?"

"Miscellaneous things like manicures, facials, massages. You wouldn't want me to look bad during our randy road trip, now, would you?"

Benton grinned. "Everything is a negotiation with you."

Skyler returned the grin. "Yes. Including the fact that Kyle gets some perks, as well."

Her boss snorted. "He wears jeans, ratty shirts and shaves when the moon is full. What kind of perks am I supposed to give him?"

"He'll think of something. He always does," Skyler said, then turned and left the office.

She didn't get far. Kyle was lurking in the hall. He looked up the minute she emerged. Judging by the amused look on his face, Kyle had probably been listening at the door.

"Thanks for including me," he said. "Benton wouldn't give me squat if it was up to him."

"You date a different woman every day. Want to trade roles?" she asked with a sigh.

"But I like choosing the woman." Kyle held out his hand to her. "Right now, I'd rather have a beer."

"You buying?"

"No." Kyle grinned as he grasped her hand.

"You're the celebrity. Celebrities always buy for the little folks."

Skyler followed her friend to the Rod and Reel Tavern on the southbound side of Route 50. There were two types of bars in the area. Tourist and townie. The Rod and Reel was definitely townie. It was a plain wooden building with a wooden bar, wooden booths, a dartboard and a back room with two pool tables. If local lore was to be believed, there was a third room in the bar for a collection of illegal slot machines. Generations of Delmarvians, named for the area where the shores of Delaware, Maryland and Virginia converged, had clung to their gambling vice. They made annual treks to Annapolis to lobby for the right to bring their slots back out into the open.

Kyle and Skyler walked through the remnants of confetti from the New Year's celebration the night before, sat at the bar and exchanged greetings with Sue, the bartender, proprietor and occasional bouncer.

"I heard your show this afternoon," she said, placing a cocktail napkin on the bar. "I'd hate to be you come Saturday, Skyler."

"We can trade," she suggested to her friend.

Sue shook her head. "No thanks. After my divorce, I swore off men."

"Wasn't that your fourth divorce?" Kyle commented, his eyes twinkling playfully.

"At least I don't sleep around," Sue teased right back.

Sue poured a mug of beer for Kyle and a white wine for Skyler. When she finished, she reached under the bar and produced a small bowl of nuts. "I saved these from happy hour."

"You should open a restaurant," Skyler said. "Then you could keep people here through dinner."

"No thanks," Sue scoffed. "I like the break. This is my downtime. Gives me a chance to regroup until the bad ol' boys pick a fight with their wives and come skulking back in here. Besides, I'm still tired from last night. It was a good New Year's Eve party, if I do say so myself."

"I had fun." It took Skyler a few minutes to warm up enough to remove her gloves. Even with the fireplace roaring, she wasn't about to surrender her coat. "Thanks to you and your tales, I no longer think marriage sounds very appealing."

"It can be fun, but just wait until you find Mr. Right," Sue advised Skyler.

"They'll be lined up for the audition on Saturday," Kyle said. "Why don't you come down to the mall and watch the parade of beefcake."

"I might," Sue said with a chuckle, and tossed her bar towel over her left shoulder. "If I..." Her mouth remained open but her voice trailed off.

Since Skyler had never seen the bar owner rendered speechless, she turned and glanced over her shoulder. She saw six feet of dark, handsome perfection.

Looking away quickly, Skyler wondered why her heart was pounding against her ribs. Before she could answer that, Tall, Dark and Gorgeous took the stool next to hers. His cologne was subtle, her response was not.

"Hi," he said, greeting Sue. "Hennessy for me and, what will you have, Blayne?"

His companion ordered a merlot.

While Sue fumbled through pouring the cognac and the wine, the man next to Skyler removed his coat. In doing so, his shoulder brushed hers. It was nothing, barely a swipe, but it seemed to electrify her senses.

"I've got to go," Kyle said when he had finished his beer and pushed the empty glass aside.

"Date?" Sue asked.

"Always," he answered as he stood up.

"We're going to that seafood place in Salisbury. Want to tag along, Skyler?"

"Not on your life. Why don't you take this one to a really nice place?" Skyler suggested. "Maybe you'd have a better shot at a second date if you didn't insist on taking your lady friends to the worst the Eastern Shore has to offer."

"Surf-n-Steak is a nice place," he insisted.

She shook her head at Kyle. "Any restaurant where you have to carry your own tray and order your meal by number is not 'nice.'"

"You're both just jealous," Kyle taunted. "I'm the only one starting out the New Year with a date. Good night, ladies." Kyle tossed a couple of bills on the bar for their drinks and a generous tip before he left.

Knowing the gorgeous man next to her had to have heard Kyle's rather unflattering assessment of her social life, Skyler took a final sip of her wine. "I'm going home, too," she told Sue. "I'm trying a new recipe tonight. If it works out, I'll bring some by for you tomorrow on my way to work."

"I'll look forward to it," Sue said. "Drive carefully." She watched Skyler leave, then picked up the empty glasses and turned to the two men. "Can I get you gentlemen another?"

Derek Conner nodded. "Thanks. Was that Skyler McMasters from the radio?"

The bartender's face conveyed pride. "The one and only. You should have introduced yourself. She's a real sweetheart."

"Is she?" he asked, careful to keep his tone light and conversational.

"You bet. Are you gentlemen new in town? Visiting or just passing through?"

"We're supposed to be here scouting for land for our plant," Blayne grumbled.

"Land? Plant?" Sue's ears seemed to perk up. "Thinking of opening a business? We sure could use it around here."

"It's a possibility," Derek remarked as he turned and offered his companion a hard stare. "We haven't made any firm decisions yet."

"What kind of business?" Sue asked. "Not that it matters, really. There are several colleges here on the shore that turn out a good number of business graduates. Plus, we have plenty of men and women willing to work. Folks around here used to make a living on the water, but the waters are overfished now."

"Salisbury has a great deal of charm," Derek said. "I'm sure that includes the people who live here."

"One of my ex-husbands owns Seaside Realty,'' Sue told him as she produced a card. ''He was a lousy husband, but he's an honest businessman.''

''Thanks.''

''Can we go now?'' Blayne whispered to his friend. ''You saw her. She didn't look like a fiendish monster to me. Can we please get back to business?''

''Sure,'' Derek said. ''I think I've figured out how I can ruin Skyler McMasters.''

CHAPTER TWO

"THIS ISN'T WORTH IT," Blayne griped as Derek tied his tie. "We're wasting time and money while you try to prove something that hasn't mattered for a long time."

"It matters to me," Derek promised him. "I'm going to prove she's a fraud."

"All astrologers are frauds," Blayne said, exasperated. "But she's harmless. I listened to her show yesterday. All she does is offer common sense advice with a few planets thrown in for effect. She's actually pretty good. You should listen to her before you—"

"I have listened to her," Derek said. "I've also done a little research. She became an astrologer the same week WSHR gave her the show. Miss McMasters has no history of an interest in horoscopes, let alone the intricacies of the zodiac. She doesn't know what she's talking about."

"So what, Derek? We've got to act soon if we're going to get the land outside St. Michael's for the plant. It won't take much money for us to build what we need. We could be into production by early spring."

"It will happen," Derek promised. "I just have to take care of this first."

"Why? We need to go meet the Realtor."

"You can handle that," Derek said as he slipped into his jacket.

"I could handle it a lot better if you went along with me. We're supposed to be starting a company, Derek, not settling some ancient score."

"It won't take me long to do what I have to do, Blayne. Until then, you can handle things."

"But I'm not Derek Conner, the boy wonder. If we're going to raise capital, you've got to get back with the program."

Derek gave his friend a slap on the back. "I'll be finished with Skyler long before we get to that stage. You will be fine today without me."

"What is that for?" Blayne asked.

Derek put batteries in his microcassette recorder and slipped it into the breast pocket of his suit coat. "If she does incriminate herself, I want to make sure I've got it in her own words."

"I think that's illegal."

"I don't care."

"That's my point, Derek. You haven't cared about anything but getting at Skyler McMasters for more than a year. It has turned into your obsession."

"No, Blayne. It's my duty."

The drive to Bayview Mall took longer than he had anticipated. He found the lot full and the marquee flashing the announcement that Skyler McMasters was in residence looking for her ideal man. Parking would be a problem, but convincing Skyler that he was her dream man would be easy. He knew everything about her. Knew every button to push. The months of studying and planning were finally going to pay off.

Derek was ready to attack.

A few minutes later, he was also at the end of a very long line. Joining the men, women and children waiting patiently for an audience with the guest of honor turned out to be something of a blessing. Other than that brief encounter in the bar, Derek had never been able to observe her firsthand.

She was smaller than the huge publicity posters made her seem. As hard as it was for him to imagine, she was much more beautiful in person. Pale blond hair framed her features as it brushed the tops of her shoulders. Big, round blue eyes dominated her heart-shaped face. But it was her smile that drew him in. Skyler had one of those smiles that radiated warmth and confidence. Her navy blue suit was simple, yet exuded a classy femininity that he would have found irresistible from any other woman.

"Sir?"

Derek pulled his attention away from Skyler and turned to a middle-aged man with headphones draped around his neck. "Will you be entering the contest?"

"Yes." His answer earned him the attention of the couple in front of him. They turned and apparently made the snap decision that he was perfect for their hometown star.

"Follow me. I'm Gil Benton, the show's producer," he said as he extended his hand.

"Derek Conner."

The producer took him to an area of the mall that had been cordoned off with burgundy ropes. From the outside, Derek thought it looked like a corral, especially when he saw the dozen or so men waiting to audition for Skyler's attention. Inside, there was a table surrounded by chairs filled with prospects. He was given a release form for photographs and the use of his image should he be chosen. Next he was given a brief questionnaire about the date, time, year and location of his birth.

Then it was his turn to watch and wait, two skills he had honed during the last year. The producer controlled the flow of things, making sure fans and contestants were given an opportunity to watch the little charlatan ply her trade.

After about an hour, Derek, form in hand, was led up onto the elevated platform where Skyler would perform for him.

"Hi," she greeted him cheerfully. Her smile slipped a bit when she looked more closely at his face and asked, "Have we met?"

He flashed her a grin and took his seat. "I was in the Rod and Reel the other night."

The breathtaking smile returned. "Hello again, then. May I have your birth information, please?"

She took his form and began to make notes on a pad as she quickly digested the information. The assessment was interrupted every so often by the flash of a camera. Apparently, Skyler was going to milk every drop of publicity out of the event.

"You are strong-willed," she said with an almost shy smile. "You satisfy your desires by your determination to finish what you start."

Derek kept his expression cheerful and at

ease. His gut was anything but. He tried to tell himself that she was nothing but smoke and mirrors. It didn't mean anything if she guessed correctly about his sense of determination. It had to be an educated guess, possibly based on nothing more insightful than the cut of his suit.

"Your moon is in the eighth house, which means your financial success will be linked to your marriage partner."

"I'm not married."

He liked the fact that his simple statement had caused her lashes to flutter. Again he reminded himself not to press. Everything he knew about Skyler told him she wasn't the kind of woman who could be swept off her feet. She was much too cautious about her personal life, which meant he would have to ingratiate himself into her world.

Skyler was desperately trying to concentrate, but the zodiac symbols and charts she'd memorized seemed stuck behind the fog caused by the man sitting across from her. "You're very confident," she managed to choke out past the lump in her throat. "You have a generous spirit and a great deal of common sense."

"Thank you."

Relax! Easier said than done, since she lifted her head and found herself staring into clear hazel eyes rimmed by thick, inky lashes. His hair was black, trimmed and styled neatly, bordering on conservative. A beautiful suit in a rich, deep olive green complimented his light eyes and dark complexion. Add a designer tie, a killer smile, and Skyler was quickly becoming one big hormone.

"Is there an area of your life you'd like to explore?" she asked.

He stroked his chin, then his cheeks colored ever so slightly when he leaned closer and whispered, "I'd like to know how I could have been stupid enough to let you walk out of that bar without getting your phone number."

Skyler caught sight of Benton's Cheshire cat grin out of the corner of her eye. Immediately, she regretted her earlier rash decision to allow Benton to select her dinner companion for the evening. The way Benton was smiling, she knew he was going to pick *this* man for his publicity stunt. But Skyler didn't want him to, not under these circumstances. Derek Conner was—at least on the surface—too perfect to be real. Too perfect to be relegated to the status of a one-time dinner date. *Great! I finally meet an interesting man, and I'm being auctioned off like an old chair.*

"It seems to me as if Mr. Conner fits all the

criteria spelled out in the stars," Benton said, then made a similar announcement over the mall's loudspeaker. Then to Skyler, he whispered, "He also photographs well."

Skyler felt her cheeks burn with humiliation. Applause broke out from the crowd and flashbulbs strobed. "I guess you are going to be the guest of WSHR radio this evening."

He smiled, apparently pleased by the circumstances. Benton shook the man's hand and then presented him to the satisfied group of onlookers.

"I'll look forward to it, Miss McMasters." His voice was deep, refined and naturally sensual.

She glanced up at him. "Dress warmly."

An hour later she was safely inside her home. "Dress warmly? What a moronic thing to say!" *The guy probably won't show after a stupid line like that!*

She hung her coat on the rack, then placed her keys in a dish by the door. Skyler's home was her pride and joy. She had spent hours decorating it until it suited her perfectly. She was surrounded by her favorite things and most prized possessions.

Going up to the loft, she opened her closet doors and stared at the contents. She wanted something along the professional function line. Remembering his artfully chiseled face, mesmerizing hazel eyes and brooding sensuality, Skyler amended her decision somewhat. The choice was simple. The Little Black Dress.

Thanks to years spent inside Washington society, Skyler had quite an extensive selection of little black dresses. She opted for the most conservative one before heading into the bath.

After she bathed, Skyler debated how she should wear her hair. She could go for drama and put it up, or be more casual. She finally chose a combination of the two. Carefully, Skyler arranged her blond hair in a disorganized twist. Next, she used the tip of her comb to pull several tendrils out and shaped them around her face and neck.

When the limousine arrived at seven, she was satisfied that she was making the right statement.

"I'll just get my coat," she told the uniformed driver.

"Yes, ma'am."

Skyler took the full-length faux fur coat from the closet, slipped it over her shoulders, grabbed her gloves and followed the chauffeur out into the cold January air. He held the door for her as she slipped into the warm interior of the huge vehicle.

Limousines didn't impress Skyler. But the single white rose and a bottle of her favorite wine chilling did. "I see the station went all out," she remarked to the driver.

"That isn't from the station, ma'am. Mr. Conner arranged it."

Wide-eyed, her heart pounding with the same exhilaration of her long-ago prom night, Skyler reached out and touched the delicate petals of the rose. *It's just a flower and some wine,* she told herself, trying to quell the girlish giddiness in her stomach. *Who are you kidding?* her brain screamed. *It's just perfect!*

Perfect also described her date. From behind the safety and anonymity of the limo's mirrored windows, she watched him emerge from the house. She felt like Cinderella. Probably because Derek Conner was definitely the Prince Charming type.

His fitted cashmere overcoat sculpted his body, allowing her to ogle him as he walked toward her. He didn't swagger, exactly. It was more like a confident stride. When the door opened, the scent of expensive cologne came in on a rush of cool air. However, when Derek joined her, "cool" was the furthest thing from her mind.

"Good evening."

You bet it is! "Hello. Thanks for the flower and the wine. It's my favorite."

Derek's smile revealed dimples. "The wine or the rose?"

"The wine...I mean, both."

The sound of his soft laughter caressed her ears. "If I didn't know better, I'd think you were as nervous as I am."

He's sensitive! He's honest! I'm in love! "I've never done anything like this," she admitted.

His smiled widened. "If you're telling me you've never had dinner with a man before, I don't think I believe it." He moved closer, though at no point did any part of his body touch hers. "You are much too beautiful."

Swooning. Yep, I'm swooning. "I meant that I had never been raffled off before. I'm not quite sure of the etiquette."

His dark head inclined slightly. "Don't worry, Miss McMasters, I've—"

"Skyler."

"Skyler." He repeated her name as if sampling it. "I've never done anything this impulsive before, so we can make up the rules as we go along. Wine?''

"Please." She fought the urge to fan her heated face as he uncorked the bottle and poured the wine into two glasses. "You must be psychic, Mr. Conner."

"Derek," he corrected her as he handed her a glass.

For a split second, their fingers brushed together. The sensation of his skin against hers sent a jolt through her system. Judging by the slight waver in his gaze, Derek felt it, too.

"Psychic?"

"Th-the wine," she managed to say over the lump in her throat. "It's one of my favorites."

Derek's intense eyes held hers. "I'm rather fond of it myself."

"Good," she said awkwardly.

"It is," he agreed as he took a sip. His gaze remained locked on her face. "So, then—" he sighed as he sat casually back against the seat "—we have more in common than the contest."

"Possibly," she agreed.

"I can hope."

CHAPTER THREE

"I'LL BE ON THE PIER when the boat returns at midnight," the driver told them.

Derek was careful not to touch her as he walked a half pace behind her up the short gangplank. They were greeted by the maître d' and escorted to a table on the port side of the floating restaurant.

The faint scent of Skyler's perfume was almost as distracting as the way the other patrons stared as they made their way to a cozy table.

"Thank you," Derek said as a dismissal once they were seated and their coats checked.

He had to give the radio station credit. Not only had they provided him with the perfect ruse to get close to the woman, they'd thrown in a great setting to boot.

Skyler was even more beautiful by soft candlelight. That irked him. He had better things to do than notice the way her eyes reflected the flicker of the candle's flame, or that her skin was flawless and creamy. Or that every action, even something as simple as taking a sip from the water goblet, exuded a latent sensuality.

Luckily, the waiter arrived and saved him from surrendering to his distraction.

"May I?" he asked Skyler as he intercepted her menu from the waiter.

She nodded rather uncertainly.

Derek didn't bother to look at the menu. It wasn't necessary. "The lady will have the smoked salmon to start, hearts of palm salad and the broiled mahimahi." He glanced at her shocked expression.

"Impressive," she said softly.

He ordered the same for himself, as well as a different wine for each course.

When the waiter left, he noticed Skyler was looking at him with apprehension in her eyes. "You didn't like my selections?"

She gave a nervous shrug. "I'm not sure whether I should be flattered or scared."

"Scared?" *I blew it! I should have moved more slowly.*

"You're either a mind reader, or a stalker."

"Stalker?" he repeated with a laugh. "How could I possibly stalk a woman I only met this week?"

She studied him for a moment, then the disarming smile returned. "Sorry. I guess I just wasn't prepared for you."

"Prepared?"

Her face colored. "When the station decided to do this promotion, I was expecting dinner out with one of the good ol' boys."

He relaxed. "The rules didn't say anything about special requirements."

"I don't think Gil ever dreamed he'd find someone like you."

"Is that good or bad?"

She held her answer until the wine steward presented the bottle for Derek's inspection.

"Good. You're very photogenic, which means Gil will milk this one date for all it's worth. Too bad you aren't a slob with a Peterbilt hat and a beer belly."

"You would have preferred that?"

Smiling, she leaned across the table and whispered, "It probably would have put an end to Gil's latest promotion idea."

Derek was surprised, and he was sure his expression gave him away. "I'm the first of many?" He was glad that had come out tinged with disappointment. He didn't care if she dated a different man every night. He just meant he'd have to put a little more effort into it if there was competition around.

"They're sending me out on a series of these dates. I'm doing seven cities over the next few months."

"Is that safe?"

"You tell me," she said. "I can't believe so many people showed up this afternoon."

"I guess you're more popular than you give yourself credit."

Her eyes sparkled. "Something like that. So, where are you from?"

"Why?" he asked. "Do you think I'm from out of town?"

Why is it so unnerving to have her ask me a personal question? Because this wasn't about being personal. It couldn't be. He couldn't allow himself to be swayed by the kindness in her expression. Or the way she seemed to give him her full attention. He had to tell himself that it was all part of her fraud. He had to ignore the fact that Skyler McMasters seemed—on the surface—to be a pretty decent person.

Her smile faltered somewhat as she explained, "The limo picked you up at the Garrison place. It's a short-term rental property, which I kind of took to mean you were new to the area."

Some of the anxiety left his body. Apparently she wasn't probing, merely asking. That was good; it meant she suspected nothing. "I'm originally from upstate New York. I'm down here looking into a business venture."

"Business venture?" she asked. When he didn't respond, she added, "Never mind. It was really rude of me to ask you that."

He shook his head. "You were hardly being rude. Like the rest of the world, I'm into computers."

"Now I'm really impressed. I have one, but so far, all I've been able to master is freezing the screen."

"What about you? When did you know you were an astrologer?"

She lowered her eyes and said, "You don't wake up one day and realize you're an astrologer. It takes some study and an appreciation for astrological signs and influences."

"So you think the stars dictate our future?"

She shrugged. The action caused the fabric of her dress to pull snugly across the outline of her body. Derek told himself he didn't care if she had a small but perfectly proportioned shape. He did not want to feel this strong attraction. He wanted her to pay.

"I think astrology is a kind of faith. Not the religious kind of faith, but a more tangible thing."

"I don't follow."

"People follow their horoscopes because they want answers or motivation or comfort. An astrological chart is something tangible that people can hold in their hands and read."

"You create the charts that give those answers?"

She smiled. "I prefer to think of it as facilitating." Lifting her head, she studied his face, then frowned. "I take it you skip the horoscope section in your newspaper."

He sighed. "I'm afraid so. I've never put much stock in something that can't be proved."

"A logical mind, eh?" she asked as the first course was served. "Astrology isn't about logic, though the consequences of following the ancient study of the stars usually results in a logical outcome."

"Are you sure?"

"I'm *sure* that I have to pay taxes. Other than that, I don't make guarantees."

"I do," he said. "I guarantee that you'll love the smoked salmon. It's wonderful."

She surprised him. Most women, especially those on a first date, didn't eat with enthusiasm. It amused Derek. Did women actually think he would believe they never ate anything but parsley garnishes? But not Skyler. She seemed to savor every bite. Watching her made him feel like a bit of a voyeur. She was really enjoying the meal.

That is what you wanted. Right?

Ignoring that little pang of conscience, Derek enjoyed his own expertly prepared meal. They continued to chat, mostly about benign topics. So far, she had said little he could use.

As Skyler savored her last bite of dessert, she couldn't help but be amazed that the evening had gone so well. Derek was a gentleman in the truest sense of the word. He was a good listener, stayed away from potentially awkward topics, and he complimented her. He was definitely a dream date.

"Would you like to dance?"

"Sure," she said. Her pulse rate quickened at the mere thought of being held in his arms.

The gentle sway of the ship provided an instant rhythm as she stepped onto the dance floor with him. She had fully expected—no, make that looked forward to—the experience of being close to him.

Apparently, he had other ideas.

Derek was a perfect dancer. He led without hesitation, cradling her hand in his without ever really grasping it. His right hand never slipped from its proper position at her waist. He was graceful...from a distance.

An annoying distance. Skyler silently berated herself. Here she was having a lovely time and she was irked because he was being *too* nice? It had definitely been too long since she'd been out.

When the music ended, Derek led her from the dance floor with an elegant swipe of his hand. She was aware of him behind her, conscious of even the smallest detail of her own movements. She reminded herself to walk correctly, no slouching. Her arms were at her side for balance, ready to reach out should the boat suddenly lurch.

Maybe we'll hit a swell and I'll be tossed into his waiting arms. Or maybe I should have the waiter toss cold water on me, she thought as she took her seat.

Unexpectedly, Derek came around next to her, bent so that his head was even with her own, and rested one arm on the back of her chair.

Skyler went perfectly still. His warm breath washed over her neck. The sensation caused a knot of anticipation to form in the pit of her stomach.

"Look." It was a soft, gentle command.

Following the direction he was pointing, she saw the shoreline coming closer. The lights danced and reflected off the calm, cold waters.

It was almost over. Cinder-Skyler knew she had about an hour before it was pumpkin time.

"It's beautiful," she remarked, mortified when her voice came out helium-high.

"I've always loved the water," he said.

Each word he spoke spilled a fresh wave of warmth over her exposed neck. "M-me, too."

"I love good food, as well. Tonight's was excellent."

"Very excellent," she agreed. *Was he moving closer to her ear, or was she moving closer to his face?*

Skyler would never have her question answered since the boat began to rock and shudder as it maneuvered closer to the pier. Derek had no choice but to take his seat until the boat docked.

Ever the gentleman, Derek retrieved their coats and held hers while she slipped her arms inside. Somehow, his knuckles grazing her neck as he assisted her was more sensual than if he had kissed her.

The limo driver greeted them as he held the door. Skyler got in and slid across the seat. Derek followed her but made no move to get close.

She assumed he was sending out an I-Can't-Wait-to-Get-This-Over-With signal. Then he rummaged around under the seat and produced a gold-foil box with a simple red bow.

He presented it with a smile that was a treasured present in itself. "I hope you like truffles."

She nearly gasped. "I *love* truffles. They're the only kind of chocolates I eat. Thank you."

He sighed as he leaned back and crossed one leg over the other. "I should thank you. This has been a very nice evening for me."

Skyler placed the gift in her lap. "It has been wonderful." *I don't want it to be over.*

But it was, all too soon. On Derek's instruction, the driver took her home first. Seeing her own front door was a disappointment, and it presented quite a quandary.

Derek walked her to the door. *Do I ask him in?*

They reached the threshold. *I want to ask him in.*

She placed her key in the lock. *Will he think I'm offering more than coffee? Am I offering more than coffee?*

Derek reached out and took one of her gloved hands in his. Tilting her head back, she peered up at him through the veil of her lashes. She tried to muster the nerve to invite him inside.

"I—" they said in unison.

Derek smiled down at her and said, "I really want to thank you."

"I was going to say the same thing." *Be brave. Just invite him in!*

Just as she opened her mouth, Derek let her hand slip from his grasp and said, "Good night, Skyler."

What? No kiss? No 'Can I come in'? No nothing. In fact, Derek didn't even wait for her to respond before he turned on his heel and went back to the waiting limo.

Once inside, Skyler leaned against the door, clutching her truffles to her chest and feeling her heartbeat. "Did I do something wrong? Say the wrong thing?"

By the time she had removed her dress and replaced it with a well-worn flannel nightgown, Skyler was trying to figure out Derek Conner. After lighting the fireplace in her room, she climbed into her four-poster bed and did what any normal woman would do. She ate the truffles and thought about the man who had given them to her.

CHAPTER FOUR

"YOU'RE SMILING," Kyle teased when Skyler
entered the office area next to the broadcast
booth.

"It's a beautiful day out," Skyler said.

"It's ten degrees, cloudy and they're pre-
dicting a nor'easter tonight."

She shrugged. "Details. How was your
weekend?"

Before Kyle could answer, Gil came rushing
in. "The pictures are great," he announced.
"But you could have been a little closer when
you were dancing. Man, you and that Conner
guy look like Ken and Barbie. This is too perfect."

Skyler picked up the photographs, surprised
that she hadn't even noticed the fact that their
entire evening had been chronicled by the station. Kyle came up behind her to look over her
shoulder as she went through the pictures. It
pained her to agree with Gil for once. But he
was right. Derek's tall, dark perfection was a

striking contrast to her petite figure and blond hair. Their chemistry showed even in the black and whites. They almost looked like royalty.

"You just sighed," Kyle remarked. "Or swooned. Which is it?"

She elbowed him. "It was neither. I was simply exhaling."

Gil and Kyle looked at each other, then turned to her and said in unison, "Swooning."

Skyler ignored their adolescent teasing and went about getting ready for her show. She gathered her charts and the newspaper's daily horoscopes just in case. At thirty seconds before airtime, she entered the broadcast booth and took the seat being vacated by Stanley the Sports Fan. After tossing Stanley's doodles in the trash, she put on her headphones as Kyle played the announce for her show.

If she thought Kyle and Gil were childishly curious about her date, it was nothing compared to her first seven callers. When she took her first break, Skyler was fuming.

"Inquiring minds want to know," Kyle said once the commercial began. "So do I."

She glared at him. "Discussing a date cost me my last job."

Kyle chuckled. "Boring Senatorgate."

"Not funny," she warned.

"Very funny," Kyle pressed. "I don't know why you're so testy. All you did was tell a few hundred thousand listeners that Senator Greely was a boring, conceited fool."

Between clenched teeth, she said, "I didn't know my microphone was open."

"The senator said you were just getting even with him for spurning your advances after a dinner date," Kyle said in a perfect imitation of Greely's thick Southern drawl.

"Thanks for reminding me, Kyle. Can we get back to work, now? Or would you rather discuss how devastated I was when my mother died?"

To his credit, Kyle dropped the subject and managed to act contrite as the show dragged on. The nearly four hours seemed more like four years as she dodged caller after caller demanding to know if Derek Conner was *the* man for her.

"Would anyone out there care to discuss something other than Mr. Conner? If so, the phones lines will be open for another ten minutes." Skyler cut her mike as a brief public service announcement began, and blew a frustrated breath to her forehead.

"What are you doing?" Gil demanded as he burst into the room.

"My job," she responded without looking up.

"Give the folks out in listener land something to think about," he suggested. "The way you were grinning when you came in, there must be something nice you can say about your dinner."

Skyler glared at him before he left the booth, then stuffed the headphones back in place. "Welcome back," she said. "I'd like to thank everyone who expressed their interest in my date Saturday night, but—"

"Mr. Conner is on line three," Kyle cut in.

"That would be our third Mr. Conner of the day," she said over the air. "And which Mr. Conner would you be?"

"The one who gave you the rose and candy."

Skyler knocked her water bottle to the floor as his deep voice echoed in her ears.

"The one who had a wonderful evening and hopes you'll agree to have dinner with him again."

"Derek!" she yelled into the mike, then frantically signaled Kyle to go to commercial.

He simply grinned and shook his head.

"Um, thank you, Derek. Perhaps you could call me when I'm not at work."

She heard his laughter. "I was going to, but it wouldn't have been terribly chivalrous of me to let you continue to dodge questions about our evening."

"Thanks, Derek. I appreciate the kind gesture. I'll let you get back to whatever you were doing."

"You haven't answered me," he said.

"Answered what?"

"Will you have dinner with me tonight?"

"I don't think this is the right time to discuss this."

"Why not? Your listeners obviously feel they have a vested interest in our relationship."

The ten other phone lines were flashing simultaneously. "Then when we have a relationship, I'll keep them posted."

"I wasn't trying to push you, Skyler," he said apologetically. "In fact, I haven't called you because I didn't want to come on too strong. But hearing your voice this afternoon made it impossible for me to wait any longer."

She leaned against the desk, torn between being thrilled that he had finally called and furious that he had chosen to do so publicly.

"The phones are jammed," Kyle interjected. "So far, everyone wants you to say yes, Skyler."

"Then I can't disappoint," she said. "But tonight isn't a good idea, Derek. There's a nor'easter coming up the coast. We'll be buried in snow by morning."

"I'll risk it."

Kyle annoyed her by playing a sound effect of a cheering crowd. "Hang on, Derek," she said as she pressed the hold button on the phone. Then, firmly but pleasantly, she said, "That's all the time we have for today. Remember to keep your radio tuned to WSHR for the latest weather warnings and traffic updates."

She removed her headphones and stomped from the booth in spite of Kyle's desperate plea that she answer Derek on the air. She ignored Gil's barking request that she stay a little longer since the phones were jammed with callers waiting to hear her answer.

"You can't leave the guy on hold," Gil insisted.

"Really? Watch me."

"YOU SCREWED UP," Blayne said.

"I made a small tactical error," Derek conceded as he continued to pack ingredients into the cooler.

"It's snowing. Warnings to stay off the road

have been scrolling across the television for two hours. Doesn't that tell you something?''

"Yeah, you watch too much television."

"Cute, Derek. Is destroying Skyler McMasters worth killing yourself?''

"I'm not going to kill myself. In Albany, this much snow wouldn't cause a panic. Besides, I've got four-wheel drive.''

"You've also got a business plan to do," Blayne said. "I agreed to come here to set up shop because I thought you were committed to starting up our own company.''

"We will," Derek said.

"Not if you're too busy playing with Miss McMasters's head.''

Derek smiled. "You're nagging, Blayne."

His friend gave him an exasperated look. "I'm committed, Derek. I want to own my own business. I want to prove I'm not a failure."

"No one thinks you're a failure but you, Blayne.''

"Really? Ask my father."

Derek put his hand on the younger man's shoulder. "When you get a few years older, maybe you won't allow your father's opinions to rule your life."

"I'm twenty-five and I've failed at everything I've ever done."

"Failing isn't a crime, Blayne. The crime is not learning from your failures."

"That would make a good fortune cookie," he whined. "I need to use what little money I have left wisely. That will happen if you're my partner. I can't lose. But I can't start a software design firm by myself. I don't have the knowledge or the track record you have. We need each other."

"You sell yourself short," Derek said as he slipped the microcassette recorder into his pocket. "You have the ability, Blayne. You really don't need me."

"Very funny, Derek. I do need you, but I need you one hundred percent. How much longer are you going to play this game with her?"

"As long as it takes."

"Takes to do what?" Blayne demanded.

"Once I get proof that Miss McMasters is a fraud, I'll send it off to the newspapers. When that happens, it's over."

Blayne shook his head. "Remind me never to get on your bad side," he grumbled as Derek headed out into the bleak winter night.

His talk with Blayne didn't exactly improve his mood. He was growing tired of the young man's insecurities. A part of him felt sorry for the kid. Blayne's charmed childhood had left him ill prepared for the real world. He should have known that Blayne's business proposal was too good to be true. Except at the time, he had only thought about the fact that Blayne's urgent desire to set up a business would enable him to seek his revenge on Skyler McMasters that much sooner.

It took him a while to make it to her house. It took a few minutes longer for him to put on his game face.

"Hi," he said when she opened the door. Holding up the cooler, he said, "I brought dinner."

"What are you doing out on a night like this?" she demanded softly.

Trying not to let her apparent concern for his safety bother him, Derek just smiled and said, "I was hoping to impress you by bringing you a gourmet meal."

Her expression evolved from concern to surprise until finally she seemed to settle on a reserved form of happiness. "I can't believe you did this, considering the fact that I left you on hold this afternoon."

As he politely waited for Skyler to usher him inside, he said, "That was this afternoon. I should have known better than to interrupt your work that way.''

After a second's hesitation, Skyler opened the door wide and gestured for him to come in. Old torch songs were playing, and he decided his plan had been a sound one. Skyler was taken completely off guard.

''I'll take your coat,'' she said as he brushed the snow from his hair.

She was wearing an oversize pink sweatshirt and matching leggings. Thick, heavy socks covered her feet and bunched at her ankles. It was a dramatic change from her polished appearance for their date. Derek wondered why he found her almost more interesting—sexier—dressed down. Maybe he was just tired.

''You didn't have to bring me dinner.''

''I didn't, technically.''

She stared up at him, battling a smile. ''You wormed your way in here with an empty cooler as bait?''

''That would be dishonest,'' he said. ''I brought food to prepare for you. I hope you don't mind.''

''Depends,'' she said. ''Can you cook?''

''I'll let you be the judge. Take me to your cutting board.''

She led him into an impressive kitchen. It

was large, well laid out—a space designed for cooking. The walls glistened with decorative, hand-painted Mexican tiles. There was an island, as well as about ten feet of usable counter space around the built-in cooktop and dual ovens.

"I'll turn down the music, and then you can tell me how I can help."

"Don't bother," he said. "I happen to like torch songs."

"Okay, so what can I do for you?"

He glanced around at the layout. "Are there stools on the other side of this counter?"

"Yes. In the dining room."

"Good. You find a bottle of wine to complement poultry, then sit and supervise in case I can't find something."

Skyler opened a small wine chiller next to the sub-zero refrigerator and grabbed a bottle from the second shelf. "I can do more than this," she insisted. "I'm a pretty decent cook."

"Which you will have an opportunity to prove when it's your turn." Taking the lid from the cooler, he used it to shoo her to the other side of the counter.

"What is that?" she asked.

Derek held up a small, notepad-size computer with a paper roll attached. "This is where I keep all my recipes. It holds an ingredients list as well as a schedule, so that after I program in what I'm going to make, it gives me a printout and automatically sets timers.''

"Neat gadget. Where did you get it?'' she asked as she uncorked the wine and poured it into two glasses.

"It's homemade,'' he admitted, wondering why he would feel proud that he'd impressed her. It wasn't part of his plan to care one way or the other. Just as he shouldn't care that she looked incredibly beautiful as she quietly watched him set up.

"Is something wrong?'' she asked.

"No, why?''

"You were frowning,'' she told him. "Are you sure I can't help?''

"Positive. Just direct me to the nearest chef's knife.''

She pointed to a magnetic strip along the wall above the porcelain sink. Attached to the strip were knives in every possible shape for every conceivable purpose.

"Careful, they're sharp.''

He gave her a sidelong look.

She shrugged. "Hey, any man stupid enough to drive around with Cornish hens in the middle of a snowstorm probably shouldn't be trusted with sharp objects.''

"Very funny, Miss McMasters. Let's hope that a delicate beurre blanc will dull the edge of your sharp tongue.''

"Beurre blanc, huh?'' she said, sighing. "There's more to making a butter sauce then having your computer spit out the instructions.''

"Really?'' he asked, amused at her skepticism.

"Really,'' she answered with a hint of laughter.

Derek rose to the challenge. In fact, he rendered her speechless as he chopped the ingredients for the stuffing like a pro. He watched her out of the corner of one eye, feeling rather pleased with himself when the taunting little curve at the sides of her mouth was replaced by a look of genuine respect for his culinary skills.

That was echoed in her praise when they had finished eating. "You've convinced me,'' Skyler said as she cleared the dining room table. "You are a great cook, Derek.''

"Thanks. You're a good eater.''

She returned a few minutes later with a tray of coffee, which she carried to the informally arranged furniture in the adjoining living room. "I like to eat. It's not my most feminine trait.''

He joined her on the overstuffed sofa. Silently, he agreed. Her most feminine trait had to be the sultry way she moved. Derek had to concentrate to keep his mind from going places it had no business going. There was no way he was going to admit that she had a definite appeal. He wasn't interested in the fact that her hair glistened in the firelight, or that the gentle slope of her neck was so attractive.

"Want some?"

"What?" he snapped.

"Coffee?" she asked uncertainly. "Is something wrong?"

That was stupid! Derek shook his head and made a production out of checking his watch. Standing abruptly, he said, "It's getting late. I should clean up your kitchen."

"Don't you dare. In my house, the cook isn't allowed to do the dishes."

"Then I should be going."

"Going? It's been snowing for hours," she reminded him.

Derek was so spooked by his reaction to her that he didn't care if he had to jump through a ring of fire to escape. He just knew he had to get out of there. He tried to blame the single glass of wine. Then he tried telling himself he was just tired. The alternative was scary. He had come to Maryland's eastern shore for one reason—and it wasn't to fall under the spell of the woman who had taken everything from him.

CHAPTER FIVE

"IS HE GAY?"

Skyler rolled her eyes as she cradled the cell phone against her ear. "I don't think so," she told Sue.

"So what are you going to do?"

"I'm going on the road," she answered. "It's not like I have choices here. He hasn't called me in three weeks. I can't tell Benton I won't do the week-long promotions in other cities because I'd like to continue holding a vigil by my phone."

"That's probably just as well. Any man dumb enough to drive through a blizzard just to cook, then not hang around for...*dessert,* doesn't have all his oars in the water. And he keeps sending you flowers or candy all the time. Maybe one of these out-of-town guys will be the one. At least they won't ask the station for your travel schedule, then send gifts instead of showing up in person. If you ask me, this Conner guy is weird."

"I'll admit he's a little unorthodox, but I think the flowers and candy are romantic. I feel like I'm being courted."

"Yeah," Sue grumbled, "courting disaster. I can't believe you can't find a normal man out there. The world's a big place."

"How many Derek Conners do you think there are?"

"One too many," Sue answered flatly. "By the way, it's no problem, I'll be happy to check your place and take in the mail. Try to have fun, Skyler. At least you'll be warm."

"There is that." She sighed. "Want anything from the Big Easy?"

"No thanks. Maybe you should pick yourself up a voodoo doll and punish Mr. Conner for not calling or dropping by in person."

"Good idea," she said as a car horn blared. "I've got to go."

Skyler spent the remainder of the day in various forms of transportation. It was almost dark when she and Kyle arrived at the hotel in downtown New Orleans.

"I'm looking forward to a week of café au lait and Southern hospitality," Kyle said as they crossed the lobby. "I just love the way women talk down here. Did you hear that lovely stewardess on our plane? She just happened to mention her address.''

"If you're going to hunt the poor woman, at least be politically correct enough to call her a flight attendant. I swear, Kyle, do you ever have a thought that doesn't originate below your belt?''

"Excuse me,'' he said, clearly hurt.

She touched his sleeve. "No, I'm sorry. I guess I'm suffering from jet lag.''

"Derek lag is more like it,'' Kyle remarked as they gave the desk clerk their names so he could find their reservations. "This is the nineties, Skyler. Put yourself out of your misery and call the guy.''

"Sue thinks he might be gay.''

He snorted. "And Sue is such a great judge of men. I guess that's why she's been divorced four times.''

Skyler laughed. "Point.''

"How about we do the town tonight?''

She shook her head. "How about you do the town and tell me about it. I'm going to take a long bath and go to bed.''

"You aren't any fun,'' Kyle chided.

"Won't having me on your arm make it difficult for you to pick up babes?''

Kyle stroked his chin as he nodded. "Yes.

However, I am your friend. I can make the sacrifice."

"Very sweet, but I really don't feel like it."

Kyle's hurt expression dissolved into a smile as they picked up their keys and headed for the elevator. "I'm glad. You would definitely cramp my style."

"What style?" she teased as the elevator doors closed.

Gil had done well. Her suite was small but charming, and she had a beautiful view of the city lights. Skyler unpacked and then went into the bathroom to run a tub. Just as she tugged her blouse from the waistband of her skirt, there was a knock at the door.

When she looked through the peephole, she saw a beautiful, full bouquet of yellow roses and baby's breath. Yanking the door open, she hoped Derek was holding the flowers.

She was disappointed, but only for a minute. When she plucked the card from the roses, she ripped into it and read aloud. "I'm thinking about you. Derek."

She inhaled the scent of the flowers, then put the vase on her night table. "Nice of you to mention it when I'm thousands of miles away."

Still, it was something. Hope filled her as she stripped and stepped into the huge tub. Settling so the warm water came to her chin, Skyler relaxed and thought of the yellow roses and Derek's hazel eyes.

"NOW WHAT?" BLAYNE ASKED.

"I'm searching for a plane ticket to Dallas," Derek answered, his eyes never leaving the computer screen.

"Geez, Derek, you're spending a fortune on a woman you can't stand. Don't you think the flowers did it? Or, here's a thought, why don't you try charming her when she's in town? She was home the last two weeks and you didn't even call her."

"It isn't the same."

"It's sick," Blayne insisted. "Besides, we're supposed to make an offer on the land this week. I need you here."

"You do not need me. You're doing fine on your own."

"Presenting your business plan to a bunch of bankers was hard. I was sweating bullets while those guys grilled me."

Derek gave the young man a pat on the back. "And you handled it. Just like you'll handle the negotiations for the land."

"I'll be glad when you're finished with your McMasters vendetta."

"Soon," Derek promised. "By sending her flowers and paying her a surprise visit in Dallas, I should be able to get her to open up."

"Then you send the tapes to the newspaper and it's done, right?"

Derek shut down his computer and wondered why he wasn't feeling more satisfied. His plan was working, and he was close to achieving his goal. He knew the answer: Skyler had haunted his dreams night after night. He'd watched from a safe distance as one of his bouquets had been delivered to her home. The genuine glee on her face had left him feeling shaken. His objective had been to get close enough to destroy her. Now, without his permission, that objective had altered slightly. Now he only wanted to get close to her. He raked his hand through his hair in self-disgust. This whole thing would have been easier if she'd been a shrew with a wart on her chin. But she wasn't. She was a beautiful woman with a virtuous side he hadn't planned for. He needed to stay focused. That was a laugh. How could he be focused when both his dates with the woman had left him with sweaty palms? He had to finish this, before it finished him.

"I'll be back tomorrow afternoon."

"Then it will be over, right?" Blayne pressed.

"Sure," Derek said without genuine conviction as he grabbed his garment bag and left the rented house.

During his flight, Derek was nagged by Blayne's question. Would it be over? By making her pay for what she did, would it change anything?

Cool rain welcomed him to Dallas. Derek instructed the taxi driver to stop off at a florist on his way to the hotel. He drew some attention as he arrived carrying his garment bag and a huge arrangement. After registering, Derek took out the press pass he had created on his computer and clipped it onto his lapel. He approached the youngest bellboy on staff, tipped him generously and asked to be shown to Miss McMasters's room. Luckily, the young man fell for his story about being there to interview the visiting celebrity. Derek stopped by his room only to drop off his bag, then, without hesitation, he returned to the elevator and the waiting bellboy. He was grateful that his ruse had worked, but annoyed by how easy it had been to get the information. Skyler wasn't safe. That shouldn't have bothered him, but it did. A lot.

Skyler had just returned to her room after a

short stroll in the rain when there was a knock at the door. She ran a hand through her wet hair and smiled, fairly sure that it was Derek's latest gift from afar. A quick check of the peephole confirmed her suspicions. She saw the bellboy who had brought up her bags, as well as a huge bouquet of roses obscuring the face of a deliveryman.

She opened the door, and the bellboy was brushed aside as Derek stepped forward and said, "Welcome to Dallas."

Skyler very nearly ripped the flowers from his hand when she heard his voice. Derek lingered by the door, a broad smile on his face. "I hope white roses are still one of your favorites," he said nonchalantly.

"Thank you! How on earth did you find me?"

"It was a little too easy," he admitted, holding out his fake ID. He nodded toward the bellboy, who was walking back to the elevator. "You really should report that kid to the management. He should never have brought me up here. I could have been a serial killer, for all he knew," Derek grumbled, his head bowed slightly.

"You're not," Skyler countered as she tossed her handbag onto the sofa. "I can't believe you're in Dallas. I can't believe you knew what hotel I'd be staying at.''

"That wasn't rocket science," he assured her. "Your station is plugging this hotel in exchange for the room, I guess. They've mentioned it at least a dozen times in the past two days.''

''I still can't believe you're here. I was pretty sure your business venture must be keeping you busy.''

A barely discernible stain of color rose on his high cheekbones. "You're in Dallas, so it seemed like a good place to be.''

''I don't know what to say, Derek. Thanks for the flowers, and thanks for delivering them in person.'' It was apparent that her words of gratitude were making him even more uncomfortable. Derek hadn't budged from the doorway. Their eyes met for a second in a powerful nonverbal exchange that sent electricity through her system.

''Sorry,'' she said quickly. "Come in.''

''I really should let you get back to whatever you were doing. I didn't want to intrude. I only wanted to say hello,'' Derek insisted.

''Don't you dare walk out that door,'' Skyler said. "I mean...please don't leave.''

He smiled, though it didn't seem to quite

reach his eyes. "You must think I'm nuts for coming all the way to Texas just to see you."

Skyler's heart was melting inside her chest. "No, I think it's the most romantic thing that's ever happened to me. Please stay, I'll order dinner for us. Have you eaten?"

"No," he said, closing the door behind him.

Skyler placed the flowers on her bedside table, called room service and tried to get a grip. She barely knew Derek Conner, but it didn't seem to matter. Any man who would spend weeks courting her with flowers, then show up out of the blue, was definitely worth taking a chance on.

Derek sat on the sofa, looking as nervous as she felt. "So you're not here on business?" she asked as she hung up.

"No. I came to see you."

"But I'll be home on Sunday," she said.

"And in Miami on Tuesday," he noted with a tight smile. "I've been listening to your show."

Skyler whistled. "Has it sounded as crazy as it's been?"

"Only when you discussed your date in New Orleans."

It was silly, but Skyler felt a pang of guilt. "It's just part of my job."

"I know. But I don't have to like it."

"That makes two of us," she agreed. "This is Gil's idea. He's hoping that the date contest thing will draw in listeners, which draws in callers, which he mistakenly thinks will make lightning strike twice."

"Lightning?"

Skyler kicked off her shoes and joined him on the sofa, tucking her nylon-clad feet beneath her. "The first show I did made some man a lot of money."

"Did you read the stars for him?"

She shook her head. "Of course not. I just listened to him and told him what I thought."

"I was under the impression that you consulted the stars before you gave advice."

She laughed nervously. "Well...it was my first night. You have to understand, I had been out of work for more than a year because I did something really stupid."

"I can't imagine you being stupid."

She was grateful for his vote of confidence. "I used to work at the largest public radio station in the country. I got to do real investigative reporting. Stuff that matters to people, or at least I think it should matter."

"Like what?"

"Welfare reform, health care, that sort of

thing. I take it you aren't a regular listener of public broadcasting?"

"Guilty. I tend to play CDs in the car."

She nodded as she shifted, moving slightly closer to him. He looked positively wonderful in his crisply pressed shirt and tie. She probably looked like a drowned rat after being caught in the downpour. "Anyway, I had gone to dinner with a senator. One of my co-workers asked me about it. I didn't realize my microphone was open, so I announced to the world that I thought he was a bore."

Derek laughed. "Was he?"

"Major league bore," she insisted. "But he was a senator and I was a lowly radio commentator. After his people were finished, the word around Washington was that I had thrown myself at the defenseless man, and only said what I said on the air because he had spurned my aggressive advances."

"So why did you lose your job?"

Raking her hands through her rain-flattened hair, she said, "Because the unwritten rule became if Skyler McMasters works for your station, no one from the senator's party will grant an interview."

Derek was quiet for a long time. "That isn't fair."

"Yes, well, righteous indignation doesn't pay the bills. Which is my very long-winded explanation to your question. Gil Benton offered me a job doing a late-night call-in astrology show with Kyle as my engineer. It was Kyle's first job and my last chance. Needless to say, I didn't know a horoscope from a stethoscope when I started."

"What about the guy you made rich?"

"*I* didn't make him rich," she insisted.

"Sorry, I meant your interpretation of his zodiac."

"No," she said on a breath. "I meant I had nothing to do with his success. It was my first night. Everything I said to him about the zodiac, I was reading straight out of a book."

"You were making it all up?" he asked incredulously.

"Gil would kill me if he knew I was telling you this. But, yes. Partly, at least."

"Only partly? I don't understand."

"The guy that called in was vacationing with his family. Instead of enjoying the sun and surf, he was all tied in knots about his business. You're an entrepreneur, you must understand that."

"I have some insights," Derek commented.

"That man sounded so sad, it was completely

obvious to me that he needed a break. He was proud of his business but he was burned-out, and he wanted to sell his company. He was torn between his desire to spend time with his family and his responsibility to his employees.''

"So you made some stuff up to help the guy sleep better?''

"I simply inferred that his horoscope indicated he should not hesitate to make a decision. At best, I gave him a push, but he chose the direction.''

"What about his employees?'' Derek asked.

"What about them?''

"Have you ever talked to any of them?''

She blinked. "No. Besides, what would I tell them? I'm sorry some huge conglomerate tossed some of you? I *am* sorry for the handful of people who were replaced by the company that took over, but they can get new jobs.''

"You're sure?''

"If I can learn to respect astrology to pay the bills, they can get new jobs. The man who called couldn't get a new family. He was missing seeing his children grow up. His long hours at work were putting a strain on his marriage. I just happen to think that a family is more important than a career.''

"Then why don't you have one?''

"No one's applied," she said. "My parents had a magical relationship. They were madly in love with each other until they died. I know it sounds hokey, but I can't imagine settling for anything less."

"You really are a decent person, aren't you?" Derek asked, as if the concept had just now crossed his mind. It hadn't; it was just the first time he had dared to verbalize what his heart seemed to have suspected from that first night in the bar when his shoulder brushed hers.

"Isn't that why you hopped a plane to deliver flowers?"

She could see the laughter in his eyes and found it contagious.

He moved closer, until the feel of his breath washed over her face in warm waves. Tilting her head back, Skyler searched his eyes beneath the thick outline of his lashes.

"I think I need to get this out of the way," he said, then leaned forward until his lips barely grazed hers.

Wide-eyed, Skyler experienced the first tentative motions of the kiss through a haze of surprise. As the pressure from his mouth increased, growing slightly more insistent with each passing second, she found herself bombarded with an artillery of conflicting emotions.

Derek's hands moved slowly, carefully to her small waist. His strong fingers slipped beneath the fabric of her jacket and came to rest just beneath the swell of her rib cage. She found herself filled with curiosity, desire and just the faintest bit of apprehension.

Her mouth burned where he incited fires with a gentle prodding of his tongue. An involuntary gasp rose in her throat at the heady new sensations pulsing through her system. Derek pulled her gently to her feet. When he moved yet closer, the feel of his thighs brushing hers was almost as intoxicating as the kiss itself. The heat from his mouth washed over her entire body, until every nerve ending tingled with a fierce life of its own.

Derek raised his head for the fraction of a second it took to wrap his arms more tightly around her, lifting her against him. Fortified by her newly awakened desire, Skyler moved her hands across the vast expanse of his chest, around the taut muscles, until she was able to feel the solidness of his back. Arching herself slightly, she held her breath in anticipation of something unknown.

Whatever she'd expected, it wasn't the knocking sound that suddenly reverberated through the suite. Derek all but jumped away from her, his breath coming in deep, ragged spurts.

"Room service," she said, silently cursing them for disturbing the best kiss she'd ever shared.

CHAPTER SIX

"WHAT DO YOU MEAN HE LEFT after dinner?" Sue demanded.

"He had his own room."

"Any guy who can afford to fly all the way to Texas to deliver some damned roses can afford to let a hotel room go to waste. What the hell is wrong with that man?"

"Nothing. By the way, I'm in love."

"You're in lust," Sue warned. "Trust me, I'm an expert on the subject. I've got the legal bills to prove it."

"I'm not in lust—I haven't slept with him. I know it's love because when I'm around him, I feel…magic."

"It's not magic, it's hormones."

Skyler sighed and lifted a spoonful of sauce toward Sue's disapproving face. "Hush up and taste this. It has to be perfect, and I've only got an hour before I go to the airport."

"It's wonderful," Sue said after tasting. "It's

a shame to waste it on a man who won't even take advantage of you."

"Don't be crass," Skyler warned as she shut off the cooktop and poured the sauce into a container. "I think it's very romantic that our relationship is building on a foundation of conversation and roses."

"I think your foundation is cracked," Sue said. "Why don't you just wait until you get back from Miami and invite him to dinner?"

"Because," Skyler explained for the third time, "the best way to a man's heart is through his stomach. And his stomach won't be able to resist chilled shrimp quenelles with herbed toast points, grilled duck with muscadine sauce and flan with hazelnut sauce for dessert. One bite and his heart will be mine!" she said triumphantly.

"Assuming this man has a heart. I mean—" Sue continued to preach as she followed Skyler up to her bedroom "—what kind of man *doesn't* try to have sex with a woman in a hotel room? It isn't normal."

Skyler went into the bathroom to change, leaving the door open a crack. "A man who respects me!" she called.

"I've never met a man who respects a woman that much."

"Stop raining on my parade," Skyler pleaded as she struggled with the zipper of her skirt. "Do you know how to get to his house?"

"Yes."

"Did I put the heating instructions with the food?"

"Yes. Did you put your brain on hold? Yes."

Skyler emerged from the bathroom, tossed her cosmetics in her suitcase and closed it. "Just promise me you'll take him the dinner and the wine."

"I will, if you'll promise me you will think about what you're doing."

"I haven't *done* anything," Skyler insisted, then, giving her friend a wink, she added, "yet."

"I don't think being impulsive suits you, Skyler. Please don't let yourself be blinded by him."

"Blinded?" she scoffed. "He's the one setting the tone, not me. I'd have asked him to marry me in Dallas if I wasn't sure I would have scared him off."

"You don't know anything about him."

Skyler paused. "I know he's romantic, charming and kind. I'll get to know him better. Once I finish traveling, Derek and I can get serious."

"How do you know that's what *he* wants?"

She frowned. "Why else would he be courting me?"

"Courting you?" Sue parroted. "He zips in and out of your life when it suits him. It seems kind of odd.... How do you know he isn't married?"

"He isn't." Her heart fell into her stomach. "I mean...I don't think he is. He said he wasn't."

"And men don't lie?" Sue snorted.

"MAYBE YOU SHOULD KEEP on taping her," Blayne said as he patted his full stomach. "Any woman who cooks like this can't be all bad."

No kidding, Derek thought reproachfully. Skyler's gift of an incredible meal had only reinforced what he already knew. He had been wrong about her. Dead wrong. Now all he had to do was find a way to tell her that he'd been lying to her from the start.

"So what now?" Blayne asked. "More flowers, more obscenely priced truffles?"

"I've got to go to Miami," he said, pushing away from the table.

"Not again, Derek. I'm this close to getting the seller to agree to our price on the land," Blayne said, bringing his index finger and thumb close together for effect. "Can't you stick around for one part of this venture?"

He shook his head. "No. Besides, you're doing great."

"But I'm doing it all by myself. That wasn't what we agreed on.... Hey, where are you going?" Blayne demanded as Derek turned around and walked out of the kitchen.

"I've got to pack."

"What?" Blayne followed Derek into his bedroom. "You mean you're going to Miami *now*? This minute?"

"As soon as I can get a flight out," he said as he began throwing clothes and toiletries into his garment bag. He then moved to the living room and took things out of drawers.

"Why the rush? Don't you have enough on tape yet?"

"She told me everything," Derek said.

"So why haven't you exposed her?"

"I'm taking care of it," Derek said. He zipped up his bag, grabbed his keys and waved over his shoulder before slamming the door behind him.

"Thanks!" Blayne called. "Thanks a lot!" he grumbled, then turned to survey the mess from the meal and Derek's hasty departure. As he began straightening up, he put some papers in the desk and in the process discovered an envelope addressed to the local newspaper. Lifting it, he could easily feel the outline of Derek's cassettes inside. Quickly, Blayne dashed to the door, grabbing his coat. If he hurried, he could get the tapes to the late drop box for Derek and finally put an end to this.

"WELCOME TO MIAMI," she said as she jumped into his arms. "And the flan was not overcooked. You probably screwed it up when you reheated it. I'm so glad you called to say you were coming. I've missed you."

His expression was kind and gentle, and Skyler silently acknowledged that she would have been lost without him. *God, I love you!* she thought, but didn't dare say. He kissed her, then set her down gently.

As they stepped out of the airport terminal into the warm, tropical breeze, she wondered if her life could get any better. "I didn't expect you to thank me in person," she said as she looped her arm though his and led him to a waiting taxi. "But I'm very glad you did."

"Skyler, I didn't... You don't know why I'm here," he said.

She gave him a gentle shove as the cab pulled away from the curb. "Are you telling me you changed planes twice and even battled the Atlanta airport in the middle of the night for some reason other than to make me very, very happy?'' She settled her head against his shoulder. "Derek?'' she prodded when he didn't answer immediately. "Don't get all intense on me now. I think your showing up here in the middle of the night is the most romantic thing in the world. I missed you.''

He placed his arm around her and pulled her to him. "I missed you, too. I won't get intense yet, but we need to talk eventually.'' He sighed as he drank in her fragrance and cherished the fact that she was at his side. At least for now. He knew he had to pay the piper, but it could wait. It had to. "Right now I can't think of a better reason for me to be here.''

"Good. But we have to stay out of Gil's sight. I'm supposed to be here finding a date, not having an affair.''

"Who said we were having an affair?'' he asked.

"Wait until we get back to my suite.''

A short while later, Skyler threw her hotel keys on the dresser and closed the small space between them. Reaching up, she gently ran the tip of her fingernail near the bottom of his lower lip. She could feel the outline of his powerfully built thighs where they rubbed hers.

His expression stilled and grew serious when Skyler pressed herself against him. Derek placed his hands at her waist. For an instant she thought he might push her away.

"Not this time," she beseeched. "Please don't run away from me anymore."

"But we need to talk, Skyler."

She shook her head and grew bolder as she held him against her. "We can talk later. Until dawn, if you want. I've let you set the pace for weeks. Can't you let me take charge this once?"

His hesitation lasted less than a second before his lips settled over hers, tentative and testing. She responded by allowing her lips to part, urging his sweet exploration. He groaned as his arms encircled her, pulling her so close that Skyler could feel every solid inch of him.

Her mind reeled from the blatant sensuality of his kiss. It was as if a flash fire had ignited and was quickly burning out of control. Her hands moved down from his face until she could feel the circle of his gold medallion over where his heart beat furiously. He gripped her more tightly, causing her back to arch. Derek moaned against her mouth.

Emotions and sensations melted together and coursed through her veins. Every cell in her body tingled with life, and she began to work on the buttons of his shirt. Guided by the powerful force of her desire, Skyler pushed aside the fabric and ran her palms over his warm flesh. His breath fell hotly over her forehead when he lifted his head. She was about to utter a protest when he lifted her off the floor and carried her toward the bedroom.

His lips were on her throat, tasting her skin. She felt so delicate, and yet the strength of her passion had completely obliterated his resolve to settle things before they became more complicated. He didn't want to think about it now. If he did, he knew he'd have to stop. *Not this time.*

He lowered her onto the bed and lay beside her, one leg wedged between hers. Placing his hand at her waist, Derek kissed the tip of her nose before renewing his interest in her throat. He felt her intake of breath when his fingers inched upward, then closed over the top of one rounded breast. He could feel the taut nipple pressing against his palm, and waves of urgent desire washed through his loins. Each caress seemed to make her want more, and he was more than willing to give it.

Slowly, deliberately he toyed with each button, kissing her skin as it was exposed to his hungry eyes. Her flesh was smooth, rich and pale under his hand. Derek was finding it hard to exercise discipline. Lifting his head, he looked at her flushed face briefly before turning his attention lower. Her fingers made light, feathery movements across his chest as he loomed above her, eyes fixed on her lacy black bra. His finger dipped inside, teasing the hard nipple. It wasn't enough.

Undoing the clasp, Derek peeled away the barrier. She made a small sound when his mouth closed around the tip of her breast. He felt her hands on his head, holding him against her as she arched upward, toward him. Each time he flicked the tip of her nipple with his tongue, Skyler moaned and pressed her hips against his leg.

Pulling at her skirt, Derek reached beneath it and placed his hand on her thigh. His fingertips barely brushed the sensitive inside, but he could already feel her responding. Her hands moved across his shoulders, massaging and molding, then down his back.

Heat merged with pressure in his groin when she made brief, shy contact with his belt buckle.

She explored the contours of his sex through his slacks.

He lost all control then, guided by his incredible passion for this woman. Derek lifted his head and kissed her fiercely. He found the silky edge of her panties, and his hand lingered there as he lay beside her on the bed. Slowly and deliberately he teased her through the flimsy fabric for several minutes, reveling in the response it inspired. Skyler thrust her body toward him, all the while matching his demanding kiss. He could smell the faint scent of her perfume.

Derek raised his head again, watching the stain of redness on her flushed face.

"You're embarrassing me."

He liked the husky, sexy tone of her voice and simply smiled down at her. "I don't think you have a thing to be embarrassed about."

"Why are you staring at me?"

"I'm not staring, sweetheart. I'm admiring," he said, just before lowering his mouth to capture one rosy nipple. She responded instantly. Skyler's fingers played through his hair as he lovingly taunted each rounded peak in turn. Every now and again he would hear a moan from her and respond by placing a kiss on her open mouth.

When he could no longer stand the pressure at his groin, Derek removed her skirt, then his own clothing. He pushed her back against the pillow, using his knees to wedge himself between her legs. He remained balanced above her, watching the expression on her face when his hips met hers. There was still the barrier of their underclothes, and he needed her reassurance.

"I want to make love to you, Skyler."

"I want that, too. Very much."

He moved only long enough to remove the last hindrance of their clothing. He could tell almost immediately that she was as ready as he was. Derek had to school himself to move slowly. She wasn't helping him at all as she continued to grind her slender body against his.

"Slow down, Skyler, or this won't last more than about ten seconds."

His mouth covered hers before she could speak, though he had a hunch she was beyond the point of lucid conversation. Carefully he entered her, listening, even expecting some sort of protest or hesitation. Instead he heard only words of pleasure whispered on a warm breath against his mouth.

With a single thrust he reveled in being deep inside such sweet softness. When she wound her legs around him, Derek groaned and fervently kissed her neck and shoulders before returning to the warm, pliant recesses of her mouth. The rhythm of their lovemaking increased as his hands reached beneath her hips, bringing her even closer to him.

She turned her face away from his, breaking their kiss. "Something wonderful is happening to me," she told him, her eyes wide, her pupils dilated with passion.

"Go with it, sweetheart. Trust me for now."

As predicted, he felt her body convulse with wave after pleasurable wave. The sensation of having her body grip him brought Derek to a fast and furious release, and he collapsed into her arms.

Apparently afraid of crushing her with his weight, he rolled off her, leaving Skyler to wonder at the incredible things her body had just experienced. She was also a bit surprised by the fact that she was no longer concerned about her nakedness. Turning her head, she smiled at her lover. He returned the gesture. "That was incredible," she told him. Skyler turned in his arms and placed a kiss on his chest, listening as his breathing returned to normal. They stayed that way for a long while, until the sun painted the sky a brilliant pink and gold.

"I don't want to go to work," she muttered as she glanced at the clock.

Derek kissed her forehead. "When do you have to leave?"

"I've got about fifteen minutes before I need to shower and dress. I'm supposed to be at some mall in the shape of a big alligator to do readings and auditions."

"I really wish we had more time," he said.

Hearing the disappointment in his voice, Skyler was secretly pleased by his apparent possessiveness. "We'll have time this afternoon."

"I have something I have to say to you."

He loves me!

"Me, too," she said as she lifted herself onto one elbow and looked into his eyes. "I know it's only been a short while, but I'm in love with you."

Derek's only response was a kind of pained silence. "Skyler..." he began.

She placed her finger to his lips. "I don't want you to say anything. I'm sorry that telling you how I feel makes you uncomfortable."

"It isn't that," he said on a rush of breath. "It's just that we...that you know so little about me. I've done some things I'm not very proud of."

She smiled. "So have I."

"I really need to explain a few things to you."

She sighed. "I know that making love has complicated things."

"It isn't that."

"Whatever it is, it can't be so awful, Derek. You've done nothing but make me feel wonderful and alive since the day I met you. Let's not spoil it with some rushed conversation where we set rules and boundaries. Not now," she said, almost pleading.

"We don't know very much about each other," he pressed.

"If that's the problem—" she kissed his chin "—I'll be happy to tell you my hopes and dreams while we're in the shower."

Derek groaned, then pulled her into a strong, affectionate embrace. "You're a very special woman, Skyler."

She basked in the warmth of his compliment. "I'm also a woman who has to get to work."

His hold tightened. "Okay, but—" he reached up to cup her face, then held her gaze with his sexy eyes "—we have to have a serious discussion as soon as you have some time. There are things I need to tell you."

Reluctantly, she shrugged out of his arms. *I blew it. He likes to call the shots, set the tone.*

I should have waited for him to tell me first. Stupid move, Skyler, she chastised herself, and climbed out of bed.

After pulling on his boxer shorts, Derek followed her into the bathroom.

"Aren't you going to join me?" she teased as she ruffled his mussed, dark hair.

He offered a sexy half smile. "If I get in there with you, you'll be late for work."

"Might be worth it."

"Behave," he said as he held her at arm's length. "You're supposed to be telling me your hopes and dreams, remember?"

Shrugging, Skyler slipped into the glass shower stall and turned on a hot stream of water. There was something positively erotic about seeing him through a haze of water, steam and coated glass. It made Derek seem like a dream, a fantasy. Smiling as she recalled their passionate night, she knew full well that Derek was very, very real.

"I've always wanted to open a restaurant," she yelled over the water.

"Really? Why don't you?"

"Money, security. But then I don't have to tell you how hard it is to own your own business."

"What kind of restaurant?"

"Small, intimate. Something that would make people feel comfortable and pampered at the same time. Sounds silly, huh?"

"Not at all. If the meal you prepared for Blayne and me was any indication, you'd be a huge success. Especially if you learned how to make a decent flan."

"Very *not* funny," she groused as she stepped from the shower into the towel he held out to her.

There was an instant when his eyes roamed her nakedness that Skyler thought her knees would buckle. How could he manage to thrill her to the core with a mere look?

"I wasn't criticizing," he said as he gently toweled the droplets of water from her quivering body. "I was merely making an observation."

"Derek?"

"Yes?"

She met his level gaze. "If you keep touching me like this, I'll need more than just your...*observations.*"

"Sorry," he said as he stepped back, leaning his powerful body against the shower.

"What about you?" she said to their reflections in the mirror. "Do you have dreams?"

He grinned. "X-rated ones, thanks to you."

"Be serious," she chided, laughing. "Where did you learn to cook?"

He shrugged. "The land of necessity."

"What?"

"It was either learn to cook the foods I loved or go broke eating out every night."

"I know the feeling. I love to eat. It's my favorite pastime."

"Really?" he purred as his hand started to slip beneath her towel.

"Okay," she amended as she swatted him away. "My *second*-favorite pastime. Speaking of which, since you can't behave, you'll have to leave. I really can't be late for a public appearance."

"I like watching you," he said.

The sadness in his voice touched her deeply. "I promise I'll let you watch me some other time. Right now, I have to get ready for work, and I find you more than just a little distracting."

He smiled, though it didn't seem to reach his eyes. "I hope you'll always feel that way."

"Why wouldn't I?" she asked, hoping to alleviate some of the anxiety she sensed in him.

He lowered his eyes and appeared to study the tiled floor as he moved to the doorway. "Because you don't really know me that well."

"After last night, I think I know most of you."

"Now who's the one who isn't behaving?"

"Good point. Be nice and let me get ready, and stop looking so sad, Derek. I meant what I said earlier."

"That you think you're in love with me?"

She turned and looked up at him. Her hand reached out to touch his cheek. His brow was furrowed with deep, troubled lines. "I don't think it. I know it."

"So do I," he whispered as he left the room.

"Damn," she muttered as she dried her hair. Did he mean he knew she loved him, or that he loved her in return? As much as she wanted to stay with him, she had to dress and get down to the lobby.

She emerged from the bathroom a few minutes later to find Derek standing at the window. "I'm sorry I have to run," she said, hopping on one foot as she placed a pump on the other.

"So am I," he said as he turned. "Can I have a kiss before you go?"

She went to him happily. "Only if you promise to lighten up while I'm gone. This is the beginning, Derek. Stop acting like it's the end."

His kiss was unlike the others they had

shared. It was sweet, tender, and left her feeling very cherished. So what if he hadn't said the words? She knew it, felt it.

Reluctantly, she left him in the suite and headed for the lobby. Gil was waiting for her with a reproachful expression on his face and several newspapers under his arm.

"Sorry I'm late," she apologized as she tugged the strap of her briefcase. Keeping her voice low, she said, "You don't know how much I do not want to do this date thing."

"No problem," Gil said tersely. He shoved the newspapers at her and said, "You're fired."

Dumbfounded, Skyler opened one of the papers and felt her head begin to spin when she read the blazing headline:

Renowned astrologist a fraud!

CHAPTER SEVEN

"WONDERFULLY EXECUTED, Mr. Conner," she said as she returned to the suite. "Catchy article, by the way. Was it your idea for them to print every word I told you? Never mind, just get out."

He stopped tying his tie and caught the newspaper she threw at him. "Oh, God," he groaned.

"God isn't your problem right now—I am. You have exactly five seconds to get out of here before I call security and have you thrown out."

He took a step closer. "Don't even think about it," she warned. "You have four seconds."

"I tried to talk to you before you left. Skyler, won't you please let me explain?"

She fought back tears as she met his eyes and said, "You can't. There is no explanation for what you did. Or an excuse, or a justification. Did you have your hidden tape recorder on when we had sex?"

"It isn't like that," he insisted. "I admit that I made the tapes. I just never meant for them to get out once I got to know you. I didn't mean for you to find out this way."

"I'll remember that while I collect unemployment. You have three seconds." She stepped into the bathroom, slammed the door and locked it. She stayed there on the floor, hugging her knees to her chest long after she heard Derek leave.

Following a decent cry, she emerged from the bathroom. As she did, the telephone rang. She debated answering it, afraid it might be some of the same press corps who had ripped her to shreds after her comments about the senator. Worse yet, it could be Derek.

Wiping the remnants of her tears from her face, Skyler grabbed the receiver. "Yes?"

"I knew he was a creep," Sue said. "I'm so sorry, Skyler. What can I do?"

"Nothing," she said, sighing. "Gil fired me."

"He's a creep, too," Sue offered. "I'll meet you at the Salisbury airport. But, be prepared, Skyler. The reporters and their trucks are already camped in your driveway."

"Great. Then I won't come home."

"Where will you go? You don't sound like you should be alone right now."

Skyler laughed without humor. She had never felt so alone in her life. "I'm not ready to face this yet," she said. "I need a few days to think of a way to explain the quotes in the paper."

"Did he really tape you?"

Skyler looked down at the newspaper Derek had left on the rumpled bed. Silently, she reread the out-of-context snippet.

During the conversations with Mr. Conner, Miss McMasters admitted her hoax. Referring to her show, she said on the tapes that "This is Gil's [the producer of Miss McMasters's show] idea. He's hoping that the date contest thing will drawn in listeners, which draws in callers, which he mistakenly thinks will make lightning strike twice." She explained the meaning of *lightning* as follows: "The first show I did made some man a lot of money.... I just listened to him and told him what I thought."

When asked by Mr. Conner if her advice was in any way influenced by her knowledge of astrology, Miss McMasters replied, "It was my first night. You have to understand, I had been out of work for more than a year.... Needless to say, I didn't know a horoscope from a stethoscope when I started."

"Every word," she told her friend. "Listen, I want to pack and get out of here. I'll call you."

"Take care," Sue said. "Please keep in touch with me, I worry about you."

"Thanks."

"WHAT IN THE HELL were you thinking?" Derek thundered. He struggled with a very strong urge to wring Blayne's pencil-thin neck.

"I—I thought I was doing you a favor," he stammered as he got to his feet. "Geez, Derek, you ran out of here, and I found the envelope in the desk. It was stamped and addressed. All you've talked about for months was getting even with the McMasters woman. How was I supposed to know you had changed your mind?"

Derek tossed his bag onto the sofa, completely disgusted and thoroughly heartbroken. "You should have asked me first."

Blayne's own temper flared. "You're never here! And even when you are, your head is someplace else. By the way, I closed the land deal."

"Great. I wish you the best." He sat down, closed his eyes and pinched the bridge of his nose.

"What do you mean?" Blayne demanded. "We are partners."

"*Were* partners," Derek corrected.

"You can't back out on me now—I need you."

Derek looked at Blayne and sighed. "No, you don't. You've handled this whole thing without my help."

"But you did the business plan!" Blayne argued.

"Which you could have paid any qualified business consultant to do. Look, Blayne, my heart isn't in it. Consider my very small contribution to this venture as a gift. Take it and run with it."

"I can't believe you're leaving me in the lurch like this!"

"Get used to it," Derek said.

"I'm sorry I delivered the damned tapes. What more do you want?"

"You'll do fine on your own. Have some faith in yourself. The operating system add-in design you created is sound. You've got the capital and the drive to succeed. You don't need me, Blayne. You're on your way.''

"Think so?"

Derek gave him an encouraging smile. "I do. Besides, I'll stick around for a while just in case you hit a snag.''

"If that's how you want it," Blayne reluctantly acquiesced. "What can I give you?"

"Thanks, but I only want one thing and no one can give it to me.''

"What is it?"

"Skyler."

"I have a suggestion," Blayne said. "Want to hear it?"

"I'm definitely open for suggestions. It isn't like it can get any worse.''

TWO WEEKS LATER, Derek was back in Miami at twilight. "There she is," he said as he pointed to a lone chair at the edge of the calm turquoise waters. "I can't tell you how much I appreciate your giving me a hand with this.''

His companion smiled. "I guess I owe you one, so this will make us even.''

Derek felt a mixture of trepidation and exhilaration seeing her again. These had been the longest two weeks of his life.

"Miss McMasters?"

She turned, her blue eyes shocked at first, then furious as she glanced in Derek's direction. "Go away, Derek. And take your playmate with you."

"I'm Jonathan Kemper," his former boss said, extending his hand.

Skyler blanched and looked uneasy. "If Derek brought you here for an apology, believe me, I am sorry if you feel deceived."

"Quite the contrary," Jonathan said. "I feel eternally grateful to you, Miss McMasters. Your advice—even if it was merely a guess—has made my life very enjoyable this past year. I did come at Derek's request, not for your apology, but to thank you and see how I can help the two of you."

"You can hold Derek's face in the water until he drowns," she suggested with venomous sweetness.

He laughed. "How about the two of us taking a stroll?"

"So long as the back stabber stays here."

Derek watched them walk down the beach, fairly certain that Blayne's idea would not work. Skyler was simply too hurt by his betrayal. Dejectedly, he fell into her chair and closed his eyes.

"So, DID DEREK DRAG YOU down here to plead his case? Not that he has one."

"I've known Derek for years," Mr. Kemper said. "He came to work for me straight out of college."

"That's all well and good, Mr. Kemper, but it doesn't change what he did to me."

"Call me Jonathan."

"Fine, Jonathan it is. You have to understand that Derek's tapes have made it impossible for me to work in radio ever again. My little slip at my previous job was almost impossible to overcome. Now, being branded a hoax and a fraud because of him has effectively ended my career."

"Derek didn't send the tapes."

Water splashed on her legs as she walked at the surf's edge. "I read that in the paper. But he *made* the tapes. It doesn't matter who gave them to the newspaper, Derek is still responsible."

"Derek is in love with you, and he said you loved him, too."

"*Loved,*" she agreed. "Past tense."

"That's a pity," Jonathan said. "He's probably one of the nicest men I've ever had the pleasure of knowing."

"I guess that means he never stabbed you in the back."

"Quite the opposite. I did it to him."

"You?"

Jonathan nodded and adjusted his sunglasses. "Derek is one of the best systems designers in the business."

"I saw his recipe doodad. He may be creative, but he's still a jerk."

"Like you, he knew I was burned-out. Derek came to me with a proposal to buy my company."

"Which makes him an entrepreneurial jerk."

Jonathan chuckled. "I'm beginning to see why Derek finds you so attractive. He must admire your spirit. The two of you are a lot alike."

"Not from my perspective."

"It would have taken a long time for Derek to raise the capital to buy me out. Unfortunately, I wasn't willing to wait. Derek was one of the employees let go after the sale to Computer Servers. Like you, he found himself unemployed, but he was determined to start his own firm from scratch."

"So what stopped him?"

"You."

"Sorry, but I refuse to accept blame for his

employment status. If he's as bright as you say, he should have been able to find a new job instantly.''

"He did. He started doing consulting work, and then he hooked up with Blayne Winston.''

"His friend that delivered the tapes?''

"Yes. But at the time, Blayne didn't know Derek had had a change of heart.''

"Goody for Blayne.''

"I'm here because Blayne insisted Derek ask for my intervention. By the way, thanks to Derek's mentoring, Blayne has started his own company, and I think it will be a success given time.''

In spite of herself, Skyler asked, ''Why isn't Derek in on the deal? I thought you said he was determined to start his own firm.''

"He wants you more. I think you should take a step back and try to figure out what Derek wants.''

"Wanting and having are too different things.''

"Are they?'' Jonathan asked. ''You once gave me some advice that changed my life. May I do the same for you?''

She shrugged. ''I'm listening.''

"I put my career before my marriage, my family and myself for a lot of years. I missed the important things. Take it from an expert, a successful career is a poor substitute for a successful marriage.''

''Who said anything about marriage?''

''Derek. Which ends my lecture. To paraphrase what you said to Derek, I've given you a push, now you have to decide which way to fall.''

EPILOGUE

"I DIDN'T HEAR YOU RIGHT," Derek said without looking up from his computer screen. "I thought you said Skyler was here."

"She is," Blayne said. "Which probably means I should make myself scarce."

Derek almost ran the younger man down as he barreled down the hallway. Seeing her, tanned and refreshed, standing in his living room, stopped his heart.

She looked at him with an unreadable expression. "Hello, Derek."

"Skyler." He choked out her name as raw emotion strangled his voice.

"I'll just be going," Blayne said as he grabbed his coat and slipped around Skyler and out the door.

"Can I get you anything?" Derek asked.

"Maybe," Skyler replied.

Rubbing his face, Derek remained silent until he could stand it no longer. *Might as well get it over with.* "Did you come here to shoot me?"

"I came to see if you'd be interested in explaining how your recipe computer thing works."

"Huh?"

She slipped off her jacket and tossed it on the nearest chair, then sank onto the sofa. "That thing you designed that can keep track of recipes and ingredients."

Confusion fogged his brain. "We parted on horrible terms. I don't see you for a month and you just dropped in to inquire about my computer?"

"I've spent the last couple of weeks doing a little investigating myself. Turnabout is fair play."

"I guess," he agreed, disheartened.

"For instance, thanks to Jonathan Kemper, I know that you approached him about developing computerized gadgets for the restaurant trade."

He shrugged. "I only wanted him to explore the idea of expanding into a new market. He wasn't interested."

"I am. By the way, do you remember when I read your chart at Bayview Mall?"

"Yes. But I've got to tell you, Skyler, you're losing me."

She took a deep breath. "Okay, I'll start from the top."

"That would be nice."

"I know you have an MBA as well as a degree in computer sciences. And you can cook almost as well as I can."

He smiled. "I don't burn flan."

"You'll have to prove that."

"When?"

"Once we work out terms."

"Terms for what? C'mon, Skyler.... I'm not feeling too patient right now."

She smiled that breathtaking smile, and it caused his heart to soar. "Too bad, you have to hear me out before we make any long-term decisions."

"Okay. Long-term?"

"I'm willing to overlook the fact that you got me fired."

"I'm sorry," he said earnestly.

"I know that *now*. As I said, I spent some time researching you."

"Why?"

"Because it mattered."

"Why?"

"Because in spite of everything, you matter to me."

Derek ran to the sofa and tried to embrace

her. Skyler firmly planted her hands against his chest and forcefully said, "Not yet."

"When?"

"When I'm finished."

"How long will that take?"

"Forever, if you don't sit down and keep your hands to yourself."

Reluctantly, Derek joined her on the sofa and tried to concentrate on what she was saying instead of how beautiful she was. She was like every Christmas gift he'd ever received all rolled up in one lovely, feminine, blond package.

"The stars said your financial success would be linked to your marriage partner. But I forgot," she said as she leaned back. "You don't believe in horoscopes."

He inched closer to her. "You're speaking in codes, Skyler. Please stop it, because I'm getting my hopes up, and I honestly don't think I can handle more rejection from you."

"I want us to open a restaurant, and I think if we adapted your computer thingy, it would help make the operation run smoothly."

"You came here to discuss a restaurant?"

She cast him a warning look. "Not *a* restaurant. *Our* restaurant."

"Who said I wanted to open a restaurant?"

"Me. Once I stopped being hurt and realized that Jonathan was right, I—"

"About what?"

"Following some of my own advice," she said as faint color stained her cheeks. "Which you have to do as well if you want us to work."

"Work as in *business* or work as in a *couple?*"

"Both," she said. "It's perfect. We can open a restaurant, small at first. Then after a few years we can expand or whatever."

"A few years? What's the catch?"

"You have to believe."

"In what?" he asked.

She reached out and took his hand. Ever so softly, Skyler pressed a kiss into his palm. "The stars."

"And if I do?"

"Then we follow the path charted for us."

"Which is?"

"I've already told you twice," she said in exasperation. "Your success is tied to your marriage partner, and I'm that partner. This is my year to find personal happiness, and I need a man who is driven, self-sufficient, confident, but sensitive. He's got to enjoy life to the fullest and have a sense of fun. Which means, you need me and I need you."

Derek grabbed her and pulled her into his lap. Cupping her face in his hands, he said, "I couldn't agree more...."

A very long time later, as they lay nestled in his bed, Derek said, "I love you."

"I love you, too."

"And starting today, I'll be checking my horoscope daily."

"Why?"

"To see when the stars say it's time for us to have a baby."

"I'd like to get married first."

"We'll take care of that as soon as we get out of bed."

"When will that be?" she asked as he kissed her mouth.

"Not for a long, long time."

The Perfect Match

by Judy Christenberry

PROLOGUE

"YOU'RE GOING TO HAVE a baby?" Debra asked, her voice rising in astonishment.

"No! At least, not yet. I didn't mean—" Allison Carter tried to organize her thoughts. "I've been thinking—"

"I'll say!" Debra returned, her eyes still wide.

Allison understood her friend's reaction. In the years they'd worked together, their conversations had run the gamut of business and personal issues, but Allison had never voiced a need for a baby.

"It's normal for a woman my age to want a family."

"But you've always been intent on a career. And you've just been made a vice president."

"Would you trade Jack and little Emily for a vice presidency?" Allison asked her, referring to Debra's husband and five-month-old baby girl.

"No! Of course not. But—but it's such a change for you."

Allison stood and began pacing, something else that wasn't like her. "I think I've made a mistake."

Debra gasped, as if that statement was as weird as Allison's desire to have a child. "But you've always been so sure of yourself. I admired that."

"I thought I was right. After my mother's example, the choices seemed easy." Her mother had married six times and was on the hunt for husband number seven. Allison had always believed she was better off concentrating on a career.

"But what has happened to change your mind?"

Allison sighed and faced her friend. "I succeeded. I'm well paid, independent, living in the fast lane." Then her shoulders slumped. "And it's not enough."

"Not enough? You mean you're lonely?" After Allison's reluctant nod, she asked, "That blind date didn't work out? I intended to ask, but I got distracted."

Allison shook her head. "No. He's just like me. Can talk of nothing else but his career."

"You're not like that. If you were, we wouldn't be friends."

"Thanks, Deb. But I'm too much like him for comfort. I need to make some changes, to…experiment with my personal life. I need to find my youth again."

Something about the look on her friend's face must've alerted Debra. "Who are you thinking about?"

Allison jerked her gaze back to Debra even as her cheeks flushed. "What do you mean?"

"You were thinking about someone specific, weren't you? Was there someone in your past you regret losing?"

"I think you must be psychic. There was a man. He asked me to marry him, but I wouldn't even consider it. I had too many plans. I was eighteen and thought I had my future all planned out."

"And he asked you to give that up?"

"It would've been hard to meet my goals in Wyoming."

"Wyoming? Wow! Jack loves Wyoming."

Allison grimaced. While she might regret losing the man, she couldn't picture herself in Wyoming. On a dude ranch.

"Is it too late?"

Allison stared at Debra. "Too late for what?"

"The man! Too late to, you know, get together?"

"I think so," Allison drawled, rolling her eyes. "It's been ten years."

"So what are you going to do?"

"I don't know," Allison wailed, revealing the point of her frustration.

"I have an idea!" Debra exclaimed.

"YOU'RE SURE?" ALLISON questioned, her hand on the telephone receiver. She hesitated to pick it up, to cast her fate in such a ridiculous manner.

"What can it hurt? I went to a palm reader before I met Jack, and she predicted I'd become involved with him. Since then, I'm not as skeptical about these things. This lady's radio show is really popular, and I've heard good things about her predictions."

The radio blared, "If you want the stars, call the Sky."

Allison grimaced and dialed the number.

After talking to the producer, she waited until a cool voice said, "Hello, Allison. What can the stars and I do for you?"

"I need advice about my love life."

Five minutes later, Allison hung up, more confused than ever.

Debra, however, seemed quite clear about the advice her friend had received. "Yippee! You're going to Wyoming!"

CHAPTER ONE

"THIS IS RIDICULOUS!" Allison muttered under her breath as she stared out the minivan window. The ground was covered with snow, a strong wind was blowing, and only the occasional cabin dotted the rugged landscape.

Wyoming.

She'd let Debra talk her into doing as the astrologist had said: travel to find her true love.

Travel to Jackson Hole, Wyoming, to be met by a real live cowboy named Billy, who loaded six people into his minivan to drive them to the dude ranch run by Richard McCall. Mac.

She hadn't had the nerve to ask any questions. She figured Mac was married with twenty kids by now. That had been his plan. Well, not really twenty kids, but he'd wanted a big family.

He wanted a wife who would work by his side, help with the dude ranch. He'd assumed, because they'd shared a spring on campus with hot sex and great companionship, that she would be willing to give up her dreams and goals.

Wrong.

She'd been eighteen and thought she'd known everything. She'd assumed Mac would come to New York with her when she graduated. He was brilliant. He'd be wasted in Hicksville, U.S.A.

He'd been a senior. Two weeks before graduation, he got word his father had had a fatal heart attack. He'd flown home, and when he'd returned, it was only to finish up his requirements and, he thought, to bring Allison home with him.

She'd suggested he sell the ranch, he and his mother, and come back East. After all, he'd scarcely mentioned his home and family in the four months they'd dated. He'd stared at her as if she'd suggested killing someone. Then he'd walked out.

"Not much farther now," the cowboy sang out, bringing Allison back to the present.

She drew a deep breath, hoping to steady her heartbeat. Ten years. And yet she could still remember how it had felt to have Mac touch her. How could those long-ago memories have this effect on her?

"You all interested in skiing or riding?" Billy asked, looking in his rearview mirror.

Several of the guests expressed their preferences, but not Allison. She wished her reason for making this ridiculous trek could be so simply explained.

And the closer she got to the McCall Dude Ranch, the more panic she felt.

"BILLY'S HERE," Myrna McCall sang out, heading for the front door.

Mac grimaced. His mother's high spirits always amazed him. Since his father's death, his mother had thrown herself into the work on their dude ranch and cattle operation, proving herself invaluable. Together, they'd carried on the traditions of the McCall Ranch, even making improvements and increasing their profits.

Parts of the job he loved. Meeting the dudes wasn't one of those parts.

With a sigh, he dumped the rest of his coffee in the kitchen sink and followed her. Best to get it over with.

He didn't even look at the guests as his mother was greeting them. Billy was unloading bags from the back of the van, and he joined him.

"Full load?" he asked as he took a heavy bag from Billy.

"Only six. I gotta make another trip for a later flight." Billy craned his neck to look around the corner of the minivan before he whispered, "There's a real looker in this group."

"Not interested." In addition to running the ranch, Mac was having to deal with his mother and friend's matchmaking. Myrna wanted grandchildren. Billy, who'd worked on the ranch for twenty-six years and had been Mac's father figure since Abe's death, kept pushing him to marry.

Billy grunted, his disgust evident.

Too bad. Mac had married five years ago, after those two had pushed and prodded him. It hadn't worked out. In fact, it had been a disaster. Shelly had thought she could convince him to move into Jackson. She liked the chic life, lots of restaurants, fashionable shops. And she'd wanted nothing to do with work.

Of course, she hadn't mentioned that fact until they were married. At least Allie had— He stopped himself. He'd vowed never to think of her again.

He gathered up four suitcases, two under his arms and the other two by their handles, and turned toward the ranch house. Inside, they'd connect the guests with their luggage. Myrna had escorted all the guests there, to get them out of the Wyoming wind.

"Welcome to the McCall Dude Ranch," Myrna was saying with a smile. "If you'll each give me your name, I'll…"

Mac set the luggage on the floor and hurried back outside. He'd have to meet the people later, but right now he wanted to spare Billy as much as he could. The man wasn't as young as he used to be.

"I'll get that, Billy," he called as he approached the end of the van.

"Did you see her?"

"Who?"

"The good-looking one. She's got brown hair, almost as dark as Myrna's, curves in all the right places, and blue eyes to die for."

"Sounds like you're more interested in her than I am." He looked at Billy, a twinkle in his eye. "Should Mom be jealous?"

Billy's face turned a beet red and Mac regretted his teasing.

"Don't be ridiculous!" Billy muttered.

Mac suspected Billy had a thing for his mother, but the man had never even hinted about his feelings. "You're always telling me I need to marry again. What about you?"

"I'm an old man, boy! It's too late for me. But I don't want it to be too late for you."

"Hell, I'm only thirty-two. And I figure you've got a few good years left, too. Take your own advice."

He gathered more luggage and headed into the house again. Billy followed, carrying almost as much luggage as Mac. The man was so hard-headed.

A grin grew on Mac's face. According to his mother, that was a trait he shared with Billy.

He turned back to close the door behind Billy, shutting out the cold wind, then faced the guests.

And lost his smile.

"Hello, Mac."

ALLISON WASN'T SURE what she expected from Mac, but it hadn't been the fierce frown he'd given her.

Of course, he hadn't had her advantage, knowing that she would see him. She'd had a couple of weeks to prepare for this moment. Weeks she'd apparently wasted.

"You know my son?" the attractive hostess asked with a questioning smile.

Ah. His mother.

"We were in university together," Allison said, reluctantly drawing her gaze from Mac. He looked good. His body was more mature now, his shoulders a little broader, his muscles powerful.

"Really? That's wonderful. Mac, why don't you take Allison and her luggage upstairs? She's in the Blue Room," Myrna suggested, an encouraging smile on her face.

Not that her smile had any effect on her son. He still frowned at Allison. "Which are yours?" he demanded.

She pointed out her two suitcases. Obviously she'd made a mistake coming here, she decided. Her stomach was churning because of Mac's reaction. He led the way up the stairs with nothing more than a nod.

Throwing back her shoulders, she marched after him. What was his problem? She was a paying guest. He was supposed to at least be polite.

He swung open the second door on the right and set her bags just inside the room. Then he turned his back on her and started down the stairs.

"Mac!" she called, unable to believe his behavior.

"Yes?"

"I thought—I wanted to say hello."

"Hello." Then he disappeared.

Frustration filled her. Okay, so it had been ten years and they hadn't parted on the best of terms. But that didn't mean he should be rude. Did it?

Or maybe she was expecting too much. Had her foolish belief in the astrologist's words made her think she only had to show up in Mac's milieu for him to fall at her feet? Her lips curved into a sad smile. She should've remembered that nothing was that easy... whatever the stars said.

And why did it matter to her? She hadn't really expected anything from her trip. Had she?

MAC COULDN'T BELIEVE Allison Carter was a guest. That meant she'd be here for a week.

Not that it mattered to him, unless she expected to take up their relationship where it left off, a decade ago. No one would expect that. Too much time had passed.

So why was he bothered?

Because he'd loved her and she'd thrown that love back in his face. He'd been so wrapped up in their relationship, in loving Allie, he'd ignored the real world. That spring had been like a dream, his senses filled with Allie. When his father's death had brought the world to a standstill for him, he'd believed he still had Allie. So when she'd refused to come back West with him, it had been a second blow that had almost destroyed him.

And he hadn't forgiven her. He'd dreamed of her, longed for her, but for ten years, he'd blamed her for the long nights when he'd ached to hold her.

She'd even influenced his failed marriage, since he'd tried to replace her by marrying someone who'd looked like her.

Now she'd turned up and smiled at him as if they'd only parted a few days ago. What did she expect from him?

He shoved away those thoughts and reached for more luggage. "Whose are these?" he asked, adding a smile.

"Those belong to us," a man responded. "Those two blue bags are my wife's, too."

"Mac, have you already settled Allison in her room?" his mother asked, having turned around at the sound of his voice.

"Yes, ma'am," he replied as he struggled to carry the two additional bags. But he avoided his mother's gaze. And Billy's.

"You're fast today," Myrna teased, but said nothing else.

Mac breathed a sigh of relief as he climbed the stairs again. Maybe his mother would forget that he knew Allison. Maybe she wouldn't ask any questions. And maybe the temperature would hit eighty this week for New Year's Day in Wyoming.

Yeah, right.

CHAPTER TWO

MYRNA HAD OFFERED coffee and snacks in the
gathering room after everyone settled in.

Allison changed into a long denim skirt and
a chambray shirt, not wanting to look like a
cheesy western wannabe, but also hoping to
avoid looking like a New Yorker. She didn't
want to throw "big city" in Mac's face.

Though why she worried, she didn't know.
He'd already shown her he had no interest, New
York or otherwise. As if to emphasize that
point, he wasn't among the people in the room
when she entered.

"Allison, isn't it?" Myrna asked with a smile
as she walked toward her, leaving the group of
guests with whom she'd been talking. "I hope
you don't mind that we're informal here."

"Not at all."

"It's nice to have one of Mac's friends arrive
so unexpectedly."

Allison recognized the information-seeking
in Myrna's statement. "I guess I should've

called before I made my plans. I don't think Mac is too happy with my appearance."

"Oh?" Myrna asked with a frown. "Was he rude to you?"

Shaking her head, Allison gave a brief smile and tried to change the subject. "No. You promised coffee. I have to admit I'm dying for a cup of it."

"Of course," her hostess responded, leading her to a gleaming silver urn set on a side table. Alongside it were platters of small sandwiches and other finger foods.

As Myrna poured the coffee for Allison, she said, "Mac may have just been in a hurry. He tries to relieve Billy of the heavy work."

Allison was about to agree with Myrna, though she didn't really believe the offered excuse, when Mac entered the room. He started toward the coffee urn but abruptly changed direction after meeting Allison's gaze.

Myrna stared after her son, then gave Allison a speculative look. "Or maybe you're right," she said with a smile.

"I beg your pardon?" She hadn't expected her hostess to be so frank. But Mac's behavior didn't leave much to interpretation. She should've expected his reaction after his obvious lack of interest in her when he carried up her luggage.

"Maybe my son *isn't* happy about your arrival. Do you know why?"

Allison raised her chin and glared at Mac across the room. She had no intention of discussing their past if she could avoid it. "We may have parted on unhappy terms, but that was ten years ago. I don't know why he'd still be upset."

"Hmm," was Myrna's only response as she too stared at Mac.

HE'D MADE A MISTAKE.

Though he tried to ignore the two women staring at him, he could feel their gazes even as he mingled with the other guests. He'd wanted to avoid Allie, but his mistake was letting his mother know how he felt.

Occasionally he indulged in mild flirtations with the women guests. It seemed that was what some of them expected. But a mild flirtation with Allie? No, that would be tempting fate. He wasn't willing to risk his heart again. But his mother would want an explanation.

She would worry him to death.

He sensed their approach just before they greeted the married couple he'd been talking to.

"I brought you some coffee, Mac," Myrna said, holding out a cup.

"Thanks," he said, accepting the offer.

"Steve, Betty, why don't you come serve yourselves a snack. We have some great ones," Myrna said with the warm enthusiasm that made her a favorite with the guests.

Before Mac knew what was happening, he found himself alone with Allison.

"Why are you angry?"

He surveyed the room rather than look at her. After all, he'd dreamed of her often enough. He knew what she looked like. "Angry? I don't know what you're talking about."

"You didn't exactly act happy to see me," she said.

This time Mac faced her. He was prepared and offered a slight smile. "Is there any reason I should be? I was under the impression you'd never come out West...for any reason."

He'd hit his target. Her cheeks flushed. "That was a long time ago."

"Was it? So, what brings you such a long way from home? New York City, right?"

Allison nodded, and Mac caught her stiffening at his question. She still made his heart turn over.

"A vacation."

"You suddenly had the urge to be a cowboy?" He didn't hide his scorn at her ridiculous answer. She'd never expressed any interest in his home life when they were at Princeton. Though that thought might not be fair. He hadn't talked about Wyoming that spring. He'd concentrated on loving Allie.

"No. I had the urge to be insulted. That's why I sought you out especially." Then she turned her back on him and walked out of the room.

Only one thing she'd said remained with Mac.

She'd sought him out?

ALLISON CAME SLOWLY down the stairs for dinner. She wasn't eager for another confrontation with Mac, but she wanted to see him again. Her eyes had devoured him earlier, noting the differences, the similarities between the Mac she used to know and the Mac of today.

He was still handsome, sexy, intelligent.

He still made her heart long for what she couldn't have.

He still wanted to be in control.

So did she. That had been one of the few problems they'd encountered as a couple. The first time they'd differed on something, it had caught them both by surprise. But they'd learned to compromise.

Now Mac didn't appear to have any interest in compromising...or anything else with her.

She'd made a mistake, listening to that ridiculous astrologist, traveling so far, expecting history to repeat itself. The only thing this trip was accomplishing was showing her how foolish she'd been ten years ago. She'd thought she would find someone else who would love her like Mac, who would make each day exciting, someone she would love with all her heart. She'd been wrong.

The man who'd driven them from the airport was waiting at the foot of the stairs.

"Evening, Allison. Are you settled in?"

"Yes, thank you. It's Billy, isn't it?"

He nodded with a wide smile. "Yes, ma'am. Been working here for twenty-six years. Came when Mac was six years old."

"That's a long time in one place. Don't you ever think about leaving?"

He appeared shocked by her question. "Nope. The land's beautiful, the people are the best on earth. What would I leave for?"

She had no answer. And, unfortunately, she was sure Mac would have the same response. "Which way is dinner?"

"First door on the left. We're havin' brisket tonight."

Allison headed for the dining room without comment. Her thoughts were of Mac, not the menu.

She hadn't made much progress in her quest. She didn't know if she'd be faced with some country-girl wife with six kids in tow, or not. Not that she cared that Mac might have chosen someone else, she hurriedly assured herself, ignoring the squeezing of her heart. He'd already indicated a lack of interest in her.

It wasn't that she had expected everything to be the way it was ten years ago. She guessed she'd come because—for a moment—the astrologist had convinced her that she could rediscover a lost love.

Their time together had been so incredible, so out of this world, that the thought of reliving those sensations was too much to ignore. But that time was past. And her heart ached with that knowledge.

Entering the open door Billy had pointed out, she found a larger group of people than had arrived with her. As with their group, there were couples, even several children, and singles. Most of the singles were women.

"Hi, there, I'm Marjorie Cohan from Chicago," an older woman standing nearby said, holding out her hand.

Allison gave her own name as she shook hands.

"You here by yourself? Looking for a cowboy?"

Allison's eyes widened at her no-pretense remark. "A cowboy? Why, no. Cowboys don't fit in well in New York City."

"I don't think you've seen our host. He'd fit in anywhere." Marjorie grinned and practically licked her chops. "Unfortunately, he's a little young for me. I'm going to try for Billy."

Allison nodded, but her mind was producing pictures of Mac at Princeton. Allison had scarcely realized he was cowboy material. He'd blended into the campus as if he belonged there.

"Do you want a drink? They've got another cowboy playing bartender over there. He's not as cute as Mac, but he'd do in a pinch."

Marjorie's words woke Allison from her thoughts. "Uh, no thanks," she said, even as her gaze traveled across the room. When she confirmed that the man wasn't Mac, she lost interest in him.

"I didn't come here to find a cowboy," she reiterated, reminding herself again that Mac hadn't been a cowboy when she knew him.

Then Mac the cowboy walked into the room.

MAC HAD MANAGED TO AVOID his mother until he came into the kitchen just before dinner. He knew she'd be there; she supervised the meals on the ranch. But he'd figured he'd be safe from any lectures because of the kitchen staff.

Wrong.

"Mac—I'm glad you came down early. I need to talk to you," Myrna said. She led the way into the large pantry, expecting him to follow.

He hesitated, but he couldn't be rude to his mother. When he stepped inside, she pulled the door closed behind him.

"What's going on with Allison?"

"I don't know, Mom. You'll have to ask Allison."

"I don't think so, smarty pants. Immediately after you spoke to her this afternoon, she went to her room and hasn't been seen since. Were you rude to her?"

He put a hand to his chest and tried to pretend innocence. "Me? Mom, you know I always treat the guests well."

"She said you were upset with her. Why would you be upset if an old friend turns up here?"

"Who said she was an old friend?" he demanded.

"She said you went to university together."

"I went to university with a lot of people. Besides, I'm not upset. I was just busy."

"Oh," Myrna said slowly, studying him. "So, tonight you'll be friendly, talk over old times?"

He was backed into a corner. "Yeah, sure."

"Good. I've fixed a table for two. I'll explain to everyone else that you're old friends."

With that little bomb, she smiled sweetly and exited the pantry, leaving Mac standing among sacks of flour and cans of beans, wanting to strangle his mother.

When he walked into the kitchen, his mother was heading to the dining room. He followed her. Best to get this evening over with. Once he'd made nice with Allie— The thought took his breath away. The last time he'd made nice with Allie, they'd made love all through the night.

With morning had come word of his father's heart attack and immediate death, and life had changed in a second.

He shook his head, then stepped into the other room. He wouldn't think about that last time. His gaze immediately locked onto Allie.

She was as beautiful as ever, though the softness he'd loved had disappeared.

His mother's discreet wave caught his eye,
and she nodded to a table in the corner, set for
two. With a resigned nod, he crossed the room
to where Allie stood visiting with another guest.

"'Evening, ladies.''

"Mac! We were just talking about you.
You're the handsomest cowboy I've ever met,''
Marjorie gushed.

Mac attempted a smile in return. The lady's
greedy stare was one of the reasons he disliked
this part of his job. "Did Allison agree with
you?''

"Of course,'' Allison replied, but there was
no warmth in her words.

He stared at her with a sardonic grin. He
knew better than to take her words as a compliment. "Mom thought you and I might enjoy
a chance to remember old times,'' he said, putting a challenge in his voice. "She's arranged
for us to have a table all to ourselves.''

"Oh, you lucky girl!'' Marjorie exclaimed.
"If you have any more duets in mind, I'm
available, Mac,'' she trilled, and batted some
fake lashes at him.

"Thanks, Marjorie, I'll keep you in mind.''
Then he offered his arm to Allison...and held

his breath. As much as he hated to admit it, he wanted to feel her touch again. Just so he could assure himself the woman meant nothing to him. She'd thrown him over once. She wouldn't have a second chance.

She hesitated, as if touching him was distasteful, then slid her hand onto his forearm. And a frisson traveled up his body. He clenched his fist and quickened his pace. Enough time had been given to that experiment. He was in big trouble.

He dropped his arm and pulled out her chair, leaving the chair with its back to the other guests—and his mother—for himself. No way did he want his mother studying his reactions to Allison Carter.

"How thoughtful of your mother," Allison said. Then she added, "She must have made the arrangements without consulting your preferences."

He settled into the chair across from her. "Why would you say that?"

"Because you've made your distaste for my presence quite clear."

"You took me by surprise."

She stiffened. "I beg your pardon. I didn't realize I should notify you of my desire to visit your dude ranch as a *paying* guest."

"You'll have to admit you never showed any interest in anything west of New York City when I knew you," he reminded her, as he had earlier.

"Neither did you!" she snapped.

She was right. He'd rarely talked about his home, his plans, because, he guessed, he'd subconsciously realized they had no future together. Allie had been full of her plans to conquer New York.

Mac lifted the coffeepot on the table and poured cups of coffee for both of them before he answered. "I toyed with the idea of spending a couple of years in New York," he finally admitted. "Mainly because of you. But when that wasn't an option, you made your position quite clear."

There was animosity in her blue eyes that reminded him of his own reaction when he'd first seen her this afternoon. "I didn't know you wanted— You'd never talked about coming back here all that much."

Which left them at a standstill. Finally, he asked the question that had been plaguing him all afternoon. "Why are you here, Allison? And don't give me any ridiculous answers about a vacation."

The waitress, Janie, a local girl, brought salads to them. Mac smiled and thanked her. After she left, he stared at Allison, waiting for her response.

She raised her chin and glared at him. "I wanted to see how you were doing. To meet your wife and all those kids you intended to have. I wanted to see what life was like outside New York."

He smiled, but he knew it didn't hold the warmth of his smiles a decade ago. He couldn't afford to be that vulnerable again. "Well, welcome to Wyoming. It's definitely a change from New York. But I'll have to admit, I didn't expect you to be tired of life in the Big Apple after only ten years."

"I'm not!" she exclaimed, her chin rising, a show of stubbornness he remembered.

Just for a minute, he'd hoped she had come because she'd finally realized she'd made a mistake. The ravaging hunger that had filled him with that momentary hope was disturbing. "Then I'm afraid you've wasted your time."

And his, too.

CHAPTER THREE

ALLISON TRIED TO DISMISS the coldness that filled her. Mac seemed to have drawn a line again: either she was with him or against him. Either she loved New York, or she hated it. Either she spent her nights loving Mac, lying in his arms, or she was alone and lonely in her single bed.

Mac didn't look at her as he concentrated on his salad. Then, as if remembering his duty as host, he asked, "And how's life in the fast lane? Did everything go as planned, or did you find out the world wasn't yours to conquer?"

Allison stiffened her shoulders. "It worked out just as I'd planned, thank you. I'm the vice president of computer operations at Merriweld-Gamble, Inc."

"Impressive."

"Thank you." She took a sip of water to relieve her suddenly dry throat. Her voice had remained strong, but inside she trembled. As lovers, they'd lain together, sharing their innermost thoughts. At least she'd thought they had. Now they talked as strangers.

Desperate for conversation, she said, "Your mother is very nice."

"Yeah. How's your mother?"

"Looking for husband number seven."

He frowned, probably remembering her feelings for her mother. "Wasn't she on husband number four back when...when we were talking?"

"Yes. They seem to go faster as she gets older."

"Do you spend much time with her?"

"No."

He sighed. "I'm sorry. I wish she'd— I'm sorry."

She shrugged. "I survived."

A soft, sympathetic smile lingered on his lips, one that reminded her of those times he'd held her close. She briefly closed her eyes, until he spoke again.

"I was fortunate in my parents. They had an incredible marriage. When Dad died— I was probably a little off balance then. I didn't intend to hurt you."

She drew a deep breath to shore up her response. With a brisk, no-nonsense tone, she said, "You made your choice."

His brown eyes didn't let her escape. He stared at her until she looked at him...and held her breath. How she wanted him to say he'd missed her, still wanted her, was willing to change his answer this time.

"Yeah. What little choice I had. But I love it here. It's home. I can't imagine living anywhere else. And you made your choice, too. You didn't have to go to New York."

She really had wasted her time.

THE NEXT MORNING, after breakfast, Billy was waiting to escort all those who'd chosen riding as their activity that day to the indoor riding facility not far from the house.

Allison drew a deep breath as she stepped out into a sparkling morning. Snow covered the ground and glistened in the sunlight, and the rolling hills were dotted with evergreen trees and framed by the Rocky Mountains beyond. She had to admit it was awe-inspiring.

"See, I told you the land is beautiful," Billy said, falling into step beside her.

"You're right," she agreed with a smile. It was easy to agree with Billy as he gave his congenial smile. "Though I have seen some beautiful beaches in my time," she added, just to tease him.

"Humph! Sand and little critters that run sideways. Can't compare to the mountains."

She laughed at his description of some people's idea of paradise. "I guess everyone who comes here loves the mountains?"

Billy stared at her. "Most people. But not Mac's wife."

Allison stumbled, almost falling to her knees. Mac's wife? She'd told herself Mac had probably married, but since her arrival she'd seen no evidence of another woman. She'd allowed herself to hope that Mac— She shook her head. "I didn't know he was married." She felt sick to her stomach.

"He's not. They got a divorce a couple of years ago because she wanted to live the city life." Billy's blunt response ended the conversation, and he walked on ahead of her.

Stunned by the information, Allison stared at Billy's back. The roller coaster ride of her emotions left her uneasy. Last night Mac had avoided any personal questions.

Billy was talking to Mac when she entered the building. When Mac's gaze immediately met hers, she knew Billy was confessing what he had revealed. She raised her chin.

She hadn't been prying into his business. She hadn't asked Billy any questions. He had volunteered the information. If Mac wanted to keep his personal life secret from her, well, she'd assure him he had nothing to fear.

Mac sauntered in her direction as Billy talked to the guests, finishing up what Mac had been doing—determining their riding abilities. Mac looked good this morning, she had to admit. Tight blue jeans, cowboy boots, a cowboy hat and plaid shirt all emphasized his muscular build, his square jaw suggested strength, and his brown eyes could melt a woman's heart.

"'Morning, Allie."

Her heart lurched. He'd called her Allison last night. "Good morning," she responded, at her frostiest.

"I hear you've been asking questions."

"I have not! Billy and I were chatting, and he mentioned your divorce. I don't know why you didn't say anything. I expected you to be married. Are you afraid I'm here looking for a husband?"

"Are you?" he returned, sounding no more interested than if they were discussing a cloud in the sky.

"No! I mean, I just wanted to know if you were happy."

"I am."

"Then why hide your divorce?"

"I didn't figure it was any of your business. It had nothing to do with you. Besides, I keep my personal life separate from my work. It makes it easier to steer clear of all these predatory females."

It was obvious that he ranked her among them. His response hurt. Looking for an escape, she said, "I'd better talk to Billy about my riding experience."

"You can tell me."

"That's all right. Billy—"

"Now who sounds afraid?"

"Not me!" she snapped. "I've never ridden before."

"Never? Not even in Central Park?"

"No." She realized he'd goaded her into doing what he wanted. She'd prefer talking to Billy.

"Then I reckon you get a special lesson."

"What do you mean?"

"You're our only true beginner. Wait here."

Nervously, she surveyed the rest of the group. Billy, with several cowboys assisting him, was matching riders with horses, helping them mount. She moved closer to him.

"Billy? I've never ridden before."

He looked at her, his gaze narrowed. "I thought the boss was taking care of you."

She couldn't deny that, so she didn't answer his implied question. "I don't want any special treatment."

"Hmm, well, I suppose—"

The sound of horse's hooves in the dirt of the arena drew everyone's attention. Mac was riding toward them on a beautiful black horse.

"Boss, you taking care of Allison?" Billy shouted.

"Yeah," Mac replied, earning Allison another narrowed stare from Billy before he gathered his group of riders and headed toward the open door at the end of the arena.

"What horse am I going to ride?" Allison asked, unhappy with the apprehension that filled her. She liked knowing what she was supposed to do. It had been a long time since she'd been a novice at anything.

"This one," Mac said as he gracefully dismounted.

She couldn't help but admire his dexterity. Then his answer settled in her head. "But... aren't you riding him?"

"We're going to share, so you can get used to the feel of riding."

"No! I mean, there isn't enough room."

"Sure there is. Come on, Allie. It's safer this way."

Their bodies pressed tightly together, rubbing against each other? That didn't sound safe to her. "Maybe I won't ride today. I can—"

"Of course you'll ride today. That's what you came out here for, isn't it?"

He was challenging her again. She raised her chin, squared her shoulders and stepped forward. "Of course."

"That's my girl."

"No, I'm not," she assured him.

He gave her a grin that made his appeal only greater. "Figuratively speaking, I meant. For the next couple of hours."

She frowned at the big horse as it shifted away from her. "Shouldn't we make the first ride shorter?"

"We'll see. Come on, I'll show you how to mount."

She swallowed, then gathered her courage and moved to Mac's side. In spite of never having ridden, she feared closeness to Mac more than she did the horse. She'd always been good at recognizing her vulnerabilities.

"Put your left hand on the saddle horn, your left foot in the stirrup, and swing your right leg over the back of Diamond."

It sounded simple. When she tried, however, she fell back against Mac's broad chest.

"Whoa, there! Are you all right?"

"Yes, but—but the stirrup is high," she said, panting.

"Try again, and I'll give you a boost."

She had no idea what he intended until, half-way to her destination, she found her hips cupped in his large hands as he lifted her higher in the air. She plopped down into the saddle with a small shriek that had the big horse dancing to the side, which only unsettled Allison more.

"You okay?" Mac asked with another grin.

Clinging to the saddle horn with both hands, Allison nodded.

"Good. Take your foot out of the stirrup." She did as he asked, and he stepped into the stirrup and threw his right leg over the horse. At the same time, his arm snaked around her waist and lifted. Suddenly, she found herself practically sitting in his lap.

"Mac, this isn't a good idea," she said urgently.

"Quit worrying. You'll get used to being up here in a few minutes."

It wasn't the height that was bothering her. The sudden closeness of their bodies brought a deluge of memories…and a powerful hunger to repeat them.

Mac had donned a sheepskin coat while he was fetching Diamond. Now he headed out the same door through which Billy had led the other riders.

"I don't see the others," Allison said, breathless.

"We don't need to ride with them. I'll show you some of the ranch. Horseback is the best way to see it."

Allison wasn't sure she'd be able to concentrate on the spectacular scenery while Mac was holding her in his arms.

MAC HAD LIED TO HIMSELF so convincingly, he'd believed he could hold Allie against him and not be disturbed.

Wrong.

The blood was pumping through his body in all the wrong places. Her softness, her scent, enveloped him and brought back forbidden memories of their time together.

"Mac," she said softly, and he leaned a little closer to hear her. "The ranch really is beautiful."

"I haven't shown you the best parts yet. There's a little lake just over this next hill. We ice-skate there in winter, and fish there in the summer."

They rode along in silence, Mac trying to keep his thoughts on the landscape instead of Allie's body.

When they topped the hill, he was pleased with Allie's gasp of pleasure.

"Oh, it's beautiful. Do you swim in it, too?"

"I have, but the water is pretty cold. It's spring-fed, but, of course, the winter snows make it colder. Most people find it a challenge even on our hottest days."

"It must've been fun growing up here."

"Yeah." He heard the longing in her voice. She'd told him about moving around with her mother to various cities, abruptly leaving when whatever marriage her mother had entered into had failed. Maybe that was one of the reasons he'd kept quiet about his early years. His life had been wonderful, particularly compared to hers.

He urged the horse down the hill, closer to the ice-covered lake. There were several benches around the edge, as well as a bonfire pit flanked by stacks of logs. "Tonight we'll drive here on a hay-covered wagon and ice-skate."

"When did you start operating the ranch as a dude ranch?"

"We started when I was about fifteen, but

this is the first year we've had winter guests. Mom and I decided to offer our best summer employees year-round jobs. They're happy to have the work and we're happy to keep them on. In the fall, we organize hunting expeditions. In winter we offer winter sports, plus riding, and spring and summer are standard operations."

"You must stay very busy."

"Yeah," he agreed, "but not too busy. We have good help."

He directed Diamond onto a path that led around the lake and up a nearby hill into the woods.

"Mac."

Again that soft voice. He leaned closer still, fighting the temptation to drop a kiss behind her ear.

"Why didn't you tell me about the ranch?"

Distracted by her closeness, he didn't understand her meaning. "That's what we've just been talking about."

"No. I mean, at school. Why didn't you talk about your home life then?"

He snuggled her closer, as if to ward off a chill. "At first, I was too distracted by our love-making to even think of anything else."

She shivered.

"You cold?"

"No. Just—just remembering."

"Me, too." He sighed, and tried to push aside those memories.

"I didn't understand. When you came back and—"

"Yeah," he said, cutting her off. "I'm beginning to realize that. I hadn't discussed anything with you. You were unprepared when I decided to go home." Guilt edged its way into his head. He'd blamed her for too many years. Was it possible some of the fault should lie with him?

Uncomfortable with his thoughts, he shrugged. "It probably worked out for the best. After all, you seem happy. You've reached your goals. I knew you would." When she said nothing, he added, "Tell me about your job."

The last thing Allison wanted to talk about was her job. She was beginning to understand things about Mac that he'd kept hidden from her when they'd dated. Thinking back, she began to realize she'd done most of the talking in their relationship.

Mac had done a lot of loving. Every time he had touched her, she had forgotten to ask all those questions she'd stored up about his life.

She hadn't been able to think when he'd kissed her.

Just as she couldn't think now, when he held her against him on horseback.

"Allie?" he prodded.

"Oh…well, it keeps me busy." She went on to tell him what her job required. She didn't mention what it left her with: the loneliness, the belief that she'd let something important pass her by, her memories of him.

As she chattered, they climbed higher and higher in the woods, riding through the aspen trees and evergreens. She breathed deeply of the crisp, clean air, amazed at the difference between New York City and here.

Suddenly, Mac interrupted her. "I have a problem."

"What? Did I do something wrong?" She was in uncharted territory, but she didn't want their time together to end.

"Nope. It's my fault. I thought I could hold you like this and not be affected. But I was wrong. Am I going to be trespassing if I kiss you?"

"Trespassing?" she asked, barely able to breathe.

"Is there a man back in New York?"

She wasn't going to back away. Not when

his wants coincided so greatly with hers. "There are a lot of men, but no one important."

He pulled her body around and his mouth covered hers. She almost sobbed with relief as she rediscovered the magic they'd always shared.

A sudden jolt, combined with a shrill whinny from the horse, disturbed their passion. Then she was falling, their lips as well as their bodies parting, and she landed in a snowdrift.

CHAPTER FOUR

MAC FOUGHT HIS WAY out of the deep snow. "Allie, are you all right?"

"What happened?" she asked in a dazed voice.

"Diamond tripped. A tree limb must've been buried in the snow so he couldn't see it. I need to check on him, if you're all right. You didn't hit your head or break anything?"

"No, I don't think so."

He pulled her up, and as soon as he was certain she was fine, he hurried to Diamond's side. The horse was standing still, its head down. It didn't take long to determine that Diamond had pulled up lame and couldn't carry them back to the ranch house.

"Is he all right?" Allie asked over Mac's shoulder.

"No, he's got a sprain. I should've been paying attention." He stroked Diamond's neck in a silent apology.

Calmly, she asked, "What do we do now?"

"I'm afraid we'll have to walk back to the house, leading Diamond. I'm sorry, Allie. I'd let you ride him if I could, but I'm afraid it would do too much damage to him."

"Then of course I won't ride."

"It's going to take us about three hours to get back. We won't make it in time for lunch," he warned.

She lifted her chin and gave him a determined smile. "Sounds like an excellent diet program. Let's get started, shall we?"

He shook his head in amazement. "I'm glad you're taking it so well."

"I walk all the time in the city. It's no big deal."

"Thanks, Allie. I need to wrap the leg before we head back."

"Wrap it in what?"

"I guess my shirt. I don't have anything else handy."

He shrugged out of his coat and handed it to her, then began unbuttoning his shirt. As he was taking it off, he glanced at Allie, catching her staring at his chest, her tongue wetting her bottom lip. The desire to return to their kiss, the one that had brought about their downfall, almost overpowered him.

Instead, he turned his back and finished taking off the shirt, feeling a little like a male stripper.

"Here, you'd better put this back on," she reminded him, holding the arms of his jacket for him.

"Thanks." He buttoned the coat, then turned his attention to Diamond.

"Can I help?"

"You might hold the reins. He could get a little skittish if it's painful."

After he'd wrapped Diamond's ankle, he looked at Allie again. She'd been remarkably calm about the entire incident. "Are you ready?"

"Yes, of course."

He extended his gloved hand and she willingly offered hers. Taking the reins from her, he led both her and Diamond back down the path toward home.

And remembered the question he'd asked Allie just before he kissed her.

"Why isn't there anyone in New York City?"

"There are millions of people there."

"Allie, you know what I'm asking. Have you ever married?"

"No, there wasn't time. I had an agenda, remember? Even as a freshman, I had my life mapped out.''

She didn't look at him, keeping her gaze on the path they were following. Maybe that was because of their accident.

''Yes, you did. But you made time for me.''

''Yes, well, afterward, it seemed more efficient to eliminate romance from my endeavors. In my family we don't have good luck with—with men.''

''You haven't dated at all?'' he asked, unable to believe she'd lived as a nun. When he'd held her in his arms, she'd been a passionate, demanding lover.

''No, I didn't mean that. Just...while I was in university, I didn't bother. Once I moved to New York City and started working, I dated. But right now, there's no one.''

''Oh.''

They came to a particularly tricky part of the trail, and he let go of her hand to guide Diamond down with the least strain on his leg. When they were once again walking side by side, she said, ''I'm sorry you haven't had your big family. This is a perfect place to raise children.''

''Yeah, it is, isn't it? What about you? Don't you want to have children?''

Allison thought of her talk with Debra, the one that had led to the conversation with Skyler McMasters. "Yes, I want children," she said, and stepped up the pace of their walk, but she had to slow down again as she had trouble catching her breath.

"I think the high altitude is taking my breath away," she added, not wanting Mac to realize she was thinking about carrying his child.

"Don't try to go too fast. We may get hungry, but we should get back to the house long before dark," he assured her. "Actually, I might have some granola bars in my saddlebags. I carry some in case I miss a meal."

He pulled Diamond to a halt and moved to his side to go through the saddlebags. Allison stepped up to the horse's head and rubbed his velvety nose.

"Are you all right, Diamond? I'm sorry you got hurt," she whispered, though walking all the way back to the ranch house seemed safer than riding while being held in Mac's arms. It made her want too much.

"Here we go," Mac said, pulling two wrapped granola bars out. "At least we'll have a little sustenance."

She took hers with a brief thanks.

"Aren't you going to eat yours now?"

"I'm not really hungry. I think I'll wait a little while."

"Okay. I'm as tough as you, little lady. I'll wait, too." He slipped his bar into his coat pocket.

"Was that a John Wayne imitation?"

"You bet. The guests love that kind of thing."

"So you're an actor as well as a cowboy?"

He shrugged. "Sometimes. Billy is our real entertainer. Tonight, by the fire at the lake, he'll bring his guitar and sing. Sometimes the guests join in, and sometimes they just listen. He's really good."

"He's a nice man."

"Yeah." Then he began, "Do you think— No, that's not a fair question."

Her heart beat faster. "What?"

"I think Billy's in love with my mother. I guess I wanted to know if you'd noticed anything, but you haven't been here long enough for that."

With her heart settling back to its normal speed, she thought about his words. "Well, I did notice that he keeps an eye on her."

"Yeah. After Dad died, Billy took care of both of us until we came out of the shock. I don't know what we'd do without him." They walked in silence for a minute, then he asked, "But if he feels that way about Mom, why hasn't he said anything?"

"A lot of times, people are afraid to rock the boat. He's happy here. What if she were appalled by his feelings and he had to leave, start over?"

As she'd been when Mac had walked away. Except that choice hadn't been hers.

He seemed to be thinking about her response. "You could be right. It would be awkward if Billy asked Mom to marry him and she said no."

"It wouldn't bother you if your mother married him?"

He took her arm to help her over a fallen log. Afterward, he continued to maintain contact. "No. Mom and Dad had a great marriage, but he wouldn't want her to be alone. She's only fifty-six."

"Maybe Billy will take the risk."

Allison said nothing else. She was discovering she wasn't in as good shape as she'd thought. Her steps were dragging. Maybe her weakness was caused by a combination of the altitude and the fact that she'd scarcely slept for the past two weeks, waiting to see Mac again. She'd been living on nerves.

After another half hour, she asked if they could stop and rest.

"Of course. You should've said something earlier," Mac insisted. He led them off the trail about six feet to another fallen log. Dusting the log off with his glove, he indicated for Allison to sit down. "You'd better eat your granola bar now. It will boost your energy level."

Something had better boost her energy level, because she was ready to curl up in a little ball and go to sleep.

As if he realized how tired she was, Mac leaned against a tree and put his arm around her shoulders as she finished the last of the granola bar. "Put your head on my shoulder and rest for fifteen minutes. Then we'll start again. And if we're lucky, we'll get to the lake while some of the guys are there, getting it ready for tonight."

With that encouraging thought, Allison did as he said and found herself drifting off.

MAC STARED DOWN at her serene face as sleep overtook her. She was still beautiful, but she was stronger than she'd been as an eighteen-year-old. Now she was a woman, sure of herself, self-sufficient.

And more attractive than ever.

The kiss that had dumped them in the snow should've melted everything around them. Part of the need to kiss her had come from curiosity, to see if she still lit him up, as she once had.

Now he had the answer. So, what was he going to do about it? He knew that answer, too. If she wanted, they could have an affair for the rest of the week. But that would be it. She had more to lose now than she had when she was eighteen.

He didn't want a martyr for a wife. But he wanted Allie. As much as ever. He sighed and pulled her a little closer. That's why his marriage with Sherry had ended. Even though she'd resembled Allie in looks, she hadn't been Allie.

Where Allie was strong and determined, Sherry was weak. Where Allie fought her own battles, Sherry had clung, wanting everything done for her. Where Allie had laughed, Sherry whined.

As the cold began to set into his bones, he gently shook Allie awake. "Sweetheart? We've got to get moving, or we're going to freeze to death."

"Oh. Of course. I must've drifted off."

"Yeah," he agreed with a grin. Standing, he pulled her up. "It's not much farther until the lake will be in sight. Hopefully, we'll catch a ride back the rest of the way.''

With a sigh, she started down the path, his arm still around her, saying nothing.

She might be tired, but Allie wasn't a quitter.

Half an hour later, they stepped through the last of the trees, and Mac's hopes were realized. There were a group of workers at the lake.

He shouted and waved. His men would know there was a problem when they realized they weren't mounted on Diamond. Immediately one of the cowboys ran to the pickup parked nearby and headed in their direction.

''Hold on, Allie. Help's on the way.''

''They saw us?'' she asked with a sigh.

''Yeah. Are you feeling all right? Can you feel your toes?''

''Yes, but I'll admit I'm cold and tired.''

He saw the weariness in her face, but not once had she complained.

''Soon you'll be in the pickup, and we'll have you back at the house in no time.''

They met the pickup near the bottom of the hill. Billy opened the door and got out. ''You two okay?''

''We're not hurt, but we've had a long walk. Allie here has about had it. Can you take her to the house, Billy, and get Mom to give her some lunch and then let her take a nap?''

''Sure can. Right this way, little lady.''

''Aren't you coming?'' Allie asked, her gaze going to Mac's face.

''I need to stay with Diamond. I'll be there later, I promise.'' He dropped a kiss on her lips, then gently pushed her toward Billy, ignoring his friend's surprise. ''Take care of her.''

Billy nodded and led her away.

Mac watched the truck disappear before he joined his men around the fire they'd started. He shouldn't have kissed Allie in front of Billy, but he hadn't been able to resist. Just as he hadn't been able to resist her ten years ago.

Why this one woman had such an effect on him, he didn't know. But he did know that nothing had changed. If he was only going to be given a week with Allie, so be it. He didn't want to waste the gift he'd been given. That she would return to New York, leaving him again, was understood. But for one week, he'd hold heaven in his arms.

CHAPTER FIVE

ALLISON AWAKENED, feeling more rested than she had in weeks. The semidarkened room was so peaceful and quiet she realized at once she wasn't in New York.

Slowly she remembered her ride with Mac, cradled in his arms, their bodies pressed to each other. Then the fall, and the long walk back to the lake. The conversation they'd had a decade too late.

She should get up soon, to go to the ice-skating. It sounded like fun. Fun had been absent from her life for a long time.

After several more minutes of remembering bits and pieces of the day, Allison realized the room was growing brighter. Startled, she checked the clock beside her bed.

It read 7:08 a.m.

Stunned, she stared at the clock until it changed to 7:09. It was working. Then she confirmed the time with her wristwatch. She'd slept fifteen hours.

She headed for the shower to wash away the last of the cobwebs. If she gained nothing else from her trip, she at least had caught up on rest.

A few minutes later, she went downstairs in search of food and ran into Myrna in the hallway.

"How are you feeling?"

"Like a slugabed. I'm sorry I didn't wake up for the ice-skating last night."

Myrna laughed. "There are plenty of ice-skating times left. I'm just glad you weren't hurt. Are you hungry?"

"Starved. When is breakfast served?"

"In about half an hour, but some of the staff are eating now. You're welcome to join them if you don't mind eating in the kitchen."

"I'd love to."

She followed Myrna back into the kitchen.

A man wearing a chef's hat called from across the room. "Myrna, your breakfast is ready."

"Great. I have a new customer for you, Avery. What would you like, Allie?"

"Eggs and toast."

"Give her an American-style," Billy called out.

Allison turned to greet the older man.

"Thank you, Billy. How are you this morning?"

"Not as good as you. All that sleep put some sparkle in your eyes." He grinned at her and patted the empty chair on his left. Since Myrna was taking the one on his right, Allison sat where he indicated.

"Careful, Billy, or I'm going to get jealous." Myrna's smile told everyone she was teasing.

"Aw, darlin', you know no one can hold a candle to you."

Allison remembered Mac's talk about his mother and Billy and watched the two of them out of the corner of her eye. The intimate look they exchanged made Allison think of lovers.

Mac's entrance distracted her.

"Well, Sleeping Beauty got up," he said with a chuckle, grabbing the empty seat next to her.

"Good morning. I'm sorry I slept so long."

"I'm not. I think you needed to rest."

"But I wanted to ice-skate and hear Billy sing."

"We'll do it again tomorrow night," Mac assured her.

"What's on the agenda for today?" she asked, amazed at how eagerly she awaited his answer.

"Today, we're going to try a different kind of horse," he said before he took a sip of coffee.

"You mean I get a horse of my own?" she asked.

Myrna choked on her orange juice. "What did you ride yesterday?"

Allison looked around cautiously, noticing how everyone seemed to be waiting for her answer. "Uh, Mac and I shared his horse so I could get used to being on horseback. I've never ridden before."

"Oh," Myrna said, drawing out the single syllable. "I see."

Allison wanted to know what the other woman saw, but Mac's red cheeks warned her not to ask.

He cleared his throat. "I meant we're going to take the snowmobiles today to move a herd. Anyone who wants can come along."

Allison frowned. "I've never driven a snowmobile before, so I guess I can't."

Billy laughed. "This time, all the dudes will be riding behind a cowboy. We don't take chances with our herd."

"Then I'd like to go."

"You really think you'll enjoy it?" Mac asked, staring at her.

"Why not? I enjoyed yesterday. As Billy said, it's beautiful here. I should enjoy it while I can." Even the thought of going back home cast a shadow over her high spirits.

"Yeah. While you can. It's a long way to New York City."

"Have you always lived in New York City?" Myrna asked.

"No. I've lived in Chicago, Kansas City, Washington D.C. and Los Angeles. Then I went to school at Princeton with Mac. After I graduated I went to New York," Allison explained.

"Good heavens, child, you've moved a lot. It must've been hard on you."

The sympathy in Myrna's gaze almost brought tears to Allison's eyes, and she wasn't a crier. "Yes, my childhood was quite different from Mac's."

"That's all right," Billy said. "It's never too late to smarten up."

"Smarten up?"

"Learn to get out of those big, stinking cities and live the good life in God's country," he explained with a grin.

Allison couldn't help but return his grin. "I don't think I'd find a job out here in the middle of nowhere."

"What kind of work do you do?" Myrna asked.

Mac answered before Allison could. "She's vice president of computer operations at a big import-export company." His voice was crisp, formal, and brought Allison's gaze to his face.

"Computers? Wow, we could use you here," Myrna exclaimed.

"Mom! I said I'd get to things soon," Mac protested. He frowned down at his plate, refusing to look at Allison.

"But Mac used to be terrific with a computer," Allison exclaimed, looking first at Myrna, then Mac.

"It's not that he doesn't know how to do the work. He's too busy. *I'm* the one who can't figure out how to turn the thing on." She shrugged. "We'll probably have to hire someone soon to get caught— Allie, we could hire you!"

Mac gave a harsh laugh. "We couldn't afford her, Mom."

"Oh." Myrna looked embarrassed.

"Actually," Allison said, lifting her chin and glancing from Mac to his mother, "if you have a couple of hours, Myrna, I'd be happy to teach you enough so that you could do some of the work."

"I'll teach my mother what she needs to know," Mac snapped, and everyone at the table got quiet.

Allison pushed her half-filled plate away from her. Suddenly her appetite had disappeared. "Thanks for the early breakfast, Myrna. Billy, what time should I come down for the snowmobile roundup?"

"But you haven't finished your breakfast," Myrna protested.

After a quick look at Mac, Billy answered, "About nine o'clock out by the arena."

"I'll be there, and I ate a lot, Myrna. Don't worry about me."

Because she certainly wasn't going to intrude into the McCall family business ever again! Once again Mac had made it clear she didn't fit into his world.

AS SOON AS THE DOOR SWUNG shut behind Allie, Mac relaxed—until his mother attacked him.

"Mac! How could you be so rude?"

"Yeah, boy, what's gotten into you?" Billy demanded, frowning at him.

Even Avery, who usually had little good to say about the guests, complained. "She seemed like a nice lady."

"She is a nice lady!" Mac roared, rising from the table. "But she's a New York lady who makes a lot more than all of us put together. It's ludicrous to offer her a job here!" Without waiting for more complaints, he stalked out of the kitchen.

What was wrong with everyone? Did they think he wanted Allie's pity? Didn't his mother realize a woman with Allie's credentials would scorn the two-bit job of inputting information into their computers? He wanted the week with Allie. But he didn't want their differences rubbed in his face. He just wanted to love her as he used to.

He was halfway to the barn when he realized someone was following him. Spinning around, he faced Billy. "What do you want?"

"Your mother is worried about you. It's not like you to act that way. She's afraid you're coming down with something."

Mac cocked his fists on his waist, prepared to blast Billy. Then he let out a long breath and his shoulders slumped. "I am. Rampant stupidity."

"What are you talking about, boy?"

"Ten years ago, I—I fell in love with Allie."

Billy frowned. "Was that the same year your dad died and you finished school?"

"Yeah."

"So what happened?"

Mac inhaled deeply. "I assumed—I wasn't thinking clearly. I expected her to drop her studies and come home with me, to marry me."

"She said no?" Billy asked, his surprise soothing to Mac's aches.

"She suggested I sell the ranch and take Mom back to the East Coast."

Billy was shocked. "No!"

"Yeah."

"Didn't you explain about the ranch, the tradition, the…everything?"

Mac started walking toward the barn, irritated that he'd let his emotions control his tongue. "No."

Billy caught up with him and grabbed his arm. "What do you mean, no?"

"I walked out." He looked into Billy's gaze and then away. "It was too much," he said in a low voice. "I'd just lost Dad. Life was going to change so much. I wanted Allie with me. But—I couldn't fight for her. I didn't have the strength."

"And now?"

Mac crossed to the corral fence and leaned against it. "It's too late. The lady has a killer job, what she's worked for all these years. You think she's going to give it up now when she wouldn't ten years ago? When it was all just a dream?''

''I don't know, but I'd be asking if I felt the way I think you do.''

Billy made it all sound so simple. It angered Mac. The years he'd ached for Allie. Not just her body, but her mind, her laughter, her love. ''Yeah, like you've asked Mom!''

Billy froze. Finally he said in a monotone, ''I asked her. She said no.'' Then he walked away.

Mac stared after him, his brain unable to function. Finally, he shook his head and turned toward the barn. Hell, the way he was going, he figured he'd have no friends at all by lunchtime.

ALLISON SQUARED her shoulders, opened the back door and hurried after the other guests who had decided to ride snowmobiles this morning. She'd considered staying in her room to avoid Mac, but she wasn't a coward.

She'd paid for her week at a dude ranch and she was going to get her money's worth.

Even if it killed her.

When she caught up with the others, she smiled brightly and aligned herself with several single women. They walked over to where the snowmobiles were lined up and Billy and four other cowboys were gathered. Allie relaxed when she realized Mac wasn't in sight.

Until he spoke from behind her.

"You're on the last one, Allie."

She spun around to stare at him. "Why?"

"Because that's the one I've assigned you."

The lady beside her, Marjorie, asked, "Which one is mine, Mac?"

Allison's gaze narrowed as he blinked in surprise, then said, "I think you're on number three, Marjorie. Check with Billy, though."

As Marjorie walked away, Allison demanded, "Why don't I have to check with Billy?"

He put his hands on his hips and stared at her, his jaw squared. "Because you're riding with me."

She stiffened. "I'd rather ride with someone else."

"Tough."

Stunned, she sputtered. "B-but that's not—"

He caught her chin between his fingers. "Sweetheart, I didn't mean to hurt your feelings at breakfast. I was embarrassed by Mom's offer. But I've only got a few days with you, and you're gonna put your arms around me, not some other cowboy."

There was a lot to consider in his response, but the last part caught her attention. "Why would I put my arms around you?"

"So you won't fall off." He took her hand and guided her toward the last snowmobile as Billy sorted out the other guests.

Something about Billy caught her eye as she followed Mac. "Is Billy all right?"

"Nope. You're not the only one I offended this morning."

More to think about.

"Did you bring gloves?" Mac asked as he straddled the machine.

She nodded. "Should I put them on?" she asked. "It feels almost warm out here." The sun was shining brightly, with almost no wind in the shelter of the barn.

"Yeah, put them on, and your helmet, then climb aboard."

She swung her leg over the back of the machine after donning her gloves. Then she discovered there wasn't a lot more space between their bodies than there'd been on Diamond. She suppressed a groan at the thought of being pressed against Mac for several hours.

Over his shoulder, Mac ordered, "Snuggle up and wrap your arms around my waist. You're going to need to hold on tight."

Allison hadn't quite forgiven him for their early morning disagreement and assumed he was exaggerating. She took hold of his jacket.

"Ready?" Mac called out to the others after starting his snowmobile.

Then he roared off across the snow.

Allison was almost left behind, but she grabbed his body with both arms. Forget keeping some distance between them—she opted for survival. With her eyes closed.

She was relieved when he slowed to a stop about fifteen minutes later. Fearing she'd left a permanent imprint of her face on his back, she lifted her head and opened her eyes.

"Are we finished?" she asked, wishing her voice sounded stronger, but she was having trouble catching her breath.

"Finished? We're just getting started. There's the herd we're moving. You need to really hang on tight now. We'll be doing some extra maneuvering."

Allison gulped. More maneuvering? "Maybe I should get off and watch."

"Get off? Aren't you having fun?" He twisted to look back at her.

How could she tell him the truth? Even if she was mad at him, she didn't want to disappoint him. "Oh, yes," she said, hoping he wouldn't notice she was clenching her teeth through her smile. "I'm enjoying it."

"Good." He turned his attention to the other snowmobiles that had pulled up beside them. "Everybody okay? We're ready to start moving the cattle, so hold on tight. We'll stop about halfway back and have a picnic."

Allison almost groaned aloud. Great. Food in her stomach. She didn't think it would stay there if she rode on the snowmobile much longer. How would Mac react if she threw up on him?

With a cowboy whoop, Mac, unaware of her misery, dashed across the snow, with Allison holding on for dear life.

She didn't know how long they rode, urging the cattle back toward the ranch house. Sometimes, she actually found herself relaxing as Mac slowed the machine behind some particularly lazy cattle. During those times, she lifted her head and took in the clean, cold air, the beauty of the snow, complemented by the evergreen trees and stately leaf-bare aspens.

Then he'd rev the motor and she'd take her death grip around his middle. Off they'd go, chasing some stupid cow that decided to go in the opposite direction.

When he finally came to a stop, Allison

looked up, assuming it was time for the picnic lunch he'd promised everyone.

But as the herd moved away, the other snowmobiles continued their pursuit.

"Why are we stopped?"

He killed the motor and looked over his shoulder at her. "We need to talk."

CHAPTER SIX

SHE'D BEEN UNABLE to think about his earlier remarks, not when she feared for her life. "Now?"

"Where else are we going to talk without being interrupted? If I go to your room, someone will see me and start rumors."

Rumors she wished were true.

That thought came unbidden and she quickly drew her arms away from him and climbed off the snowmobile. "Of course," she said briskly, trying to sound businesslike. "What do we need to talk about?" She stood with her arms crossed, staring at him.

"First of all, I wanted to apologize for my rudeness at breakfast."

"Please—"

"No, I need to say this. Mom doesn't understand what kind of job you have. She didn't realize how inappropriate—"

"Your mother didn't embarrass me." She

kept her voice even, unwilling to admit any emotion.

He let his head fall forward, then straightened and adjusted the cowboy hat that had replaced his safety helmet. "Okay."

"And I didn't mean to intrude. It won't happen again."

"Allie—"

"Is there anything else? Because I'm getting hungry."

"Yes, there is something else," he said with determination.

"What?"

"I don't know what to do. You asked about Billy. Well, I accused him—that is, I asked him why he hadn't talked to Mom about...about being in love with her."

The abrupt change of subject caught her by surprise, but she remembered her impression of Myrna and Billy at breakfast. "What did he say?"

"He said he'd asked her and she'd said no."

"You mean he proposed marriage?" Allison asked. "And she turned him down?"

"Yeah, that's what I figure. Should I say anything to Mom?"

"Are you sure?" she asked.

"I can't think what else he meant. Why?"

"Well, they seem so close. This morning I thought—" She immediately clamped her lips shut.

"What?"

"Nothing. I'm sure I was wrong."

"I won't know until you tell me what we're talking about." He was beginning to sound irritated, as he had at breakfast.

She really regretted her slip. "Uh, the way they were looking at each other, it made me think they were lovers. But I'm probably wrong."

Mac didn't move, but Allison watched him clench his hands until the knuckles turned white. "Mac, I—"

"He's sleeping with her, and they're not married," he finally said, sounding outraged.

"He said he asked her."

"That can't be right. She wouldn't—she couldn't—"

She'd had enough. "Isn't this a little like the pot calling the kettle black?"

"What do you mean?"

"Really, Mac! I don't know about your love life the past ten years, but you certainly slept with me without—"

Wrong thing to say.

"Well, thanks for that explanation. This is

different.'' Without warning, Mac brought the motor roaring to life. "Let's go."

Allison climbed on, and they zipped over the snow toward the disappearing herd. She held on with her death grip again, fearful he *intended* to leave her behind this time.

MAC'S HEAD WAS SPINNING. Allie had to be wrong. Not that he objected to his mother— He didn't want to think about that. But he'd noticed nothing between his mom and Billy except friendship and...

He was going crazy.

When they caught up with the others, they were at the picnic site. One of the cowboys had driven out from the ranch house earlier and built a fire. The scent of chili and coffee made the air even more fragrant.

Mac parked the snowmobile. After Allie got off, she waited for him to move. He was still debating what he should do.

"Mac? Aren't you going to have lunch?" Allison asked, breaking through his thoughts.

"Yeah, I guess," he answered without smiling. Swinging his leg over the machine, he stood and marched toward the group gathering around the fire.

Hurried steps behind him told him Allison

was coming, but he didn't expect her to grab his arm. "What?" he asked.

"You're not going to say anything to Billy *now,* are you?" she asked, her eyes widening.

"I just want to know what's really going on," he muttered, unable to concentrate on anything else.

"But, Mac, you can't—"

"What now?" Billy asked, coming toward them. He was still stiff, not relaxed as usual.

"I'll go on ahead," Allison hurriedly said, and came around Mac. But this time, he grabbed her.

"No. I think you should stay. You're the one who—"

"What's going on with you two?" Billy asked. "You still fighting?"

"No." Mac stared at Billy. He'd been his friend for twenty-six years. He'd taught him a lot about ranching. He'd supported him when his dad died, and he'd worked especially hard ever since to help make the ranch a success. But, in spite of everything, Mac couldn't hold back his question.

"I want to know how long you've been sleeping with Mom."

Billy acted as if he'd slugged him. His face

pale, he stared back at him in silence. Finally. he said, "Two years."

"When did you ask her to marry you?"

"Two years ago."

"You love her, don't you, Billy?" Allison asked softly.

"A'course I do. I know I don't...I'm not good enough for her to marry, but—"

"Did she say that?" Mac asked with a frown.

Billy blew out a deep breath. "She said she couldn't marry until you were settled." He gave a shaky laugh. "But seein' as how you're a grown man and all, I figured she was lettin' me down easy."

The three of them stood there, isolated from the others, and Mac didn't know what to say. The more he thought about Billy and his mother, the more he believed she loved him, too. So why was she stalling?

"I'm going to the house," he abruptly said.

"Here now, you're not going to confront Myrna, are you?" Billy demanded, stepping in front of Mac to stop him.

"If I'm the excuse she's using, I think I have the right to know what's going on."

"But, boy, she might...might send me away. And I'd die."

Billy stood there looking so vulnerable, it almost broke Mac's heart. He squeezed the older man's shoulder. "Whatever happens, you won't be sent away. You're part of the ranch, Billy. You know *that*."

"I don't know if I *could* stay if she didn't want me," Billy replied. "But I guess you're right. It's time to fish or cut bait. I've been living in a fool's paradise." He turned back toward the machines. "I'm comin' with you."

"I'm not going to be left behind," Allison protested, running after Mac and Billy. "Billy, who rode on the back of your snowmobile?"

"Damn, I forgot. Marjorie," Billy said, looking confused.

"Tell her to ride back with the cook in the truck," Mac ordered, never breaking stride.

Billy hurried back to the fire for a brief conversation, then returned to his machine. Mac sat astride his snowmobile, with Allison behind him, waiting.

"Are you sure this is what you want to do?" Allison asked softly.

"No. No, I'm not sure at all, but I think I need to know what's going on."

"Let's go," Billy said, his voice tight with tension, and they set off on the ride back to the house.

Myrna was in her office, trying to read a

computer manual, when they opened the door. She looked up, a bright smile on her lips. "Hi. Just in time. I don't understand any of this."

Mac stepped into the office, followed by Billy. Allison hung by the door. She said softly, "I should go."

Mac reached for her hand, holding her in place.

Myrna looked at all of them. "What's wrong? Why are you all back this early? Has something happened?"

Mac didn't know how to answer any of the questions.

Billy stepped forward. "Darlin', Mac knows."

"Knows what?" Myrna asked, puzzled.

"About us."

Her gaze widened as it traveled to her son. Then with her cheeks bright red, she lifted her chin and stared back at Mac. "It's none of his business."

"It is if you're using me as an excuse not to marry Billy," he returned.

Her cheeks turned from red to pale. "My reasons are my business," she snapped.

"You mean you lied to me?" Billy asked. "You used Mac so you wouldn't hurt my feelings?"

"No!"

"Do you think Billy isn't good enough to marry?" Mac demanded. "He's a good man."

Myrna stood up. "Of course he is! I love him!"

"Then why aren't you marrying him?" Mac pushed.

Myrna moved edgily toward the window. "We first—first talked about it two years ago." She looked at Mac, as if wondering if he understood the significance of her words. Finally, she added, "You were going through your divorce. I thought it would make things difficult for you."

Guilt filled Mac. He'd been so wrapped up in his own misery, he'd never noticed anything about his mother. She'd just been there for him.

Myrna's gaze swung from her son to Billy. "And since then, he's never asked again, so I figured he'd only proposed because he thought he had to."

Billy erupted. "Woman, are you crazy? I worship every inch of you. I'd give everything I own to marry you, to care for you."

Allison tugged on Mac's hand and whispered, "I think that's our cue to exit."

Mac, fascinated with what was happening, turned to her. "What?"

"Come on," she insisted, tugging on his hand.

They stepped out into the hallway, and Allison closed the door behind them.

Mac stared at her, then broke into a huge grin. "You know what, Allie? I think I'm about to get a new daddy."

And he hoped he deserved to be forgiven for his lack of awareness of the people around him. How ironic that it took Allie's return to his life for him to awaken to others' needs. Perhaps the power of his own needs had made him more sensitive. He hoped so. And, this time when she left him, he intended to face his pain with more courage.

DINNER THAT NIGHT was a celebration. Myrna and Billy wandered around, holding hands, a dazed look on their faces. The guests, as well as everyone who worked on the ranch, were excited about the upcoming marriage.

They hadn't set a date yet, but Billy wasn't interested in any long engagement.

Allison watched them, enjoying their happiness, but feeling more alone than ever. Her gaze would wander to Mac, who was taking credit for his mother's nuptials. How she wished she had a future with him.

"Allison?"

She turned in surprise to find one of the waitresses standing behind her. "Yes?"

"You have a phone call. Do you want to take it in your room?"

"Yes, of course." She hurried up the stairs. It had to be Debra calling, of course. She'd thought about phoning her friend several times, but since she had nothing good to report, she hadn't.

"Hello?"

"Allison, why haven't you called? I've been dying to hear how you're doing," Debra said.

"Hi, Deb. How's the family?"

"Fine. I didn't call to talk about them. Did you find him? Is he married?"

"Yes, I found him. He's not married now. He got divorced about two years ago."

"You don't sound excited," Debra assessed.

"No." She couldn't let herself, because Mac hadn't shown interest in much of anything but lust.

"No fire? He doesn't turn you on anymore?"

Allison sighed. "That's not the problem."

"Then what is?"

"He's not interested. I mean, I think there's something there physically...but he loves it here. He doesn't want to come to New York."

"You asked him?"

"No, but he's made it clear."

After a pause, Debra said, "Nothing much is going on at the office, except a problem with the Neilson Group."

Allison was surprised by the lack of interest she felt. "Really?"

"You want the details?"

"Not really. I'll deal with it when I get back." Depression filled her. She didn't want to think about leaving.

"What about you staying there?" Debra suddenly asked. When Allison said nothing, Debra added, "You know I'd miss you desperately, but I want you to be happy."

"We haven't discussed anything like that."

"Would you want to?"

Allison realized how much things had changed since she'd arrived a few days ago. Yes, she'd be happy here with Mac. And not just because of Mac.

And she'd be miserable in New York without him.

"Yes," she finally whispered into the receiver.

"Then what are you going to do?" Debra asked, sympathy in her voice.

Allison relaxed, even chuckled. It was as if

she'd suddenly realized that she was in charge of her happiness. For once in her life, she would do what felt right to her, not what was on her list, not what would make her different from her mother. "I'm going to grab me a cowboy."

"That's my girl!" Debra cheered.

"It doesn't mean he'll agree. He's stubborn and...and wonderful. But I'm going to give it my all, and one difficult cowboy is going to know I've been here, if nothing else!"

CHAPTER SEVEN

ALLISON'S GOOD INTENTIONS got sidetracked by a snowstorm.

Not that it changed her mind. Having finally figured out what was important in life, she was prepared with a plan. She was going to make Mac suffer. She was going to tempt him like never before. She was going to love him.

As soon as she could find him.

The storm kept the guests in the house the next day and the cowboys out working, feeding the cows, rescuing them from snowdrifts, until late. Myrna and the household staff were left to entertain the guests.

Avery taught the ladies how to weave bread baskets. One of the waitresses gave a class on needlepoint. A waiter taught some guests how to make lures for fly-fishing. Allison created some puzzles and games on the computer for the children and printed them up.

"Allie, these are wonderful," Myrna said with a big smile. "It's sweet of you to help."

"I enjoy it. I'll be glad to input some of that data you mentioned, too, if you'll show me what you want done."

"But you're a guest! I can't let you work."

"I hope I'm a friend, too," Allison said. Myrna looked at her, a question in her gaze, and Allison smiled.

"Do you think you could ever live outside New York?" Myrna asked, her smile matching Allison's.

"I think so. It depends. I've been giving it some thought."

"The snowstorm doesn't scare you?"

Allison let her gaze drift to the window. "If you can survive it, I can, too. But I might like it better if certain people could stay inside with us."

"Me, too. But that's part of the life, you know. It may be a little harder than life in the city, but the rewards are great."

Allison grinned. "It's not easy in the city, either."

"Well, come on. I'll show you what I'm supposed to do on the computer, and will be eternally grateful if you can help me with it."

After dinner that evening, Allison was frustrated. She'd had a productive day, but she'd seen nothing of Mac. She refreshed her lipstick and perfume and went to the kitchen.

"Avery, have the cowboys come in?"

"All but Mac and Billy. I've got their supper in the oven."

"Why don't you go on to bed? I'll serve them and then clean up," she suggested. It would give her a good excuse to stay with Mac while he ate.

Avery looked shocked. "I don't think Myrna would—"

"Myrna would what?" that lady asked with a weary smile, entering the kitchen.

Allison explained. "I offered to serve Mac and Billy and clean up so Avery can go ahead and rest. He's had a long day."

"Are those the only two who haven't come in?"

Allison nodded.

"Allie's right, Avery. You've put in a full day's work and more. Go on. We'll take care of those two."

With a relieved sigh, he left the kitchen.

"That was thoughtful of you, Allie."

She grinned. "Don't give me too much credit, Myrna. My motives were selfish."

Myrna grinned back. "Mine, too. Want a cup of decaf while we wait?"

MAC AND BILLY FOUGHT their way through the storm to the big house almost an hour after they'd sent the rest of their staff to dinner. The fierce wind seemed to blow through their clothes, and they were thoroughly chilled when they stumbled into the kitchen—to find two ladies waiting for them.

Mac heated up at once.

"What are you doing here?" he asked, more gruffly than he'd intended.

To his surprise, she didn't get angry with him. "I offered to clean up after you and Billy eat. Avery was beat."

He frowned. "You're a guest."

She was already on her way to the oven. Myrna responded as she poured them hot coffee. "If you want to eat, I wouldn't look a gift horse in the mouth."

Two plates filled with roast beef, potatoes and beans had Mac closing his lips at once. He wasn't going to chance getting his food dumped in his lap.

As hungry as he was, he still noticed when Allie leaned close to put the plate before him. Her elusive scent mingled with that of the roast beef. If he turned his head, his lips could've clung to hers, as Billy's did to Myrna's.

"Thank you," he said stiffly.

"You're welcome," she returned, and sat down beside him.

"We can clean up after ourselves," he added, still frowning. It had been a long day, and his resistance was low.

"Speak for yourself, boy," Billy urged. "I'm about done in."

Myrna rubbed his shoulders. "You worked too long today."

"Yep. But the storm's playing itself out. And tomorrow will be an easier day."

"Will we get to have the ice-skating tomorrow evening?" Allison asked.

"I didn't know you liked ice-skating that much," Mac growled. He wanted to be friendly, relaxed, but she tied him up in knots. As tempting as her body was to him—and it was almost irresistible—her waiting for him, sitting beside him, caring…made him ache with want. With the need to have her in his life, not just his bed.

"I enjoy it. And tomorrow's New Year's Eve, the day before my birthday."

Damn. He'd forgotten that. It was also the anniversary of the night they'd met. He'd been at a New Year's Eve party at a friend's apartment, bored. Sipping a beer, he'd been watching the foolishness going on, thinking about leaving, when Allie had entered with a girl-friend. For some reason, his body had immediately come to attention. The other women had ceased to exist. He'd cut her out from the herd before she knew what was happening.

They'd spent the evening talking. She'd told him her birthday was New Year's Day. He'd teased her about being a New Year's baby.

"Your birthday!" Myrna exclaimed. "We'll have Avery bake you a birthday cake. How exciting!"

Allie smiled, then turned to look at Mac. "It's my favorite time of the year because of the good memories I have."

He stared at her. Was she trying to tell him something? He didn't think her mother played in any of those favorite memories. Was she talking about her years in New York? Or could she be referring to their time together?

"I guess you celebrate big-time in New York," he said, watching her.

"No, not really." She didn't duck her head in shyness. That had never been Allie's way. Instead, she smiled, letting her gaze rove over his face, making his skin tingle.

"How old are you gonna be?" Billy asked.

Myrna protested. "You're not supposed to ask a lady."

"Hell—I mean, heck—she's not old enough to care," Billy protested.

"I'll be twenty-nine."

"That's very young to be a vice president, isn't it?" Myrna asked.

His mother's question reminded him why he didn't grab Allie and head for the nearest bedroom. Because she'd be going back to New York in a few days. He concentrated on his dinner.

"Yes."

There was an awkward silence. Mac kept eating.

"Well, we'll certainly celebrate your birthday," Myrna finally said.

The two ladies smiled at each other, and Mac wondered at their friendship. "What did y'all do today?"

Myrna and Allie told funny stories about their day during the rest of dinner, entertaining the men with mishaps. Particularly the treasure hunt they'd arranged for the children. The kids had loved it, but one little boy had gotten a little too enthusiastic and discovered one of the older ladies in the shower.

They'd had to go over the rules again.

Mac chuckled as Allie described the screaming and panic that had followed. Since the little boy was only four, the lady forgave him. He explained he'd heard the water and thought the fish on his list would be there.

"Fish?" Billy asked.

"We had in mind the stuffed one on the wall in the dining room. Andrew wanted to find a live one," Myrna explained.

Mac had gradually relaxed, telling himself he was treating Allie like a friend. One who visited once every ten years.

Until she laid her hand on his shoulder. Then he almost jumped out of his chair.

"Do you want some dessert?" she asked, leaning toward him again.

Damn it, what was wrong with the woman? It was as if she wanted to touch him. As enticing as that thought was, he knew better. He'd thought he could handle an affair with Allie, but the way his body reacted to hers, that would be a foolish idea.

Even worse, if he came to depend on her presence, to need her in his life to survive, as he had felt tonight when he'd found her waiting for him, how could he go on when she left him? The best thing to do was to avoid her. Starting now.

"No! No dessert. I've got things to do." He

shoved himself from the table and hurried out of the room.

A cold shower would be number one on his list.

THE STORM WAS OVER by noon the next day. With Mac's testiness last night, Allison believed she was making progress. At least he hadn't ignored her.

She began to prepare for the evening.

New Year's Eve. The day before her birthday. The time to begin a new life.

The anniversary of her meeting with Mac.

When the hay wagon pulled up in the barnyard that evening, ready for the guests to board, she searched for Mac and found him standing a few feet away.

"Aren't you going to ride on the wagon?" she asked, stepping close to him.

"I usually go ahead on one of the snowmobiles to be sure everything is ready," he said, and moved a step away.

"Oh. Can I ride with you? I think I'm allergic to hay," she added as he started to shake his head.

He frowned. "I don't remember you being allergic to anything."

"We didn't have a lot of hay at Princeton,"

she reminded him. In fact, she wasn't allergic, but it was a good excuse to ride with him.

"You could go with Billy. He's going to drive the wagon, and you'd be on the front seat, not in the hay."

"I think Myrna's planning on sitting with Billy."

"Oh."

She waited for him to give in, saying nothing.

"All right. You can ride out with me. Did you find a pair of ice skates that fit you?"

She lifted her hand to show him the skates she held.

He reached for them, and she made sure his fingers covered hers, hoping that touch affected him as much as it did her.

"I'll put these on the wagon," he muttered, and hurried away from her.

When he returned, she was standing by the snowmobile, waiting.

"Are you sure you don't want to ride on the wagon? The guests really enjoy the hayride."

She smiled at his hopeful expression. If she didn't know better, she would think he disliked her. But she knew. He might not have marriage in mind, but he wanted her.

After he got on the snowmobile, she slid into place, loving the way his body heat spread to her. This time she didn't hesitate to wrap her arms around his strong body.

Without speaking, he started the machine and shot across the barnyard for the path to the lake. Allison laid her cheek against his back, content for the moment with her place in life.

When they reached the lake, several cowboys were already there, with a roaring fire lighting the area. They'd swept snow off the ice and the benches, and Avery had coffee and hot chocolate warming on the edge of the fire.

Several spotlights lit the ice so the skaters wouldn't stumble and fall, and a stereo system played romantic music.

"I had no idea you'd be so well prepared," Allison said with a smile. "Will you skate with me?"

"I didn't bring any skates," Mac said abruptly. "I have to supervise everyone."

She noted that the cowboys were surprised at his answer. "Oh. Well, I'm not ready to skate yet. Is there anything I can do to help?"

"No," he replied, looking away.

Avery, however, had another answer. "Could you get the cups for the drinks out of that box?"

"Sure." Since she wasn't making any progress with Mac, she spent the few minutes before the arrival of the wagon assisting a grateful Avery.

Once the guests arrived, she donned her skates and joined the others gliding over the ice, listening to Billy sing love songs, Myrna beside him. But she kept her eye on Mac. And noted that he kept his eye on her. Especially when she accepted invitations from some of the cowboys to skate.

As the evening began to wind down, she took off her skates and came up behind Mac, seated on one of the benches, the farthest from the fire, in the cold shadows.

Sliding her arms around his neck, she whispered, "Remember when we went skating?"

He grew very still before answering. "Yeah. You've improved."

She kissed his cheek. "Yes. I skate because I enjoy my memories."

"What are you up to, Allie? That's the second time you've referred to memories. What memories are you talking about?"

She rounded the bench and sat down beside him. "The times we spent together. Don't you enjoy those memories?"

"No!"

His determined coldness was getting to her.

"You seemed to be enjoying yourself at the time."

"Of course I was! You were...a terrific lover."

"Do you think I've forgotten?" she asked daringly.

He shifted away from her. "No. Your kisses still light me up as much as they ever did."

"So why have you been avoiding me?"

"You're trying to seduce me, but I don't understand why. We still have the same differences we always had."

She stared at him in the shadows. Time to lay her cards on the table. "Okay, I'm trying to seduce you. Is it wrong to wonder if we still have that magic?"

Instead of answering her, continuing to resist her, as she expected, Mac suddenly pulled her into a bear hug, his lips covering hers in a kiss that held all the magic of ten years ago.

CHAPTER EIGHT

SHE SHOULDN'T HAVE tempted him.

Mac lifted his lips from Allie's, his head spinning. It was as if no time had passed. He pulled her closer and slanted his lips across hers again, seeking what he'd wanted since he'd first seen her a few days ago: a return to their love-making.

As he kissed her, he unzipped her ski jacket, his hands eagerly searching her warm flesh. The soft sweater, silky to his touch, that he discovered under her jacket only urged him on. He slid his hands beneath it to stroke her breasts.

"It's cold, and someone might see us," she whispered as she pulled away.

Damn. He'd forgotten they weren't alone. The woman was dangerous. "Come on." He didn't bother explaining where they were going. He knew he should resist Allie because she would leave him soon, but he couldn't. His coldness toward her the past few days had kept her from touching him, but it hadn't relieved his needs, his hurt.

She'd pushed him past his limit tonight. He had to share this time with her, even though he knew she would leave him, hurt him, make his craving for her almost unbearable. What they had was too powerful.

He paused to whisper to Billy that he and Allie were going back to the house, then continued on to the snowmobile. When her body pressed against him and her arms held him, he wondered if they'd be able to reach his room before he burst into flames.

Leading her up the back stairs, behind the kitchen, Mac managed to avoid seeing anyone. Those guests who'd opted to watch a film and remain in the ranch house never knew they'd returned.

Outside his door, he paused. "Allie, are you sure? Because once you go in there with me, I'm not going to be able to stop. I've wanted you too long."

She smiled serenely at him. "I've wanted you, too."

He didn't need any more encouragement. Opening the door, he turned and swung her into his arms. She wrapped her arms around his neck and let him carry her into his room.

Into paradise.

He kicked the door shut, then moved to the foot of his bed. When he let her body slide down his, he almost shouted at the agony of wanting her so much. He pushed off her jacket, then slid his hands under her sweater. "Are you cold?" he whispered, trying to restrain himself.

"No," she whispered back. "I'm hot. All I can think about is you," she muttered before her lips sought his.

He took that as an invitation and began disrobing her, while their lips worked to make new memories that would rival the old. Or even be better.

She didn't hesitate to help him rid himself of his clothes, either. Her hands touched all of him, as if relearning his body. And he loved every excruciating minute of it.

They sprawled on the big bed, arms and legs entangled, lips seeking and loving, erasing ten years of longing. He couldn't believe how easily they came together, with no awkwardness, no stumbling. They were perfect together, as they'd always been.

"Now," Allie cried out, pulling him toward her. He'd been attempting to kiss each inch of her.

"Shh, baby, in a minute. I haven't had the chance to love you in so long…"

She tugged on him again. "Now, Mac, now. I can't wait. I want you so badly."

He couldn't resist those words. He positioned himself over her and entered, closing his eyes as he felt her warmth around him. "Oh, Allie," he said, sighing.

She hugged him close, her lips seeking his, and talking was forgotten. They mated, as they always had, with the passion of lovers who would be together forever. And it still wouldn't be enough.…

ALLIE LAY AGAINST MAC in the afterglow of their lovemaking, reveling in the beauty of the moment. She'd sometimes wondered if she'd imagined the perfection of their time together.

When he'd left, she hadn't understood how special their loving had been. In her anger, she'd been sure she would find someone else who could give her what Mac had. Someone who wouldn't walk away. Someone who would conform with her agenda.

She'd discovered her mistake.

No one even interested her. After she'd moved to New York, she'd tried to find a man who could take his place. She'd never even come close. A few times she'd encouraged men she'd found mildly attractive, hoping to rediscover the bond she'd had with Mac.

It hadn't worked that way.

Finally, she'd given up. As she'd approached her twenty-ninth birthday, she'd once again told herself she'd imagined the magic they'd shared.

Now she knew she hadn't.

With tears in her eyes, she snuggled against him, allowing her hands to continue to smooth their way across his muscular body.

"You keep doing that and I'm not going to let you rest," he growled.

She loved the burr in his voice after lovemaking. She'd forgotten his sexy whispers. With a smile, she answered his warning. "Okay," she said, and continued to stroke him.

"A definite invitation," he murmured, and pulled her on top of his heated body.

He still knew how to communicate.

WHEN ALLIE AWOKE the next morning, the sun was shining brightly through the windows. And she was alone.

She stretched under the covers, remembering Mac covering the two of them after loving her again. He'd been gentle and tender. Vaguely there was a memory of his kissing her this morning before he went to work.

When they married, she wouldn't be able to sleep in as she had this morning. She'd have duties, also. She smiled as she imagined her life, so changed from a week ago. The prospect of living on the ranch delighted her now.

Last week she couldn't imagine changing her life so completely. But she knew now that the love she and Mac shared wasn't something a person should ever give up. The most important things in life were not careers, theaters, things. People were what was important.

Here in Wyoming, she'd have Mac, and their children, if possible. And Myrna and Billy. A family. And a family was worth more than anything.

Even so, she'd still have her work. Oh, not the power and prestige on her vice presidency. But she'd discovered how empty those things were. When she was inputting data for Myrna, however, she'd recognized several different applications of the computer she could use to the ranch's benefit. An excitement had filled her as she'd envisioned charts and comparisons that would make decisions easier.

An excitement she hadn't felt for her work in a year or two filled her. She was beginning to realize that the higher she went in the company, the more structured and less creative her work became. Here she'd have a lot of freedom, and she'd be helping Mac.

Encouraged by her thoughts, she shoved back the covers and headed for Mac's shower. The hot water eased the stiffness of her body, unused to the lovemaking that had occupied their night. When she returned to the bedroom, wrapped in a towel, her spirits soaring, she discovered a note Mac had left her on the dresser.

She was thrilled at the evidence that he'd thought of her that morning. Opening the envelope, she eagerly read his message.

Happy birthday, baby. Why don't you move your things to my room until you leave? I don't want to sleep without you.

Mac

She frowned. Of course she was pleased that he wanted her in his bed every night. Until she left. That was what upset her. He hadn't dropped any hint that she might extend her stay. He didn't mention any desire for her to stay.

Just sex until she left.

She crumpled the note in her hand. Quickly pulling on her clothes from last night, she hurried to her own room. But not to pack. She wasn't leaving. And she wasn't moving.

Not until she had a conversation with Mac McCall.

NONE OF THE GUESTS were up early on New Year's Day, which left the cowboys plenty of time to take care of chores. Mac did his work with a satisfied smile on his face.

"Enjoying the day, boy?" Billy asked.

"Yeah, sure," he returned, not paying attention to Billy's question.

"You seem a mite more content than you were yesterday," Billy continued.

"More content?" Mac realized what Billy was driving at, and his cheeks flushed. "It's a beautiful day."

Billy chuckled. "Yeah. Beautiful. Want to make it a double wedding when your mom and I get hitched?"

Mac dropped the tack he'd been mending and stared at Billy. "What are you talking about?"

"I'm talking about that grin on your face, like a cat with a bowlful of cream."

"Billy, you're barking up the wrong tree. Allie and I— We may have enjoyed ourselves last night, but it's temporary. She'll be leaving tomorrow, like the rest of the guests." He frowned, hating to think of her departure, but he'd never hidden from the truth.

"You're a fool if you let her go," Billy stated.

"I don't have a choice."

The rest of the morning, he argued with himself, knowing Billy was right. What he had with Allie was special. He'd tried to find the same feeling with Shelly, hoping that because she looked a little like Allie that lightning would strike twice. He'd been wrong. Both of them had suffered because of his mistake.

And he would suffer when Allie left. But he'd known that before he'd taken her to bed last night.

He wasn't going to beg and plead for her to stay. He'd be matter-of-fact. Tell her goodbye. Tell her to look him up if she ever wanted to visit the West again. Tell her he might come to New York in a few months.

But he wouldn't tell her his heart would break when she left. He wouldn't tell her that he didn't expect to sleep well until she was in his arms again. Or that he loved her more than life itself.

Because he wouldn't ask her to sacrifice her dreams.

Suddenly the day didn't seem so beautiful.

WHEN ALLISON CAME DOWN to lunch, she didn't go near the kitchen, where the cowboys usually ate. She figured the longer she stayed away from Mac, the more time she had to prepare her attack.

Because she wasn't going to let him walk away from her.

Not like the last time.

She was prepared to fight for her happiness now, with whatever it took. If she could convince him to let her stay a little longer, she hoped he would recognize what they shared.

She hoped he'd agree, and tomorrow she'd call her boss, the president of her company, and ask for a leave of absence, giving her some extra time. He wouldn't be happy, but Allison couldn't worry about that. They'd find someone else to replace her. In fact, the man down the hall, who'd felt he'd been passed over when Allison got her promotion, would eagerly step in.

The only person who couldn't be replaced was Mac. She'd proved that to herself. Now she had to convince him.

After the noon meal, Myrna surprised her with the birthday cake she'd promised. Allison had assumed it would be a small celebration, but all the guests and cowboys were included.

Mac came to stand behind her chair, taking her by surprise. His touch sent a flood of heat through her. It was the first time she'd seen him since last night.

He squeezed her shoulders gently. "Blow out the candles, Allie," he suggested after everyone had sung the traditional song.

She did so, then, at Myrna's suggestion, began cutting the cake and passing out pieces to everyone. Mac never left her side. Finally she offered him a piece, after everyone had been served but the two of them.

"Cut yours, too, and let's go upstairs to eat ours," he whispered.

Her heart began beating faster. What did he have in mind? Would he offer her her heart's desire?

She did as he asked, noting Myrna watching them. She smiled at her, but her lips trembled. "Myrna, thank you for the cake. Tell Avery it's beautiful."

"I will. Are you two going to celebrate privately?"

Allison's cheeks grew even hotter. Did Myrna suspect what Mac had in mind? Allison was sure the tall cowboy beside her wasn't just planning on eating cake.

But she had a surprise for him, too.

She didn't intend to let herself be swayed by his touch until they had settled some things. But it would be hard....

Mac took her hand and led her to his room. As soon as they'd entered and he'd closed the door behind them, he took her plate of cake and put it on the dresser, along with his own.

"I see you got my note," he murmured, drawing her into his arms. "Did you move your stuff?"

"No," she said, her voice calm.

He frowned. "Why not? Are you worried about what people will say? You never used to worry about that."

"No, I'm not worried."

His arms fell away and he stepped back. "I don't get it. Tired of me already?"

"No."

"Allie, you're not giving me much to work with. What's going on?"

"I thought maybe you'd ask me to stay," she whispered, moving a little closer. Near enough that he could touch her by leaning forward. Tempting him.

"No," he protested hoarsely. "I'm not going to do that. You've achieved your dream. I'm not going to ask you to sacrifice it."

She surprised him by turning away. But instead of leaving, she kicked off the loafers she was wearing, unbuttoned her jeans and slid out of them. Then, without looking at him, she began unbuttoning the silky shirt she wore.

"What are you doing?" he demanded, his frown fierce. If he didn't concentrate hard, he was going to dive onto the bed, pulling her with him. After all, he hadn't come upstairs just to eat cake.

"I assumed you wanted to make love." She smiled at him as if she'd said it was a sunny day.

"Yeah," he whispered, his gaze never straying from her hands as they undid the last buttons.

"Okay." She slid out of the blouse, standing before him in lacy panties and bra. "Did you intend to remain dressed? It makes it more difficult."

"No, but—"

She interrupted him. "Do you want to remove the rest, or shall I?"

Her come-hither look was effective. His fevered brain told him he needed to ask her something, but his body didn't allow him time to think. The only words he could utter were "I'll do it myself."

His hands stroked her silky shoulders before

gently sliding her bra straps down. As if that act released all his inhibitions, they were both naked on the bed in seconds, repeating all the delights of the night before.

When their passion was spent, at least momentarily, he pulled her against him, holding her close. As long as he held her, he could keep at bay the despair that filled him when he remembered she'd be going home tomorrow.

"Mac?"

"Yeah, Allie?" he asked before briefly kissing her again.

"How much would it cost me to stay awhile if I slept in your room? I mean, I shouldn't have to pay full price, since I wouldn't be occupying a guest room. Of course, I'll pay for my meals, but—"

He kissed her. What she was saying didn't make sense, but he couldn't resist playing along. "How long would you want to stay?"

"As long as you want me."

Her quiet answer, ringing with sincerity, stunned him. He pulled away from her, staring at her beloved face, fighting the hope that rose in him.

She moved out of his arms and sat on the edge of the bed, her back to him. He knew he'd hurt her with his silence, but he didn't know what to say. "Allie, I—"

To his surprise, she stood, whirling to face him. Her magnificent beauty almost distracted him from her words. But not quite.

"Mac McCall, unless you're a lot stupider than I think you are, you'd better take what I'm offering. What we have doesn't come along every day. It hasn't come along in ten years, and I don't expect it to do so in the next fifty. Except with you!"

Her words angered him. He clambered off the bed to face her. "Do you think I don't know that? I married another woman because she looked like you! It didn't work. But the longer you stay here, tempting me, giving me a chance to believe in a future, like I did once before, the more it's going to hurt when you leave."

A smile tilted the corners of her lips, startling him. She lifted her hands to his chest and stroked his skin. "Who said I was going to leave?"

He almost believed her. Then he shook his head. "Allie, I can't go to New York."

"Not even for a visit? I'd like to show you around."

"Allie, I'm not talking vacation plans here.

I'm talking about our futures. Yours is in New York, living your dream. Mine is here.''

She pressed her lips against his collarbone. "Do you know what I discovered when I achieved my dream?" she asked conversationally, as if they weren't standing naked, pressed against each other.

"No, what?" he asked, trying to concentrate, but his hands were sliding up and down her spine, cupping her hips, pressing her against him.

"I didn't have the right dream."

He stilled.

"What did you say?"

"I didn't have the right dream. I had no one to share it with. And the one person I wanted to tell hadn't contacted me in ten years."

He buried his face in her neck. "Allie, I'm trying to explain that you can't have me *and* your dream." It hurt to say those words, but he wouldn't mislead her. And as much as he loved her, he couldn't live in New York. Not happily.

"Yes, I can."

His body had been ignoring his head, and his arousal was obvious to both of them. But he pulled away from her and strode to the window. Parting the curtains a little, he stared out at his snow-covered world.

Could he leave? Could he give up his home, his family, his occupation, to move to New York? Would it be worth it to be with Allie? Could he strike a compromise? Five years in the city, then five years here?

Her hands slid around him as she pressed herself to his back. "I can, because my dream has changed."

"Changed? How?" he demanded hoarsely, turning around to hold her.

"My dream is you, Mac. You and our children. Our family together." She took a deep breath and stepped away from him, leaving his arms empty.

"I'll go home tomorrow, if you can tell me you don't want me. If you can tell me that the magic we share doesn't matter. If you can tell me that you don't want my children."

"But, Allie," he whispered as he pulled her back against him, "are you sure you can be happy here? I don't want you to be a martyr."

"Mac, I haven't been this happy since we were together at school. I'd shunned any romantic links because of my mother. I'd placed my faith in my career and in things. You're the only one who's ever taught me about the value of people. I think we must be the perfect match, because you give me more joy than I could ever imagine.''

He kissed her, wanting to believe her, but he had one more question. Raising his head, he asked, ''But your work? Allie, I know you're brilliant. And you'd miss your work.''

''That's what you think, cowboy. When I finish getting your business in order—and you'll be thrilled with what I can do to help you—I may teach some classes in Jackson. I bet there are other people who need to know about computers.''

''That would satisfy you?''

''Yes, because I could pass on my love for the computer. I've lost my enthusiasm for the corporate world. I've discovered it here again. So I can be happy with my work, which pales in comparison to my happiness with you. We're too good together to ever part again.''

Joy filled Mac's heart. He believed her, finally. And he wasn't passing up a second chance. ''You're right, Allie. We are the perfect match. I knew it ten years ago. I should've fought for us, but I was too overcome by my father's death.''

He kissed her, then asked, ''Will you marry me? Will you live here with me in Wyoming and raise little cowboys?''

"Only if we have some little cowgirls, too," she whispered in return before her lips met his.

"That's a deal," he agreed after lifting his head. "Shall we go down and tell Mom and Billy that we want a double wedding?"

"I think we should get dressed first," she suggested with a beautiful smile.

"Hmm, I think we should work on those cowboys and cowgirls first. After all, we're properly clothed for that activity," he insisted, pulling her naked body even closer to his.

"Okay. We don't want any wasted motion," she agreed.

Several hours passed before Mac and Allie joined his mother and Billy downstairs. After accepting their excited congratulations, Allie and Mac wandered out to the barn. He had chores to do, and she refused to be separated from him.

She stared up at the wide blue sky of Wyoming as they crunched along in the snow, Mac holding her hand. But she wasn't seeing the blue of the sky. She was imagining the bright stars that shone down at night.

Stars that had brought her to Wyoming.

Her reluctant call to an astrologist had brought her true happiness. Never again would she scorn such romantic beliefs. After all, the stars had led her to her lover, her cowboy, her heart.

Now she knew why the stars in Wyoming were so spectacular.

The Arrangement
by Margaret St. George

CHAPTER ONE

Capricorn: This is not the day to be practical. Loosen up, let yourself go with the flow. Opportunity knocks at your door tonight. You'll be lucky in love and business.

Gemini: A period of change is beginning for you. Trust your instincts to see you through. Visit friends tonight and be open to a surprise coming your way.

Smiling, Michael folded the newspaper and laid it in the booth beside him. He didn't believe in astrology, of course, and only read the daily horoscope for amusement. In his opinion, horoscopes were seldom correct. His business was doing well, but that was due to hard work, not luck, and he knew he wasn't going to be lucky in love tonight. But he did plan to loosen up and enjoy the evening.

Leaning back in the booth, he looked up as C. J. Wald dashed through the restaurant's door. Pausing to shake off the cap of snowflakes clinging to her dark hair, she scanned the warm, fragrant interior until she spotted him, then her face lit up and she waved and started toward his table.

Her dazzling smile was the first thing he'd noticed when they'd met ten years ago at a fraternity party. Her smile and a catch-your-breath figure. Her warm, bubbly personality had also captivated him that first night, and it still did. She was one of his oldest and best friends.

Watching her move toward him, noticing the attention she attracted, he sat a little straighter, feeling a flash of pride that tonight he was the focus of C.J.'s unique combination of style, intelligence and charm. And her wonderful smile. When C.J. smiled at a man, he felt as if he were the only male in the world.

Sliding out of the booth, he stood, kissed her cold-pink cheek and helped her off with her coat. "What perfume are you wearing? You smell like cinnamon rolls."

"Several passengers said the same thing," she said with a grin, then slid into the booth. "Sorry I'm late. We had a surprise check-ride today, which means that after the flight we had to spend an hour going over our review. I'd hoped to go home and change before I met you, but ended up coming directly from the airport."

"You look great."

Her flight attendant's uniform was classically

elegant and trimly tailored in contrasting tones of cocoa and cream, set off by a burgundy tie. Everything conformed to TransWest's regulations, including brown pumps and her coat and gloves, except her earrings. Being C.J., she had to find a way to express her individuality. Today she wore smiling Santa faces in each ear.

"Did your supervisor bust you for the earrings?" he asked, smiling.

"She was more forgiving than usual, being that it's only three weeks until Christmas." Folding her hands on the table, she smiled and studied him across the candle and silver. He noticed she wasn't wearing an engagement ring. "You look fabulous, Michael Court. How long has it been? We had dinner right before my birthday. That would be in June, much too long ago." She glanced up when the waiter arrived, taking a moment to order wine and stuffed mushrooms. "So. Tell me everything you've been doing since spring, but jump to the important stuff first. Did you pop the question to Melanie, and when do I get to meet her?"

"Melanie and I called it quits a couple of months ago," he said in a level voice.

"Oh. I'm sorry." Reaching across the table, she pressed his hand, her slender fingers still chilly from the outside air.

"Don't be. It wouldn't have worked. Melanie couldn't arrive anywhere on time if her life depended on it."

"Oops. Maybe I should apologize again for being late."

"If you're late, it's for a better reason than being unable to decide what to wear. What's even worse, Melanie never balanced her checkbook. Can you imagine?"

C.J. blinked and her lips twitched, then she burst into delighted laughter. "Oh Michael. If you could see your face. You're actually shocked! Only you would end a relationship because your lady didn't balance her checkbook."

After a minute he managed a grin. "Okay, smart ass. Maybe it doesn't seem like a big deal to you. Now it's your turn. What's going on with Hank What's His Name? I expected to see a diamond on your finger."

"You and my mother." Sighing, she tossed back a wave of glossy dark hair and took the glass of wine the waiter handed her. "Last summer was crazy. Mom had a kidney removed—cancer—and she stayed with me for almost a month after the surgery. My relationship with Hank didn't survive Mom's shameless hints about marriage. She'd have a copy of *Brides Magazine* on the coffee table when Hank came over. She'd remind him that I get free passes for travel, like a honeymoon, for instance.'' She shrugged and spread her hands. ''She all but offered to go with Hank to pick out rings. Unfortunately, Hank and I were a long way from being ready for a commitment. Couple that with a sudden lack of privacy and Mom's full-throttle matrimonial press, and it was goodbye, Hank.''

''I'm sorry, C.J.''

''Actually, Mom was more heartbroken than I was. I tell you, Michael, I love her dearly, but she's driving me crazy.''

''She's still living with you?''

''No, she's back in her own house, thank God. It's this marriage thing.'' Frowning, she gazed down at the mushrooms on her plate. ''There isn't a week goes by that Mom doesn't remind me that I'm coming up on thirty, and other women my age have started families. She's positive that cancer is going to get her, and her only desire in the world is to see me happily married before she goes.'' She rolled her eyes. ''The doctor swears Mom is healthy as a horse. But to hear her tell it, she's on her last gasp and I'm ignoring her dying wish. She even asked if I was gay.''

Michael laughed, enjoying her company.

''Go ahead and laugh,'' she said, grinning. ''But I've decided to marry the next guy who asks, just to get my mother off my back.'' They interrupted the conversation long enough to order steaks, then talked about people they knew in common. Over salads, C.J. asked, ''How's your grandfather? I meant to ask the last time we met, but I don't think I did.''

''Granddad died in July.''

''Oh, Michael. Why didn't you call me?'' When she reached for his hand again, he noticed how soft her palm was and how well shaped her fingers were. She had expressive, capable hands with gently rounded nails painted a light, clear red. ''This seems to be a night for saying I'm sorry.''

''I still miss that old man.'' A half smile curved his lips as he pictured his grandfather's face. ''Granddad left me more than a million dollars.''

''Good Lord,'' C.J. said, staring. ''I can't imagine that much money.''

''The bad news is, like your mother, Granddad was obsessive on the subject of marriage. He left me enough money to pay off my office building with a lot left over, but I inherit only if I'm married before my thirtieth birthday.''

C.J. leaned back in the booth. ''Well, friend, you're going to have to work fast. Your birthday is December 31.''

He nodded and drained his wineglass. ''I have

three weeks to meet someone, sweep her off her feet and marry her." He shrugged and lifted his eyebrows. "It's not going to happen."

The firm had taken off this year, and he'd added two additional architects to handle the bids and commissions flowing in. He hadn't forgotten Granddad's stipulation, but he'd assumed things would work out between him and Melanie. Then, after he and Melanie stopped seeing each other, there hadn't been time to develop a new relationship, let alone meet someone interesting, which he hadn't.

"And I thought my mother was over the edge on this subject. What happens if you don't marry according to your grandfather's schedule?"

He could hardly bear to tell her. "The money goes to establish a pet cemetery."

"You're kidding! If someone left me over a million dollars if I were married by the end of the year, I'd be proposing to every man I met." She looked around the room, eyeing the women in the restaurant as if sizing up candidates. "Seriously, you're wasting time having dinner with me. You need to get moving on this."

"C.J., honey, slow down. I've accepted that I'm not going to inherit Granddad's money."

"Something must be wrong with my hearing. I never thought I'd see the day when Michael

Court would leave a million dollars on the table.'' She was gently teasing him, but she was right.

And so were the astrology gurus when it came to money. Financial security had always headed his priority list. He'd opened a savings account when he was eight years old. He'd started an investment club in high school. For the last eight years he'd worked ten-hour days, six days a week to establish and build his architectural firm and his reputation for talent and excellence. His goal had been to pay off the mortgage on his office building by the time he was thirty. He wasn't going to reach that goal, but he would have if he had married and thus inherited his grandfather's bequest.

''I've thought about it, and there's no way I could ask someone to marry me under these circumstances. You're the impulsive one, not me.'' He smiled at the candlelight glowing on her face. ''And a marriage at this point would certainly be impulsive.''

''Did your granddad leave Bill a million dollars, too?''

He nodded. ''With the same condition. But that wasn't a problem for him, being married already and only twenty-eight.''

''So Bill receives a million dollars, but you don't. That's not fair,'' C.J. said, bristling on his behalf. "Relatives should mind their own business and stop trying to manipulate the younger generation. It makes me so angry. You and I both know your grandfather wanted you to have that money. So why didn't he just leave it to you outright instead of attaching strings to your inheritance?"

"Probably for the same reason that your mother didn't realize she was driving Hank away instead of turning his thoughts toward marriage and family. She had the best intentions, but she went about it the wrong way. So did my grandfather."

"You know something?" C.J. put down her fork and stared at him across the table. Candlelight gleamed in her brown eyes and highlighted smooth skin. If Michael hadn't known they were the same age, he would have guessed her several years younger than he knew she was. "We ought to call your grandfather's bluff."

"We?" he asked, smiling. It was like C.J. to make his problem her problem, too. She had helped him study for finals during college, had nursed him through the breakup of his first real romance, had helped him shop for an office building, had been a steadfast and loyal friend for ten years. There were long periods when they didn't see or talk to each other, then he'd pick up the telephone and it was as if he'd talked to her just yesterday. In his opinion, that was the mark of a true friendship. "Just how are *we* going to call Granddad's bluff?"

"We teach him a lesson."

Michael laughed. "Remember how this conversation started? Granddad is beyond lessons."

She waved a hand. "There's a way you can get your rightful inheritance and still not let him push you into a hasty marriage that you might regret later."

"And how is that?" he asked, taking a bite of salad.

"We elope. We get married, you and me."

Choking, he hastily put down his fork and pounded his chest. "Have you lost your senses?"

"Wait a minute.... Yeah, this would work." Pursing her lips, she narrowed her eyes and gave him a thoughtful look. Triumph sparkled in velvety eyes the color of chocolate. Leaning forward, she continued talking while he stared at her. "Michael, listen. Getting married would solve both our problems. My mother will be ecstatic. She'll stop worrying about dying, stop bugging me. And you'll get your grandfather's inheritance, like I'm sure he wanted you to."

"You and me? Married?" He had never

thought of C.J. as a girlfriend, let alone a potential wife.

She waved a hand. "It wouldn't be a *real* marriage. It would be what they used to call a marriage of convenience. We'd get divorced in, say, six months or so. That will give Mom time to move to Florida like she wants to do. She's afraid I'll never get married without her nearby to urge me on, so she's been putting off the move. And you'll meet your grandfather's criteria…or do you have to stay married for a certain length of time?"

"No," he said slowly. Now that the first shock had passed, his mind raced. She was right. He genuinely believed his grandfather had wanted him to have the inheritance, but the old man couldn't resist attaching conditions. He'd been up front about it. He had told Michael of the marriage stipulation years ago, and constantly teased that time was growing short for both of them.

"Great." C.J. clapped her hands and laughed. "I love this. Let's do it. I've got three days off next weekend. We could elope to Las Vegas and get married in one of those Elvis chapels. If we're going to do this, we might as well have some fun with it. We could wear something out of the fifties, dance down the aisle and let an Elvis impersonator help us thumb our noses at interfering relatives. What do you think?"

"I don't think people decide to get married on a whim between the appetizer and the entrée." He leaned back in the booth. "Next weekend? C.J., slow down. We need to talk about this. Think about it."

Suddenly, she looked different. In a ten-minute span, C.J. had changed from his old pal into a beautiful stranger. It wasn't that he failed to notice how lovely she was, more that he'd donned a pair of blinders years ago.

When he had first met C.J., she'd been dating his best friend. A man didn't look at his best friend's girl as a girl, not exactly. He'd made himself consider her only as a chum, a pal, a friend. And that's how they had continued. Years after his college buddy had drifted away, he and C.J. remained close friends. He attributed the staying power of their friendship to the wisdom of not permitting the man-woman thing to rise between them.

Suddenly, the man-woman thing was there.

He studied her with fresh eyes and discovered that C.J. had matured into an excitingly beautiful woman. Until now, he hadn't let himself notice the lush shape of her full lips or how long her lashes were. The sweep of dark hair coiled in a loose knot at her neck no longer impressed him as elegant as it had a few minutes ago. Now the wispy tendrils floating around her oval face seemed sexy. And he wondered how long her hair was when she wore it loose. How it would look spread across a white pillow. Like a midnight cloud? And what surprises were concealed by her tailored uniform? He hadn't let himself look—really look—at her figure since the first night he'd met her.

He blinked and cleared his throat uncomfortably. "I appreciate what you're suggesting, and I'm grateful. But a marriage of convenience, as you put it, isn't what Grandfather had in mind. It would feel like cheating."

"That's his fault, not yours. Michael, you agree that he wanted you to have the money, right? So let's do it," she said, her eyes sparkling. "We could invite a few close friends to join us in Vegas, and after the ceremony, we'll have a great party, then hit the casinos."

He spread his hands and smiled. "Is this how it works? The bride is more interested in the wedding than in the details of the marriage?"

"In this case, absolutely," she said, giving him that wonderful smile.

It was tempting to agree, but he wasn't the type of man to make big decisions on the spur of the moment. "One of the things I admire about you is your sense of adventure and spontaneity," he said after a minute. "But adventure and spontaneity aren't two words that I generally associate with getting married."

"Actually, I do," she said.

"C.J., you're my oldest friend."

She pretended to be wounded. "You don't have any friends over thirty?"

"You know what I mean. Look. We both know instances where marriage has hurt a good friendship, and I don't want that to happen to us. Keeping you as a friend is more important than the money."

A shine of moisture jumped into her eyes. "Michael, that's one of the nicest things anyone has ever said to me. And I love you for it. Our friendship is important to me, too. I wouldn't suggest getting married if I thought for an instant that living together would injure our feelings for each other."

"Living together." He rubbed a hand across his forehead. "You're way ahead of me. I suppose we'd definitely have to live together."

"Married people usually do," she said, laughing. "Your place or mine, big boy?"

"You haven't seen my place. I moved into temporary quarters four years ago—about the size of a closet. I bought ten acres near Evergreen, but I haven't found time to design the house I want

to build. Some day, when things slow down..."
He spread his hands and shrugged.

It occurred to him suddenly that work had taken over his life. He hadn't found time to develop a serious relationship even though his inheritance hung in the balance, hadn't found time to design or build the house he wanted, didn't have time to ski or attend the symphony. He'd let his season tickets to the Bronco's home games lapse. Couldn't recall the last social event he'd attended that wasn't work related. Frowning, he considered his crowded business schedule and wondered how he could clear a three-day weekend to get married.

"Sounds like my town house, then. I have two bedrooms, but we'll have to share a bathroom. Let me think. Do you work at home?"

"I work all the time," he said slowly, troubled by the realization of how limited his life had become.

"We could set up your drafting table in the basement." She tapped a finger against her lower lip. "We'll work it as if we were roommates. Share expenses and so forth."

"Absolutely not. You're doing this to help me. The least I can do is pay our expenses."

"Michael, I'm also doing this for me. The marriage issue is driving a wedge between Mom and me. We've always been close, but now I dread seeing her because I know we're going to argue about when I'm going to settle down. I really hate what's happening to our relationship. Mom had a great marriage, and she wants that for me, too— wants it badly. Maybe one of the reasons I'm single is that I want a marriage like my parents had, so I'm picky. And frankly, it's hard to meet terrific guys in my job. Usually the good-looking guy in seat 18A is getting off the plane in Chicago, but I'm going on to New York City or Baltimore, or, or, or, and we're geographically incompatible. It's frustrating."

"My parents had a good marriage, too. And that's what I want."

"We're lucky. But our expectations are high and neither of us has been willing to lower our standards. We know good marriages are possible. Speaking for myself, I'd rather remain single all of my life than settle for second best. I don't know why Mom can't understand that." Smiling, she pushed her plate away. "Which is the long way of saying that you aren't the only one who will benefit from this arrangement. My mother will be happy, and my relationship with her will improve. You don't know how guilty I feel knowing she wants to move to Florida but won't until I'm safely married."

"If you're doing this to please your mother... how will she feel when we get divorced?"

"Disappointed, I'm sure. But by then she'll be in Florida, where she wants to be. Too far away to nag me almost daily about finding another husband." Lifting a slender hand, she smoothed a tendril behind her ear. "I'll worry about Mom. She's not your problem."

For several minutes neither of them said anything. Michael assumed C.J. was considering the idea, as he was. Impulsiveness wasn't in his nature, and his instinct was to walk away from anything that didn't allow time for thought and analysis. "Marry in haste, repent at leisure" was an old saying that impressed him as absolutely true.

On the other hand, Granddad's money would pay off his office building. He'd meet the goal he'd set. Goals didn't mean anything unless you were willing to do whatever was necessary to achieve them. In this case, it meant getting married within the next three weeks. And that certainly wasn't going to happen, unless...

"I don't believe it," he said. "I'm actually considering this."

"An Elvis impersonator. A great party afterward. You get over a million dollars." She grinned. "What's not to like?"

"I need to really think about it."

She leaned back as the waiter served their steaks. "Michael, honey, you drive me crazy. But okay, it's your inheritance on the line. Just give me three days' notice, so I'll have time to get our passes to Las Vegas."

It was impossible to eat or to think of anything but her suggestion. C.J. talked about her flight schedule this month, and a recent skiing weekend. He didn't hear a word she said. Suddenly a lot of things were possible that hadn't been an hour ago. He could pay off his office building. Slow down his life. Start taking weekends off again.

"I can't believe you're willing to do this," he said as they left the restaurant. He walked her to her car and kissed her on the cheek.

"And I can't believe that you're hesitating," she said, smiling. "Hey, what are friends for?"

What she was offering to do went far beyond the expectations of friendship. "I'll call you."

He'd been a fool to think he could just go home, watch a little television and go right to sleep. His mind was running a mile a minute. At one o'clock, he gave up and called her.

"Hullo?" a sleepy voice answered.

"You're amazing. I figured you'd be up, pacing and thinking about getting married."

"As far as I'm concerned, it's a done deal," she said, yawning in his ear.

"Okay. Let's do it." He'd thought about it for hours and still couldn't quite believe that he was agreeing. Going with the flow, as his horoscope had stated. This could not be more unlike him. "We should have a prenuptial agreement," he heard himself say.

"Keep it simple, all right? We leave the marriage with what we brought into it, nothing more, nothing less. What else do we need to talk about? Do we need to set up some rules?"

They hadn't mentioned sex, but he assumed the rule there was a given. To preserve their friendship, they wouldn't let sex become an issue. C.J. had mentioned having two bedrooms in her town house; they would be roommates, nothing more. They weren't talking about a real marriage.

"I think we should agree that we won't date while we're married," he suggested with a smile.

"Oh, Michael," she said, bursting into laughter. "I love your sense of humor."

The odd thing was that most people weren't aware that he had a sense of humor. But C.J. brought out the best in him. She challenged him intellectually, made him feel as if he was interesting company, and she laughed at the same things he did.

"If I know you," she said, "you're standing next to your desk. Find a pen and paper. We need

to make a list of everything we have to do."
When he was ready, she said, "First, we need to
find out if there's a waiting period on the marriage
license. Book an Elvis chapel. And a hotel. Let's
see, you need to arrange for a moving company
and start packing your stuff. I need to clear the
closet in the spare bedroom, and I'll request the
passes to Las Vegas immediately."

"I'll have to reschedule my Friday and Saturday appointments," he said, cradling the phone
between his ear and his shoulder, splitting the list
into His and Hers columns.

"We need to decide who we'll invite. I doubt
very many people will jump on a flight to Vegas,
especially at this time of year, but there are a couple of friends I'd like to ask, anyway. And we
probably should have some wedding announce-
ments printed, you know, to send to other friends
and associates, distant relatives. What else?"

"We need to decide if we're going to do this
in fifties attire or regular dress or a tux and
gown," he said, getting into it himself. "I like
the idea of the fifties."

"So do I. Jot a reminder to me to find a poodle
skirt. Where do I start on that one? A costume
shop?"

"I'll need to notify the post office of an address
change." The list was growing. "I'm invited to

several holiday parties, and I imagine you are, too. Shall we go to a few of them together?''

"Damn." He heard her draw breath. "Put this item at the head of my list. Cancel dates with Mark and Steve. I guess we shouldn't date during our brief engagement, either."

"Who are Mark and Steve?" he asked curiously. Earlier today, he wouldn't have cared who they were. Now suddenly he did.

"Just friends. Nothing romantic."

"Rings." He scribbled the word on his side of the list. "We need to buy rings."

"An engagement ring isn't necessary—that's a needless expense. Just plain gold bands, don't you think? I wear a size six and a half."

He noted her ring size. "I should probably add you to my auto policy."

C.J. laughed. "Trust you to think that. But it's not necessary. I wouldn't dream of driving your Explorer, and believe me, you won't want to drive my old junker. But there is something, and I hate to ask you to do it, but..."

"Your mother?"

"Yes. If this were real, the first thing I'd want to do is take you to Mother's and tell her the news."

"I'd like to see your mother again—it's been years. Let's do family tomorrow night, agreed?

We'll see your mother, then we'll stop by my brother's house.''

His gaze dropped to the photos arranged in a line along the back of his desk. His parents, his granddad. Sometimes he missed them so much the emotion rose up like a tidal wave and blindsided him.

When Michael hung up, knowing that the decision was made, he felt a rush of relief and happiness. He would get what he wanted, and so would Granddad. He only wished it didn't feel as if he was cheating. He gazed at his grandfather's photograph for several minutes before he went to bed.

CHAPTER TWO

*CAPRICORN: YOU ARE entering a phase of change.
Plan a trip, consider a new direction. Financial
prospects are excellent now. Neptune's influence
will bring a confusing new romance.*

*Gemini: Impulsive decisions made now could
backfire. But family relationships are smoothing
out. This is an ideal time for that vacation you've
been putting off. Prepare for a change in living
arrangements.*

C.J. glanced at her car radio and laughed. She
was listening to an astrologer named Skyler
McMasters whose program was broadcast from
back East. She tried to catch McMasters's program whenever she could because the woman had
an uncanny way of seeming to speak directly to
C.J.

She was certainly about to experience a change
in living arrangements—that was on target. And
the vacation she'd been putting off was to a wedding chapel in Las Vegas. She was on her way to

meet Michael at her mother's house, and she supposed the decision to marry him could indeed backfire. But it wouldn't.

Frowning, she looked at her gas gauge. Full. But her eight-year-old Ford was coughing a bit, acting as if it was almost out of gas.

Car years were like dog years. An eight-year-old Ford was more than fifty years old in car and dog time. Regardless, she was going to drive it until it shook apart, or until she'd saved enough to buy an extravagant, impractical, hopelessly expensive Cadillac. She'd scrimped to get by for most of her life, and just once, she wanted to own something that was top of the line, something wildly luxurious. A Cadillac.

The Ford sputtered across the intersection, and the wipers brushed at a light fall of snowflakes as she headed toward Wheat Ridge, an older section of Denver. Tonight would be a happy occasion for her mother.

And for her, too. Seeing her mother happy would make her happy. Her problem was solved, and she felt good about helping Michael. Plus, it was fun to think about the Elvis chapel and the lights and flash of Las Vegas. If they could muster a small wedding party on short notice, they'd have a reception at the hotel-casino where they were staying. She'd ask Michael if he thought they should arrange dinner for the guests or just have hor d'oeuvres.

The funny thing was, at the back of her mind she'd always suspected that someday she would decide to get married just like this—quickly, impulsively. She'd even fantasized about eloping. But she'd never imagined the groom would be her old friend Michael.

Oh, there'd been a few times when she'd looked at him and wondered. After all, he was great-looking, ambitious and charming. When her friends met Michael, they rolled their eyes in disbelief when she insisted there was nothing romantic between them. She liked to explain that she and Michael were proof that a man and woman could be friends without romance or sex getting in the way. When fantasy intruded, she told herself that Michael would make someone a fantastic husband. Not her, but someone.

It was going to be her, after all.

Of course, it wouldn't be a real marriage, she reminded herself as she parked behind Michael's Explorer and waved at him. It was just two good friends helping each other out.

Michael walked toward her car through the falling snow, his handsome face illuminated by the porch light shining above her mother's door. Something tentative about his smile reminded her of the first time they'd met. She had noticed him immediately, as he was taller than most of his frat brothers and better-looking. And suddenly she remembered wishing that she'd met Michael before she started dating his best friend. Odd how things worked out.

Michael stood with his hands thrust in the pockets of his overcoat, frowning at her car as she opened the door. "I could have picked you up at the airport."

"But then I'd have had to leave my car there and how would I get to work tomorrow?" She grinned. "Or are you dying to get up at four in the morning to drive me back to the airport?"

"Since you put it that way," he said with a smile that vanished as he inspected her car. "At what point do you replace this junker? When you start leaving pieces of it on the road behind you?"

"Nope," she said, sliding out and glancing toward the porch. The curtains twitched beside the door, and she smiled. She suspected her mother had guessed the reason for this visit. "I'm saving for a Cadillac."

"You're kidding. Wouldn't a four-wheel drive be more practical?"

"Michael, honey, some people make decisions based on criteria other than practicality."

"I don't believe it," he said, laughing. At the door, he paused before pressing the bell. "C.J., are you sure you want to go through with this?" he asked softly, his blue eyes searching hers. "Once we tell your mother and my brother, there'll be no going back. We're committed."

Before she could answer, her mother opened the door and beamed at them.

"Michael Court! I haven't seen you in—what?—three years. Not since C.J.'s New Year's Eve party, way back when. It was your birthday, too, I remember that. Come in, come in." Stepping back, she ushered them into a comfortable living room. Within five minutes, she had everyone settled with a glass of wine and a tray of holiday cookies, and she turned an expectant look to C.J. "I think I know what this is about. At least, I hope I do." She smiled at Michael. "And I couldn't be happier."

C.J. had imagined this moment a dozen times, if for no other reason than to please her mother. She remembered to reach for Michael's hand, drew a deep breath and smiled. "Michael and I have decided to get married."

"Oh!" Her mother's hands leapt to her cheeks

and moisture sprang into her eyes. She gave Michael a damp smile. "You don't know how long I've waited to hear those words. Do you have a ring?" she asked C.J., her voice excited.

"I thought C.J. should pick out the ring she wanted," Michael said smoothly. He cleared his throat and touched his tie, looking so uncomfortable that C.J. almost burst out laughing. "This happened suddenly. Well, not exactly suddenly. I mean, I think we both always knew..." He gave C.J. a sidelong glance, signaling for rescue.

"Mom, since Michael and I have known each other practically forever, we don't see any reason to wait. We're going to hop on a plane next weekend, fly to Vegas and tie the knot there."

"An elopement?" her mother asked, horrified. "To Las Vegas?" A long shudder rippled down her body.

C.J.'s heart sank. She'd been afraid of this. "Now, Mom, we don't want a big wedding. And we need—" she stopped and cleared her throat as Michael had done "—we want to be married by the end of the year. We're firm on that."

Her mother stared. "C. J. Wald, are you pregnant?" She didn't look as if she'd be too disappointed if the answer was yes.

"No, no, it's nothing like that," Michael said hastily, his face pink.

"It's for tax purposes," C.J. said, pulling an answer out of thin air. "See, if we're married before the end of the year, then we get the marital deduction for the full year." Michael looked at her and lifted an eyebrow, his eyes twinkling.

"I don't understand about taxes, but I do know weddings. And C.J., I've been planning your wedding since you were a little girl. You can't elope! You just can't get married in one of those tacky Las Vegas places!" She turned wide eyes to Michael. "Please, don't do this to me. A real wedding might not be important to you two, but it's so important to me."

Her words hung in the air.

C.J.'s mother was a small, soft-looking woman, but she might as well have been ten feet tall and molded out of steel when it came to getting her way. Two hours later, C.J. and Michael stepped onto the porch and both drew a deep breath of frigid night air.

C.J. threw up her hands. "When we walked in there, it was our wedding. Now it's her wedding. I'm sorry, Michael. It won't be a quickie ceremony or the fun of an Elvis impersonator. But at least she agreed to meet the deadline." And if anyone could throw together a wonderful wedding in three short weeks, it was her mother.

"It's all right," Michael said, placing his hands on her shoulders. "One of the reasons you came up with this idea was to make your mother happy. So a formal wedding it is."

She stared up at him. "You were right about being committed. If we backed out now, she'd kill me. And you, too."

Michael grinned at her, flashing white teeth. "I like your mother, I always have." They walked toward their cars. "Are you ready for my side of the family?"

"I'll follow you to Bill's house."

Michael's father had died of a heart attack when Michael was ten, and two years later lightning had struck the golf course, where his mother was playing, killing her instantly. His grandfather had finished raising Michael and his younger brother, Bill. It occurred to C.J. that maybe Michael's grandfather had insisted on Michael and Bill being married before age thirty because he believed they needed to start families of their own while they were still young.

That's what she was thinking when she parked behind Michael in front of his brother's house. "Quick, I need a refresher course on your brother.

I haven't seen Bill in five years." She glanced up at an impressive two-story featuring lots of glass and varying roof lines. "Did you design Bill's house?"

Michael nodded. "Bill's practicing law, and I think I told you that Susan is a nurse. They're expecting their first baby." He took her arm and led her toward a wide porch lit by coach lights. "We won't stay long."

"C.J.!" Bill swept her into an exuberant embrace immediately after opening the door. He grinned at Michael and slapped him on the shoulder. "Congratulations to both of you! Susan?" A smiling brunette stepped forward and clasped C.J.'s hands. "This is C. J. Wald, soon to be my brother's blushing bride." He beamed. "She's too good for you, Michael. You don't deserve this gorgeous creature."

Bill and Susan gave C.J. a tour of the house Michael had designed, then served eggnog and canapés before a cheerful fire in the family room. C.J. liked them both and felt a rush of gratitude that they welcomed her so warmly into their family and made the evening so comfortable and easy. She also liked watching Michael and his brother. They had an easy bantering manner that didn't hide their closeness and love for each other.

By the time she and Michael got up to leave, C.J. felt as if she'd known Bill and Susan all her life.

"Please tell your mother if she needs help, she can call on me." Susan smiled. "I'd love to be involved in the wedding."

"Thank you. And I won't forget to send you the book we were talking about." She glanced at Susan's slightly rounded stomach beneath a red velvet dress, and felt a pang of envy that surprised her. Babies were a long way off in her future and wouldn't have anything to do with Michael.

Bill gave C.J. another hug. "I couldn't be happier. I always thought you and Michael would be perfect together. I don't know why it took you both so long to see it, but I'm glad you finally did."

"Me, too," C.J. said. Good Lord. She was falling right into this as if their marriage would be real. Thinking about babies and liking it that Bill and Susan would be part of her life. She needed to get a grip on herself.

Silently, she and Michael walked arm in arm down the sidewalk. "I like your brother and his wife very much," C.J. said when they reached her car.

"They like you, too."

Leaning against the car door, she rubbed her

hands together. The air was damp and cold, and a light snow was still falling out of the night sky. "Michael?" she said in a wondering voice, looking up at him. "We're really going to do this."

"We're really going to get married."

They stared at each other, then burst into hysterical laughter.

SITTING ON THE BED surrounded by papers, C.J. looked at the radio playing in her hotel room, then rolled her eyes. The astrologer Skyler McMasters had just mentioned that practical Capricorn and impulsive Gemini were not an especially compatible match.

"Just what I needed to hear," she said to her friend and flying partner, Cindy Wheeler. They were on a layover in Baltimore, and it was driving C.J. crazy as she kept thinking about all the things she needed to do at home.

"You don't believe in that stuff, do you?" Cindy asked.

They were poring over C.J.'s January flight schedule, looking for trips she might trade to gain a few extra days for her honeymoon. Repaying the trades would make for a busy first month of marriage, and she'd be gone a lot. Not that it mattered.

"No," C.J. said uncomfortably, turning off the radio. "But it is uncanny how often my horoscope seems to match what's going on in my life."

"You could drop the trip on the fifteenth," Cindy suggested, peering at her copy of their schedule. "That's a three-day with two layovers. Not too great for a newlywed. No, wait. Dropping the three-day would take your monthly hours below sixty-five. Sorry, that won't work."

"I'm so tired I can't think," C.J. said, tossing her schedule on the bed and yawning. "It's time to send you back to your own room so I can get some sleep."

Surprised, Cindy glanced at her watch. "It's only nine-thirty. Boy, are you slowing down. And we didn't even talk about the wedding."

C.J. groaned. "The wedding has taken over my life. I have another gown fitting an hour after we get back to Denver tomorrow, then Mom wants me to go over the choices she's made about the cake, the flowers, and on and on and on."

"You're on the final countdown," Cindy said at the door. "Ten days from now you'll be basking on a beach in Hawaii with a handsome new husband."

"Frankly, I'd rather be eloping to Las Vegas."

Cindy frowned. "C.J....are you all right with

this? Somehow you don't seem...I don't know... starry-eyed and excited enough.''

That bothered her, too, although it shouldn't have. "I'm fine. Just tired, that's all."

In fact, nothing was turning out the way C.J. had hoped. First, the guest list was growing by leaps and bounds. Second, the wedding would be held in the morning, not her favorite time of day, but her mother didn't want the wedding to interfere with New Year's Eve plans people might already have made. Third, the honeymoon had shifted to Hawaii, and it had stretched into five days instead of a weekend. Instead of being whimsical and as much of a farce as the marriage would be, the wedding was beginning to feel very, very real.

Sighing, C.J. let her shoulders slump. Her mother was in her element, putting a wedding together in record time, but C.J. felt worn to a frazzle. And lately she'd felt moody and out of sorts.

The holidays were not a good time to be feeling tired and distracted. Every flight was crowded, and it seemed more and more people ordered special meals, which meant additional headaches if the special meals were overlooked and not loaded into the galleys. On the trip into Baltimore, the serving cart had broken, and she and Cindy had to run the meals out the way flight attendants used to do before carts were put into service. If it wasn't one thing, it was another.

She had hoped to finish her Christmas shopping during this layover in Baltimore, but a storm had moved into the area and the pilots had to circle for almost an hour before landing. By the time the crew reached the hotel and had dinner, the snow had thickened again, and C.J. was too tired to shop, anyway.

There was too much to do and not enough time. Christmas was going to be a blur this year, she already knew that. At least she had Michael's gift taken care of. She'd bought him a leather garment bag to take to Hawaii.

It amazed her that she and Michael were actually going to get married. At least she assumed he hadn't changed his mind. They had talked by phone, of course, but she'd been too busy to actually see him last week and their phone conversations had been brief. That was all right, she supposed. They'd have plenty of time later to get acquainted on a deeper basis.

Unexpectedly, it bothered her to realize there were a lot of things she didn't know about Michael. She didn't know what kind of music he preferred, how he spent his weekends, if he was tidy or sloppy. She hadn't even asked her favorite test question for all dates: How many times had he seen *Casablanca*?

A tiny niggling feeling of doubt crept into her mind. This was a lot of trouble to go to just to gain a roommate, especially as she had always said she didn't want a roommate. And she hadn't anticipated how crummy she'd feel about deceiving her mother and Bill and Susan, not to mention a lot of good friends.

Was she going to regret doing this?

"I CAN'T BELIEVE YOU'VE put off buying C.J. a Christmas gift until the last minute."

Michael frowned at his brother, then checked the price tag on an efficient-looking vacuum cleaner. "She probably already has a vacuum cleaner," he muttered. He was starting to feel desperate.

"You don't know?" Bill took his arm, turned him around and marched him out of the appliance store. After peering through the crowds of holiday shoppers, he led Michael to a coffee shop with tables facing into the mall. They placed their order, then carried the steaming cups to a table. "You're worrying me, bro."

"Why is that?" Michael asked irritably. He hated shopping. Had no idea what to get for C.J.

"Don't take this wrong, I'm delighted that you and C.J. are getting married. But you and I had lunch a week before you phoned about the wedding, and you didn't mention a thing about this. It isn't like you to suddenly decide to get married, and I would have bet anything you'd have a long engagement." Bill stared at him with eyes very like his own. "What's equally puzzling, when you talk about C.J., it's like you don't know anything about her except surface details."

"That's ridiculous. I know her values, what kind of person she is. And you know how long we've been friends—this isn't sudden."

"Michael, when you mention C.J. you always say what a great friend she is and how loyal and so on. But you haven't said anything about love."

"I care about her, of course," he said stiffly.

Bill stared at him across their coffee cups. "Great. I'm glad. But you don't marry a woman because she's a pal. You marry her because you can't live without her and you want to spend the rest of your life loving her. That's how I feel about Susan. I can't imagine a life without her. Is that how you feel about C.J.?"

Suddenly, Michael wished he had never agreed

to the wedding. He hated deceiving his brother, and never had before. For one crazy minute he considered telling Bill the truth, but discovered he wasn't very proud of the truth. And he felt guilty that it hadn't even occurred to Bill to ask if he might be marrying C.J. to receive Granddad's inheritance. Obviously, as far as Bill was concerned, that was so unthinkable that it wasn't worth mentioning. Actually, he thought Bill would understand if he knew the truth, but he couldn't bring himself to explain.

"Look. I want to marry C.J. and C.J. wants to marry me. End of subject." He glanced at his watch and then at the crowds. Time was wasting. He needed to finish his Christmas shopping.

"In other words, butt out."

"Put your energy toward helping me think of a gift. What do women want?"

"Not appliances. How about a piece of good jewelry, or a negligee?"

Those choices sounded too intimate. He had in mind something more practical and useful. He just didn't know what she needed. A blender? A toaster? A microwave oven?

As he continued shopping, his thoughts kept returning to Bill's comments. His brother was right. Marriage ought to be about love and forever and happily ever after. Instead, he and C.J. were making a mockery of the institution, and deceiving a lot of nice people in the process. Things weren't working out the way he had envisioned.

If C.J.'s mother hadn't already booked the church and bought C.J.'s gown, he would have been tempted to call the whole thing off.

"I wonder what shape her washer and dryer are in," he said glumly. "Or would that kind of gift be too extravagant?"

Bill shook his head. "You'll learn, big brother. I'm telling you, women don't like gifts that have a plug attached."

"OH! You look so beautiful!"

C.J. stared into the bridal shop's full-length mirror. Like her mother, standing behind her, sudden tears moistened her eyes. She hadn't known it until now, but on some level she'd always imagined this moment: trying on her wedding gown.

She'd feared that leaving the choice to her mother might end in a bouffant explosion of skirts and sleeves. But her mother's unerring taste and instinct had led her to a wonderful gown that was perfect for C.J.'s tall, slender figure.

The gown was a white sheath, beautifully beaded on top, with draped satin below. Sleeveless, it hugged her throat in front, then scooped low in back, almost to her waist.

"This is a fabulous gown," she murmured in a choked whisper.

And suddenly she felt depressed.

This was the gown of her dreams. It was everything she had ever wanted a wedding gown to be. And her mother's face, filled with love and joy and pride, was exactly as C.J. had known it would be when this day came.

But it was all a sham.

"Oh, Mom," she said, sitting down abruptly. "I wish you hadn't gone to all this trouble and expense. I wish Michael and I had just eloped to Las Vegas."

It wouldn't have seemed real if they'd said their vows in front of an Elvis impersonator. She and Michael would have laughed and slapped each other on the back, and they would have made jokes about interfering relatives and helping each other out. They would have mugged for their friends, had a great party, and then played blackjack until the wee hours. It would have been a grand joke, nothing serious. With a beginning like that, they could have continued easily with their plan.

But this was serious, she thought unhappily,

lifting her head to stare at herself in the mirror. This gown, her mother's joy—this was serious and it was real. And it made her wish she was worthy of the moment, made her wish that she was *really* getting married to someone she loved deeply and passionately.

If it hadn't been for Michael's million dollars and her mother's feelings, she would have called the whole thing off.

"These slippers are pinching a little," she said instead, then turned to the saleslady. "Do you have the same style in a half size larger?"

MICHAEL CARRIED the last load of clothing into C.J.'s town house and hung it in the closet of her guest room. Next, he put his toiletries in the bathroom they would share. C.J. had cleared some space for him, but he noticed she had more room for her stuff than he did. Well, it was her house, he thought, lifting a perfume bottle and sniffing the top. It was his favorite, the perfume that smelled like cinnamon buns. He set her perfume bottles in a nice row, tidied up the area, aligned the hems of the towels, then went downstairs.

"There's a beer in the fridge," C.J. said, looking up from a pile of papers. "We have sixty-five acceptances so far. And people are sending gifts.

I'd forgotten about that. It doesn't seem right to accept the gifts, but..." She smiled. "We've received four blenders so far. But I like yours the best."

He'd given her a blender for Christmas. And despite her loyal comment, he didn't have a feeling that she was particularly thrilled about his present. He suspected Bill was right about women wanting gifts other than appliances.

"Thanks," he muttered, reaching into the refrigerator and popping the tab on a Coors. "I think I'm moved in. I set up my drafting table in the basement as you suggested." He walked into the combination living-dining room. "It feels funny not to have my own stuff here." There was no reason to attempt to blend their possessions since their arrangement was temporary. Still, he felt like a houseguest without his own things.

"If you want to bring some furniture over, I could put some of my stuff in storage."

"No, it's okay." He sat at the dining room table and skimmed a quick look over her red sweater and the red ribbon tying back her hair. She wasn't wearing makeup today and looked fresh and about twenty. There was something incredibly sexy about a woman's bare lips. C.J.'s mouth was a little wide and her lower lip was full.

She had a mouth made for laughing. And kissing. He cleared his throat, then looked away and took a long swallow of the beer. And it occurred to him that thinking about her kissable lips was not a good habit to fall into.

She pulled another paper from the pile. "I had a key made for you. It's on the kitchen counter." She ticked off one item on her list. "I'd like to stock the fridge so we'll have something to eat when we return from Maui. What kinds of frozen dinners do you like?"

He smiled, tilting his head. "I take it you don't like to cook."

"I don't know. I don't have much experience," she said with a shrug, leaning back in her chair. "It hardly seems worthwhile to cook for one person, so I buy prepared foods or I eat out most of the time. Do you like to cook?"

"As a matter of fact, I do."

She stared, then laughed. "I had no idea. I'm not sure I can picture you cooking."

"Tell you what," he said after a moment's thought, "while we're married, I'll do the cooking. It's the least I can do."

The words *while we're married* seemed to hang in the air and vibrate with meaning.

C.J. cleared her throat, then waved a hand.

"Okay, I won't argue with a man who wants to feed me. But I'll do the cleanup. Seems like a fair trade."

For the first time since he'd known her, he couldn't think of anything to say, and the conversation died. But the old man-woman thing was operating in high gear.

He was very aware of her fresh-soap scent, couldn't stop looking at her bare lips. When she leaned forward, her sweater pulled tight across her breasts, and he sucked in a sharp breath. He kept remembering the intimate glimpse of her perfume bottles and lipsticks and bath powder. He'd even taken a long glance into her bedroom.

She had done her bedroom in vivid tones of rust and navy, which he didn't usually think of as feminine colors, but in this instance it was very much a woman's room. The strong colors were softened by ruffles and flower arrangements and a bookcase crammed with brightly colored jackets. A collection of snow globes sat in front of the books. He hadn't known she collected snow globes. He could have gotten her one for Christmas. If they were still married in June, he'd get her a snow globe for her birthday.

"Thanks for the garment bag." He knew she didn't have a lot of extra money and wished she had chosen something less expensive. He would have been happy with a box of handkerchiefs.

"You're welcome," she said, smiling. "We'll exchange the extra blenders." Her smile faded. "How do you want to handle this gift situation?" Bright color rose from her throat. "I mean, who keeps what?"

"I suppose the practical way to do it would be to return the gifts for cash, then split the cash."

"No offense, but that sounds a little crass, don't you think?"

He did. And he didn't like it. "What else can we do?"

"I guess you could keep the gifts sent by your family and friends, and I'll keep the gifts sent by my side." Leaning back in her chair, she tapped the pencil against her cheek and studied him. "Michael...how many times have you seen *Casablanca*?"

"I don't know, four times? Maybe five?" Suddenly he understood this was a test question, and he grinned. "How many times have you seen *Rollerball*?"

She laughed. "Three times, and I still don't understand the scene where they set the trees on fire."

"I don't, either." Smiling, he relaxed a little.

Maybe this would be all right, after all. "Do you mind if I get another beer?" he asked, crushing the empty can in his hand.

"Michael, honey, if you're going to live here, you don't need to ask permission to get something out of the fridge."

In the kitchen, he looked around for a recycling bag, then popped his head out and asked her where it was.

She gave him a sheepish look. "I know I ought to recycle, and I started to last summer. But..." Her shoulders lifted in a charming shrug.

"Okay. I'll set up a recycling system in the garage," he said lightly, tossing the crushed can in the garbage bag, although it pained him to do it. "If that's all right with you, that is."

"Sure. Just remind me to use it. I'm great at starting projects, not so hot at finishing them."

That didn't sound too good. It sounded, in fact, like something that was likely to drive him crazy. But only temporarily.

After they reviewed their lists one last time, had a pizza for dinner and wrote some thank-you cards, Michael stood and stretched. He waved as he headed toward the door.

"See you at the rehearsal tomorrow night." Suddenly the moment was on top of them.

"Don't forget to pick up your tux tomorrow morning," she said, following him. When he lifted an eyebrow, she smiled. "Sorry. I figure since I need reminders, everyone else does, too."

She stood beneath the light in the foyer, her hair glossy and floating around her shoulders. For one crazy moment, he felt like taking her in his arms and kissing her. Really kissing her. Not a peck on the cheek, as usual. A moment passed before he realized she was staring at his lips as if the same nutty thought had occurred to her.

Suddenly she stepped back, wet her kissable lips and thrust out her hand. "Good night... friend."

He clasped her hand and resisted an urge to apologize for wanting to kiss her. And it occurred to him that being married to her wasn't going to be as easy as merely taking on a roommate. "Good night, friend." His voice sounded thick and a little hoarse.

"Next stop, Maui."

"Bring lots of sunblock."

He needed to go; he still had lots of last-minute chores to do. But he didn't want to leave her.

"Bill and Susan upgraded our room to the honeymoon suite. Did I remember to tell you?"

"That's nice of them."

She laughed self-consciously and withdrew her hand from his, then made a shooing motion. "Off with you. I still have to phone Mom, pay some bills and pack."

After he closed the door behind him, he sat in his car for a minute staring at her town house. "My wife," he said aloud, testing the words on his tongue. "I'd like you to meet my wife. My wife is flying the New York run this month. My wife said..."

The words sounded kind of good, actually. Surprisingly. And somehow applying them to C.J. changed her. When he looked at her and thought *my wife,* she suddenly became fascinating to him.

He liked it that she'd seen *Rollerball* three times.

THE WEDDING BEGAN at eleven o'clock, and C.J. was a nervous wreck. She couldn't have felt more fluttery inside if this had indeed been the most important day in her life.

"I wish your father were alive to walk you down the aisle," C.J.'s mother whispered as they took their places at the back of the church. "He'd be so proud today."

C.J. blinked hard and took her mother's arm. "I'm glad you're walking me down the aisle."

The music began and people stood, turning toward them.

"Honey? Are you sure about this?" her mother asked, clasping her hand and searching her face. "Michael's a wonderful man, and I like him, but…it worries me that the two of you don't touch and hug like I expect people in love to do. Honey, it's not too late to change your mind. If you don't love Michael with all your heart and soul, we can turn around right now and walk out of here. It's okay."

And it would have been. C.J. read it in her mother's eyes, felt it in her mother's firm hand in hers. She was getting married to make her mother happy, but her mother would have called it all off to make her happy.

"I love you, Mom," she whispered, tears in her eyes. "Michael and I…we…he's my best friend."

"That's wonderful, but—"

But everyone was standing, smiling, looking at them. The wedding march swelled, and C.J.'s heart lurched, then beat a little faster. She lifted her head, squeezed her mother's hand and stepped forward. It was too late to turn back now.

Then she saw Michael and drew in a sharp, soft breath. She had never seen him wearing a tux, and he looked wonderful, the handsomest man on earth. And he was looking at her the way she would want her groom to look at her. With surprise, appreciation and a sudden deep smolder in his blue eyes that she had never seen before.

And her nervousness increased. She was trembling when her mother placed her hand in Michael's, then stepped back to sit in the first pew.

"Dearly beloved, we are gathered today to join this man and this woman in holy matrimony..."

The vows passed in a blur, and C.J. suspected her responses were all but inaudible. Then she and Michael turned to face each other while the organist played "Sunrise, Sunset." The song seemed to go on forever.

Michael gazed deeply into her moist eyes. "You are so beautiful today, you take my breath away."

She tried to think of something witty and light to say, but couldn't. "You should always wear a tux," she whispered.

His dark hair was neatly trimmed, but one unruly curl had dropped forward on his forehead. His eyes were a steady smoky blue. Not for the first time, C.J. noticed the strong sculpted angles of his face, how broad his shoulders were. His palms were as moist as hers, and they were both trembling.

"I wish we'd gone to Vegas and that Reverend Tarcher was wearing an Elvis wig," she said in a low voice. And wondered if their friends could see that her lips were quivering.

Michael smiled down at her. "Feels real, doesn't it?"

"It's real to everyone but us."

When the music finally ended, C.J. noticed her mother dabbing at happy tears before they turned back to Reverend Tarcher.

"I now pronounce you man and wife," the reverend said with a wide smile. "Michael, you may kiss your bride."

He moved closer to her, and she felt the heat of his body enfold and draw her to him. Gently, he lifted her chin, gazed into her eyes, then kissed her lightly on the lips.

Lightning jolted C.J. from her scalp to her toes. His lips were soft yet firm, his touch gentle but certain. They fit together like pieces of a jigsaw puzzle. And for the first time in her life, C.J. experienced the rocket sizzle of pure chemistry. It was as if Michael's kiss awakened a million slumbering cells deep within her body. Suddenly and amazingly, she felt more alive than she ever had before.

Michael drew back from her, a look of surprise on his handsome face. He frowned, then he bent to give her another kiss, a real kiss this time— deep, exploratory, a kiss that forgot they had an audience until the audience erupted in laughter and cheers.

"Good Lord," he said in a wondering voice, staring at her.

C.J. couldn't speak. Her lips tingled and her body was on fire. "Oh, boy," she murmured finally, raising her fingertips to her lips. "We're in trouble."

She prayed no one else had heard her.

"Ladies and gentlemen, I have the honor of presenting Mr. and Mrs. Michael Court!"

The music rose in triumphant waves, Michael took her arm, and they started down the aisle. Tears of joy streamed down her mother's cheeks. Their friends grinned and clapped.

No one knew that Mr. and Mrs. Court had just shared their very first kiss.

And what a kiss it had been, C.J. thought, sliding a glance up at her new husband. She was still shaking inside and tingling.

Her husband.

Good heavens. She had a husband.

CHAPTER THREE

CAPRICORN: NO MAN is an island, not even you. Even loners need someone, and it might be someone who's been there all along. Old friends take on special significance right now. A little patience will reap rewards.

Gemini: A change of status will solve old problems and create new ones. With Mercury changing signs, you're particularly persuasive now. Be sure you know your own mind before you attempt to convince others.

Sighing, C.J. tucked the folded newspaper into the seat back in front of her and turned her head to gaze out the plane's window. Far below, the ocean sparkled with sunset colors.

It was a little late for her horoscope to be warning her about convincing others. The deed was done. She had thought she knew her own mind about marrying Michael, but now she wasn't as sure. She didn't remember ever feeling this confused.

"Your mother not only put on a nice reception, it was a great party, too," Michael said, turning a book upside down on his lap.

C.J. strained to see the title, something about recent advances in air ducts for commercial buildings. Unreasonably it annoyed her that good old practical Michael wasn't wasting a minute of vacation time reading a novel. Not him. Even on his honeymoon, he was working.

"Several people told me the reception was a great start to the new year. Good food. Good music."

And lots of congratulations and photographs and hugs. By the time they cut the cake, C.J. had been feeling like the biggest fraud in creation. Seeing her mother beaming and happy should have made her happy, too, but against all expectations, it didn't. Instead, she felt as if she had cheated everyone. Maybe including herself.

"Is something wrong?" Michael asked softly.

Looking down, C.J. twisted the gold band on her finger. It was heavier than she had imagined it would be. "Don't take this wrong," she said after a minute, "but I feel lousy about deceiving my mother."

"I know what you mean," Michael said with a sigh, closing his book. "She spent a lot of money and more or less gave up her Christmas to give us a wedding. Bill and Susan did, too. I hope you'll help me find a way to make it up to them.'' He fell silent for several minutes. ''I've never deceived Bill in my life. It doesn't feel very good. And it doesn't feel good knowing your mother put all that effort into a wedding that wasn't real.''

''The wedding was real enough,'' C.J. said sharply. ''It's the marriage that's a sham.''

''If we'd gone to Vegas like we planned, it wouldn't have put your mother out at all, or cost her anything.''

C.J. shifted on the cramped seat and stared at him. ''If you're saying I should have insisted on our original plans, I tried. You were sitting there when we told Mom. If you didn't like the way it was going, you could have jumped in and insisted, too, you know.''

''I didn't feel it was my place to get in the middle of a family disagreement. Plus, I guess I was still stunned by the whole idea.''

''You don't think I was stunned?''

''C.J., I didn't say that.''

''If you need to blame someone, blame...I don't know, blame the situation!''

Michael's blue eyes narrowed. ''I'm not looking for someone or something to blame. I'm just saying that things got out of hand and went in a direction we didn't plan on. And neither of us feel very good about it.''

"I don't want to talk about this, okay?" she snapped. "Just read your book and leave me alone.''

"All right," he said in a tight voice. "You got it.''

Now she didn't feel good about Michael, either. And that wasn't fair. This wasn't his fault. The wedding had been her suggestion.

"Michael?" she said in a small voice. "What are we doing? We just got married a few hours ago. Why are we fighting?"

He looked up from his book and studied her face, then his own expression relaxed. "I'm sorry." Reaching across the armrest, he took her hand. "The last three weeks have been a strain on both of us. The holidays, putting together the wedding..."

"I'm not saying I regret what we did. I'm just saying there are parts of it that we didn't think through as well as we probably should have.''

"I know. Suddenly we were into it and just got swept along." He rubbed her hand between his. "Look. It's done. Let's put the worries behind us for the next few days and just enjoy ourselves.

Can we do that? I haven't had a real vacation in I can't remember when, and neither have you. We both need a vacation, wouldn't you say?"

"You're right. And you might start by picking up some pleasure reading," she said, nodding to the book in his lap.

Michael blinked in surprise. "This *is* pleasure reading."

That made her laugh, and she felt a little better. Dropping her head back on the headrest, she gazed out the window. It had been a long day of firsts.

Her first wedding. Their first kiss. And now their first argument.

"Michael? Do you consider yourself a loner?" she asked, thinking about his horoscope.

"I suppose so," he said after a minute's thought. "Why do you ask?"

"Your horoscope... Oh, never mind."

Maybe Michael had been right to worry if their friendship could survive their marriage. She was starting to wonder, too.

IT WAS A LONG DRIVE from the airport to their hotel outside Lahaina. Michael caught glimpses of moonlight on ocean waves, spotted the feathery silhouettes of palm trees. The cab driver maintained a steady flow of conversation with C.J. while Michael tried to relax and thought about the day.

He doubted he would ever forget the moment he had looked down the aisle and seen C.J. walking toward him on her mother's arm. She was simply the most beautiful bride he had ever seen. And for one fantasy moment, it was all real. She was his and he was hers.

And their kiss... All through the reception, he'd looked at her, danced with her, and remembered that kiss, stunned by his reaction and unable to put it out of his mind.

He'd almost felt relieved when they bickered a little on the airplane; it put things back into perspective for him.

"Wow, this is a gorgeous hotel!" C.J. said, leaning toward the window as the taxi turned into a torch-lit circular drive. Lush tropical greenery crowded the driveway. A livery-clad bellboy hurried forward to assist with the luggage.

And suddenly it occurred to Michael that honeymoon suites didn't have separate beds. He couldn't believe he hadn't thought of that before.

The thought rattled him enough that afterward he hardly recalled registering or following their luggage to the suite.

Frowning, he watched the bellboy carry their bags into the bedroom and set the suitcases beside the bed. One bed. He had requested two beds, but that was before Bill and Susan had upgraded their reservations to the honeymoon suite.

"I'll sleep on the sofa," he said, stepping into the living room once they were alone. He glanced at a puffy sofa done in bright splashes of color.

"Look," C.J. said, smiling. "My flight partners sent us a fruit bowl. And the hotel management gave us a bottle of champagne." She read the cards aloud, then looked around. "This is beautiful!" Throwing open a set of glass sliders, she walked out on the balcony and inhaled deeply. "Oh, Michael! Look at the moonlight on the ocean! And feel that air. It's late, but the air is still warm and it feels so soft." Turning, she hurried back into the suite. "Come on. Let's go explore. It looks like there are several swimming pools, and the beach is lit."

He raised his eyebrows and wrenched his thoughts from how lovely she looked with her eyes sparkling in anticipation. "Shouldn't we unpack first?"

"There's plenty of time for that. We're in Maui, in a fabulous hotel. Let's go see it!"

She had a point. It had been too dark to view

much of the countryside during the drive, but they could at least explore the hotel grounds. On the other hand, it had been a long day, it was late, and they still had to unpack.

"Wouldn't it make more sense to explore the grounds in daylight?" he asked hopefully, feeling the effects of the lengthy flight and an emotionally confusing day. Actually, the sofa was starting to look comfortable and inviting.

"Michael, honey, we're on our honeymoon. We can sleep late tomorrow. Take a look, it's romantic out there." She grinned at him. "I know, I know. Neither of us is particularly sentimental, and romance isn't on the priority list. Would you be more interested in exploring if I told you this place appears to have a maze of interesting-looking paths that meander through exotic greenery? Aren't you curious to discover where the paths lead?"

He suspected they would lead to the same places tomorrow in the daylight, but he didn't say so. Even a pretend marriage required compromise, he realized. And so what if they explored before unpacking instead of afterward? Even if unpacking first was more organized and orderly. Go with the flow. Wasn't that what his horoscope was always advising? Loosen up, Capricorn.

"All right, let's do it," he said, giving in to C.J.'s spontaneous nature.

For the next hour they checked out the hotel's shops and wandered romantically lit grounds, eventually ending up in lounge chairs facing moonlit waves hissing up the beach. A white-coated waiter served them huge goblets of mai-tais and a platter of interesting nibble food.

"This is the life," C.J. said with a contented sigh. She crossed trim ankles on the lounge and sipped her mai-tai in the moonlight. "Here we are eating poi and tiny Hawaiian ribs, relaxing in the lap of luxury. I hope it's snowing back home."

"I picked up some brochures in the lobby." The light was dim on the terrace, making the print hard to read. Romantic settings never had decent lighting. "I thought we'd decide on our agenda. We'll want to explore Lahaina, of course, do some shopping. There's an interesting tour of the cane fields. And I thought we'd rent a car and drive to Hana one day. Another day we could drive up to see the volcano. Does that sound interesting?"

She shrugged. "Sure. So does just lying on the beach."

"Great! Okay, let's do Lahaina tomorrow, get the shopping out of the way. Saturday, we'll tour the cane fields in the morning, rent the car after lunch and schedule some beach time for the afternoon. Sunday, we could drive to Hana—that's an all-day trip. We'll have lunch by the waterfalls. Monday—"

"Wait!" C.J. was staring at him over the top of her mai-tai goblet. "Michael, do we have to plan every minute of this trip? Can't we just take each day as it comes and do whatever we feel like doing at the moment?"

The idea horrified him.

"I spend most of my life by the clock," she continued. "Check with the crew desk at one o'clock, flight leaves at two o'clock, arrives wherever at five o'clock, there's a one-hour-and-forty-minute turnaround, then check in with the crew desk, and on it goes. All by the clock. The best part of a vacation is not having to be somewhere at a certain time, and doing what you want to when you want to do it."

Michael disagreed. He wanted to catch a cab into Lahaina at nine o'clock tomorrow morning, shop until noon, have lunch at Longi's until about one-thirty, check out the art galleries and shops until three, then stop by the replica of an old whaling village. If he had the day planned correctly, they would have time to relax in the room for an hour before dinner at the hotel's gourmet restaurant on the top floor at seven. If they relied on spur-of-the-moment whims, they could easily miss most of the island's attractions.

C.J. peered across the small table separating their lounge chairs, then laughed. "Hey, I didn't mean to throw you into a trauma. Okay, how about this? You can plan every other day. On the off days, we'll play it by ear. Does that work for you?"

Compromises never satisfied anyone one hundred percent. But if she could agree to a couple of days of organized activities, he supposed he could endure a couple of unplanned days. "Okay," he said finally, reluctantly replacing the brochures in his jacket pocket.

They sat in silence, sipping their drinks and watching the waves tumble up the beach. C.J. had been right. This was a nice, relaxing way to end a unique day. Better than sitting in the suite trying to think of something to say that wouldn't sound strained or turn into a cliché.

"You know something?" she said after a while. "I had a bit of a bummer on the plane, but I don't regret what we did. I'm glad I'm here with you, my friend. We're going to have a nice vacation. The craziness of Christmas and the wedding is over, and we have a brand-new year ahead. And you're starting it a million dollars richer. What are you going to do with the money?''

"Pay off my office building," he answered promptly. "Maybe I'll get started on building my house. Maybe I'll invest some of it." He shrugged. "Actually, we've been so busy that I haven't really had time to think much about it." It was odd how quickly he'd fallen into the habit of saying "we" instead of "I."

She shifted on the lounge to face him, curling her legs up under her. "I don't think I remembered to wish you a happy New Year. And happy birthday, too, Michael."

Humidity had made her hair curly, and a light breeze off the ocean teased curling tendrils from the elegant upsweep she'd worn for the wedding. She looked charming and adorable. "My grandfather always said that zero birthdays were milestones." He smiled and took her hand. "He was right. This birthday is going to be hard to top. We'll have to do something special on your thirtieth birthday, too."

Immediately, he wished he'd held his tongue. They had married on his thirtieth birthday, they would be seeking a divorce on her thirtieth. Tactfully, C.J. didn't point this out. She squeezed his hand and managed a smile.

"I have a confession to make," she said, lacing her fingers through his. "I always wanted a honeymoon in Hawaii. It's almost a cliché, but still… Have you been here before?"

"No, this is the first time." He'd always thought of Hawaii as a honeymoon place, too.

"Me, too. I was saving Hawaii for my honeymoon."

And now they had both wasted paradise on a pretend honeymoon. When the real thing came along, they would each have to choose another site.

"Well," Michael said, when he felt their moods start to sink, "it's been a tiring day. Are you ready to turn in?" He resisted mentioning that they still had to unpack.

Which, as it turned out, was something of a frustrating experience. He went about unpacking in a methodical and efficient manner. C.J., on the other hand, kept wandering off to admire the view in the middle of putting her things away and abandoned a pile of clothing on the bed while she poured them glasses of champagne. He finished putting his clothing away long before she did, then sat in a chair beside the bed to keep her company while she finished.

Somewhere in the middle of hanging things in the closet, she had washed her face and donned a nightgown and a white terry-cloth robe. Now she sat on the side of the bed, holding her champagne glass close to her chest and looking at the floor.

"Maybe it's too many mai-tais followed by too many glasses of champagne, but I'm suddenly having another sinker," she said in a low voice.

"Right place, wrong man?" he asked gently.

"Oh, Michael." The bedside light sparkled in the moisture that filmed her dark eyes. "I'm sorry. It's just...I always imagined... I mean, it's my honeymoon, but..."

He moved to the side of the bed and put his arms around her, guiding her head to his shoulder. "I know," he said gruffly.

On their wedding night they should have been anticipating long hours of making love and making plans for their future. It should have been a night of passion and soft laughter and whispered words of love and commitment.

From where he sat, he could see into the living room, could see the sofa. This wasn't going to be his ideal wedding night, either.

"If you feel like crying, go ahead. I understand

perfectly." He felt the soft curve of her breasts against his chest, inhaled the lemony fragrance of her hair. And he remembered that electric kiss at the altar and became very aware that they were sitting on the bed, holding each other. When he felt an instant stirring, he stared at the sofa over her head and wondered how well their arrangement would actually work out. He suspected it would be harder to live with her than he had imagined, because he no longer saw her the way he used to. There was a kiss between them now. A passionate, electrifying, unforgettable kiss.

C.J. lifted her head, bringing her kissable lips within inches of his own. "I'm sorry. I swore I'd think of this as only a vacation, not a honeymoon. But the *H* word keeps popping up." She gave him a wobbly smile, then her gaze dropped to his lips, and she inhaled softly.

For an instant neither of them moved. Michael didn't think he breathed. He felt paralyzed by the realization that he wanted to kiss his old friend, his pal, his best buddy. He wanted to kiss her until she was breathless and mindlessly whispering his name. He wanted to bend her backward on the bed and open her terry robe to reveal the delights beneath. He wanted a real wedding night with his wife, with C.J.

C.J. was the first to pull away. She lifted her fingertips to a fiery blush spreading across her cheeks. Then she covered a yawn so patently fake that he almost laughed. "Well. Good night, pal," she said abruptly. "Do you need any help with the sofa?"

"There's an extra pillow and some sheets in the closet." He made himself walk to the door. "Sleep well."

"You, too," she said, standing beside the bed, giving him a strange look that he couldn't interpret. Desire? Sadness? Both possibilities disturbed him. Desire was against the rules. Sadness wasn't the tone either of them wanted for this vacation.

He should have known that he wouldn't fall immediately asleep on his wedding night. For starters, the sofa wasn't all that comfortable, after all, and it was too short for him to stretch out. He lay in the soft darkness with his arms behind his head, his feet dangling off the upholstered sofa arm, and he listened to C.J. tossing and turning. Apparently, she was having difficulty going to sleep, too.

He wondered what it would have been like if their marriage had been real. Would they have been compatible sexually? He decided there wasn't any doubt about compatibility. A picture of C.J. naked in the moonlight flashed through his mind, and he smothered a low groan. He absolutely could not allow himself to think about her that way. He'd go crazy.

He had to keep in mind that this was not a real marriage. They didn't love each other except as friends. This was simply an expedient and brief arrangement between two people thumbing their noses at interfering relatives.

But he kept coming back to the astonishing realization that he had a wife and they were on their honeymoon, but he was sleeping on the sofa and she was sleeping in the wedding bed. The picture was all wrong.

C.J. SAT IN BED DRINKING her morning coffee and pretending to watch the early news on TV. Actually, she kept sliding glances toward the bathroom, where Michael stood over the sink, wearing only a towel wrapped around his waist, leaning toward the mirror to shave.

There was something intimate and arousing about watching a man shave, she decided, frowning slightly. She'd been watching him shave for four mornings now, and instead of getting used to the sight, it continued to fascinate her. But watching him made her speculate about things she shouldn't be thinking about.

She ran an admiring eye over his smooth bare back and muscled thighs, then resolutely turned her gaze back to the television set.

This honeymoon was driving her bonkers.

Sharing a bathroom meant they were continually running into each other in various stages of undress. Then there was the beach, and more naked chests, legs, thighs.

Yesterday, they had rubbed suntan lotion on each other, and before they'd finished, C.J. was in a fever of arousal. She had stared at Michael's glistening skin and wanted him in a way she had never wanted any man in her life. Michael. Her friend. She'd wanted to drag him up to their room and spend the afternoon in bed. And there had been a moment when he paused, his hands on her sun-warmed back, silky with lotion, when she'd wondered if he was fighting the same desire. It was crazy.

She almost preferred his structured days. At least then they were running here and there according to his schedule. Busily doing things that kept her mind off the nearness of him. The way he smelled of spicy after-shave and sun lotion. His blue, blue eyes and long, dark lashes. The electric tingle she felt when he accidentally brushed against her.

Sighing, she leaned back against the pillows and thrust her fingers through her hair. "What's on our schedule for today?"

Bending over the sink, he splashed water on his face, then patted a towel over his jaw and throat. "The missionaries' museum this morning. Lunch at the Blue Lobster." He came to the bathroom door and skimmed a slow glance over the nightshirt she'd bought in Lahaina. "I'm concerned that you've only bought that nightshirt and some perfume—nothing lasting."

C.J. wasn't certain that he particularly liked the painting he'd bought in one of the many galleries, but he was convinced it was a good investment. Investment potential wasn't among her criteria for an ideal souvenir, and she found it amusing and very like Michael that appreciation in value was his souvenir priority.

"Would you like to do some more shopping this afternoon?"

"Actually, I'd prefer more beach time," she said, looking past his bare chest and the arrow of dark hair that pointed to the towel tied at his waist. "Look, if you'd rather shop you could go without me. We don't have to spend every minute together.'' She was surprised by how snappish she sounded. "I'll be fine right here."

A thoughtful, almost surprised look lifted his eyebrows. "I'd rather spend time with you. But if you're tired of my company..."

She wasn't. She didn't think she'd ever be tired of his company, and she told him so. "I was just concerned about you," she explained. She wished to hell that he would get dressed. It felt strange to be sitting in bed in her nightshirt, talking to a handsome, exciting man wearing only a towel. And knowing her longings were going to go nowhere.

"I'm not tired of your company, either," Michael said. "Sex is out of the question," he blurted suddenly. The statement seemed to surprise him as much as it surprised her. He looked irritated with himself.

"Absolutely," she agreed, feeling heat rise in her face. Oh, Lord. He was thinking about it, too. "No sex. That's the rule. And like you said at some point, a very sensible rule."

"Plus, we've always said we wouldn't let the man-woman thing get in the way of a good friendship."

She stared at him. Wanting him. "Sometimes

that's hard, but we've managed." She hesitated. "It's the right thing to do."

"Absolutely. No question."

"I agree. Sex would only complicate things."

"In a big way."

"It would be hard to go back to just being friends after the divorce. I mean, if sex was in the way."

They studied each other for a long, tense moment, then both burst into laughter. When C.J. recovered, she grinned at him. "Should we talk about this unexpected problem? Or just continue to try to ignore it?"

Michael's smile warmed her all over. "We'll just keep telling ourselves that we're friends and we don't want to do anything that would endanger that friendship." His smile turned rueful. "I've never known any couple that actually stayed friends after ending a sexual relationship."

C.J. thought a minute. "Me, neither."

But holding to the no-sex rule was not going to be easy. Michael was looking at her in a way that smoldered and burned and set her skin on fire. She suspected she was looking at him the same way, because he made a sound deep in his throat, then quickly turned away.

That old man-woman thing was going to be a big problem.

THEY ENJOYED THE MUSEUM, had a fabulous lunch. But shopping in the afternoon pointed out their significant differences. C.J. was drawn to silly, frivolous items, or novelties that had no practical use whatsoever. Michael was pulled toward sensible, useful things, items he could just as easily have bought at home for less money.

"You could have bought that clock anywhere in the world," C.J. pointed out, losing patience. "It's beautiful, but nothing about it says Hawaii." She was tired of walking, and now it was too late to sun on the beach. According to Michael's relentless agenda, they had reservations for a buffet dinner at their hotel, followed by a Hawaiian stage show. She glanced at her watch and headed toward the rental car.

Michael fell into step beside her. "I'll have this clock the rest of my life. How long will that hula doll hold up?"

"Okay, it's a silly souvenir. But maybe I don't want to remember this fake honeymoon for the rest of my life." The minute the words fell out of her mouth, she regretted them. Stopping, she lifted a hand to her forehead. "I'm sorry. I don't know what's wrong with me."

But she did know. And when she raised her head and gazed into Michael's eyes, she understood that he knew, too. Things were changing between them in both obvious and subtle ways. Plus, they were seeing each other with greater clarity than they ever had, learning each other's personal habits and deeper personality traits.

C.J. had discovered that Michael was a considerate and thoughtful companion. His light humor defused potential trouble spots. He was generous but not frivolous with money, and part of his frustration about her hula doll was due to the fact that he had wanted to treat her to something more expensive and lasting. He also drove her a little nutty with his tidiness and practicality and a need for order in his life. He'd even started picking up after her.

And there was that problem of wanting him. That especially drove her crazy. She found herself thinking about him all the time, absolutely all the time. Thinking about him in a way she must have suppressed all these years.

If the honeymoon was this arousing and emotionally confusing, how were they going to live together for five or six months?

C.J. WAS THE MOST disorganized person Michael had ever seen. He hadn't known that about her. And yet, she somehow managed to get herself together despite his certainty that she wouldn't. She would start to put on her makeup, then interrupt to smooth on her nylons, then fiddle with her hair, then return to her makeup. It amazed him that she ended up looking like a million dollars and was ready to step out the door right on time.

He was grateful that she was punctual; punctuality was important to him. Time was money. But the way she wandered off in the middle of things made him feel crazy inside. Her delight with the silly hula doll charmed him, yet he didn't understand it for a minute. He resisted her impulsive suggestions, yet he had surprised himself by enjoying every minute of their unstructured days. The contradictions in his own responses gave him a headache.

"Take a look at that ice sculpture," he said while they were moving through the dinner buffet line. "It occurs to me that it illustrates our differences."

"Odd, I was thinking how different we are, too." But she grasped his point immediately. "I see something beautiful," she said, smiling. "You see something frivolous, a waste of money.

Right? It doesn't plug in, doesn't do anything, it's just going to melt.''

Laughing, he nodded, his gaze sliding over her tanned bare shoulders. Tonight she wore a stunning halter-top black dress that had caught every man's eye. He was proud to have her on his arm, and he felt his chest swell every time she gazed into his eyes and smiled just for him.

"Right. You see the world in terms of beauty and novelty. I see it in terms of usefulness and practicality. That's a big difference in philosophy.''

"Maybe we'll learn something from each other," she said lightly. As usual, she put a positive spin on things.

It was hard not to feel positive on a gorgeous evening like this. Their table was ocean-side, a hurricane lamp cast a romantic glow over their hands and faces, and the air was as warm and moist as honey.

Michael smiled when C.J. laughed at something he'd said, and a forbidden thought flickered through his mind. It would be so easy to break the rules and fall in love with her. They had their differences, yes. But what couple didn't? For the first time since he'd met her, he permitted himself to wonder if they might become something more than friends.

That's what he was contemplating when a half-dozen hula dancers undulated onto the stage and the dinner show began.

"You're supposed to watch the dancers, not me," C.J. whispered, digging a playful elbow into his ribs after he moved his chair next to hers and dropped his arm around her.

But the dancer's swiveling hips weren't nearly as fascinating as the seashell curve of C.J.'s small ear.

"We will!" she called, raising her hand. Standing, she tugged Michael to his feet.

"We will what?" he asked, smiling uneasily at the people turning to look at them. He hadn't been paying attention to the show.

C.J. started toward the stage, pulling him along. "We'll volunteer to learn the hula."

He was mortified. "In front of all these people?" Heat flooded his face, and if there had been any graceful way to decline he would have done so instantly. But C.J. was already climbing the steps to the stage. The audience cheered and applauded. Why wouldn't they? They weren't the people about to make fools of themselves: he and C.J. were.

One of the dancers dropped a plumeria lei around his neck, another took his jacket. C.J. was laughing and trying to swivel her hips. She was getting into it and having fun. Damn. He was stuck, and he hated this kind of thing. But there was no way out. Nothing to do but go along.

"Well, look at this, ladies and gentlemen," the lead dancer said into the microphone. "Sexy guy, huh? Look at those hips!"

The audience whistled and cheered, and Michael managed a weak grin. C.J. swiveled around him, cute as hell, and to his astonishment, he managed to ignore his self-consciousness and swivel right back. After a few minutes he relaxed, and he and C.J. started doing something that was a mixture of the macarena and the hula. The audience laughed and cheered. C.J. giggled and blew him a kiss.

"Let's have a big hand for this couple. They've been good sports."

Still swiveling their hips, he and C.J. danced down the steps and did the hula back to their table, semihysterical with laughter. A bottle of champagne was waiting for them, along with Polaroids of their stage performance, compliments of the management.

"Oh, Lord. If you could have seen your face when you realized we were going up there!" C.J. wiped tears of laughter from her eyes. "And when you started doing the macarena, I thought I'd die!"

"Then you started doing it, and one of the other dancers." He fell back in his chair and grinned.

Never in a million years would he have gone on stage if she hadn't dragged him up there. Now, here he sat, suspecting that tonight would be the night he remembered most vividly about the trip.

They drank the bottle of champagne, then walked in the foam of moonlit surf, holding hands and watching their sandy footprints disappear. They had a nightcap on a torch-lit terrace, decided against a midnight swim, then returned to their room near one o'clock, intoxicated by a perfect evening and each other.

Michael shut the door behind them and didn't bother to turn on the lights. It seemed the most natural thing in the world to take her into his arms and kiss her. The perfect end to a wonderful evening, when their bodies pressed together in a deep and passionate, champagne-tasting kiss. Which led to another and another, each deepening in urgency and need.

C.J. moaned softly and wrapped her arms around his neck when he swept her up and carried her through bars of white moonlight into the bedroom. After standing her on her feet beside the bed, he kissed her again and again and again until they were both breathless and feverish and tugging at each other's clothing with mindless fingers.

There was one moment of fleeting clarity when he thought, We can't do this. Then her dress slipped to the floor and he sucked in a sharp breath, forgetting all the reasons why they couldn't.

She was as beautiful and as lushly perfect as he had imagined she would be. With a trembling finger he traced the tan line curving over her breasts, and when he touched her naked, silky skin he was lost. He couldn't have stopped if he had wanted to. He needed her. Wanted and needed her as if she were the only woman in the world.

"Oh, Michael," she breathed when he placed her on the bed and bent to kiss the rosy tips of her magnificent breasts. "Yes. Yes, yes, yes."

Then she framed his face between trembling hands and kissed him, wildly, deeply. Her body lifted to his.

She was everything he had dreamed of and had ever wanted a woman to be. Enthusiastic, uninhibited, passionate, responsive. His wife was the most exciting woman he had ever been with or could have imagined....

Much later, he gazed down at her tousled head nestled against his shoulder and whispered, "My wife." She murmured something in her sleep and smiled. He held her until his arm tingled painfully, but he didn't want to wake her, didn't want her to move away from him.

He suspected that tomorrow he would deeply

regret their making love, and so would C.J. But right now, Michael was as happy as he had ever been.

FOR A MOMENT, C.J. thought she must have dreamed last night. Then she opened her eyes and found Michael watching her, his head on the pillow next to hers. They were both naked.

"Ohmigod," she murmured, sitting up and grabbing the sheet to her breasts. "We...Michael, we..." Fire burned her cheeks, and she couldn't quite catch her breath. "Good grief. How much champagne did we drink?" Her mind raced.

Okay, there was no sense flogging herself or him. It was the situation. The ocean, the moonlight, paradise. A lot of champagne, flirtatious glances, holding hands. People came to Hawaii because it was romantic. Stronger people than she had probably succumbed to the ambience. And she and Michael were, after all, married. None of the rationalizations helped.

"I owe you an apology," Michael began, sitting up.

She glanced at his naked chest and felt the hot pink deepen on her throat. "I don't recall protesting," she murmured, "so no apologies are necessary. But we've just added a huge complication. Huge."

"Damn it." He pushed a hand through a tumble of dark hair. "I'm sorry, C.J. Things just...got out of hand."

Things, as he termed it, had been fabulous. Wonderful. And now they were in serious trouble.

People didn't embark on an affair knowing in advance that it would end on a certain day. That wasn't their agreement.

And knowing they were terrific together was going to place an inevitable and unavoidable strain on their situation and on their friendship. How did they go back to being just friends after a stunningly wonderful night like last night?

C.J. hit the bed with her fist and explained what she was thinking. "Damn it, anyway. How do we get past this?"

"The only answer is not to let it happen again," he said, hastily slipping out of bed. He dashed for the bathroom.

"I know it." And she hated it. Because C.J. was falling in love with her husband.

And that was very much against the rules of their marriage.

CHAPTER FOUR

CAPRICORN: AVOID overreacting to someone near who's on a different wavelength. Knowing what you want is necessary for your long-term goals.

Gemini: Make sure everyone is on the same page or you could make a mistake. A sense of confusion is no reason not to finish what you started.

Michael paused near the coffeepot to hear the daily horoscope on the radio station C.J. usually listened to. C.J. teased him about listening to his horoscope only so he could ridicule astrology. She was right, of course. That's what he usually did. But today his horoscope came uncomfortably close to the truth.

He'd been impatient lately, a little irritable. But who wouldn't be? C.J. wasn't just on a different wavelength, she sailed an entirely different ocean.

Or could it be that he was nit-picking, looking for differences between them instead of similarities? Seeking out areas of incompatibility instead of letting himself notice how well they got along most of the time.

Frowning, he opened the fridge and added cream to his coffee, then studied the Polaroids clipped to the front of the refrigerator door. As he had sensed at the time, the night they had danced the hula on stage was his most vivid memory of Hawaii. He'd found himself studying the photographs often during the snowy months of January, February and March, and remembering their honeymoon.

Oddly, the days in Maui he had enjoyed most were the unstructured ones when they had followed the whims of the moment. Doing spur-of-the-moment things was also what he secretly most enjoyed about living with C.J., which surprised the hell out of him.

Occasionally she suggested a movie thirty minutes before it was scheduled to begin, which meant they had to make a mad dash for the theater. Instead of resenting the last-minute change in plans, Michael discovered it was like being handed an unexpected surprise. When C.J. was home, life became unpredictable and a lot more exciting than his scheduled existence.

Last week they had impulsively decided to go skiing and headed into the mountains without a hotel reservation, relying on luck, something he wouldn't have dreamed of doing before they married. Nor would he have imagined himself making an adventure of staying in a Motel 6, as they had ended up doing. To his bewilderment, these spontaneous decisions had become moments he treasured, perhaps because they were so unlike him.

Of course, there was another reason that he thought so often of the Hawaiian stage show. That was the night he and C.J. had made wild, passionate love. It was a night he would never forget.

He opened the refrigerator again and took out a bottle of wine, then glanced at his watch. Her flight would be landing about now, then she'd stop by the attendant's lounge and check her company mail before she came home. That gave him an hour and a half to fix dinner, a couple's chore that he enjoyed.

She'd been gone for two days, and he missed her. Badly. The house seemed too quiet, too tidy, too lonely without her. He didn't bother cooking when C.J. was on a layover, didn't sleep well, didn't quite know what to do with himself.

The truth was, he genuinely enjoyed being married. He seldom worked late anymore, feeling he should be home when C.J. was. He liked cooking and was eating better and more sensibly than he used to. He liked hearing about her flights and the people she met, enjoyed telling her about the projects he was working on. Because of her spur-of-the-moment suggestions, he was involved in more leisure-time activities than he had been in years.

Most of all, he enjoyed C.J. She was even-tempered, usually in a good mood. He'd gotten sort of accustomed to the clutter that she created but didn't seem to notice. They never ran out of things to talk about. He appreciated her insightful comments about his work, loved her sense of humor. It was the best of all worlds, living with his best friend.

Except he wanted her every waking minute of his life. Every time he looked at her, he remembered that night in Hawaii, remembered the satiny glow of moonlight on her naked body. Remembered feverish kisses and clinging arms.

Maybe without that night, it would have been easier to live with her. As it was, he bent over backward not to catch a glimpse of her running from the shower to her room, a towel wrapped around her moist body. He tried—and failed—not to think of her sleeping in the room next to his. Tried—and failed—not to remember the silky smoothness of her skin and the yielding warmth of her lips.

She was driving him crazy.

"Damn." He glanced at his watch again, then stared into the refrigerator.

He knew what he was getting out of their arrangement. Companionship, a comfortable home, a congenial and exciting roommate. And, of course, he'd received his inheritance.

In comparison, C.J. had gotten the short end of the stick. In fact, their arrangement worked against her. What if she met Mr. Right on her current flight? Knowing C.J., she'd let Mr. Right walk off the plane without so much as a wink. She would honor her promise to Michael, and their vows, however brief. That wasn't fair to her, and he felt guilty about it.

He slammed a skillet down on the stovetop, detesting the image of some guy flirting with her. On the one hand, he cared deeply enough to want her to meet her Mr. Right. On the other hand, a possessive tiger rose in his chest and roared, *That's my wife and you can't have her. She's mine.*

But that wasn't their agreement, and he had no right to feel that way. He had promised to walk away at the end of a few months. C.J. wasn't his. She was just doing him a favor, that's all. Undoubtedly, she'd be appalled if she knew he experienced flashes of possessiveness.

And heaven knew what she'd think of him if she ever guessed how much time he spent remembering making love to her.

But that night was very much between them. He tended to divide their relationship into the time before he made love to her and the time afterward. And he knew he would never look at her the same way again.

"I'M GOING TO MISS YOU, Mom," C.J. said, giving her mother a hug. They stood in the kitchen, surrounded by the boxes they were packing. "I know how long you've wanted to move to Florida, but now that the moment has finally come…"

Her mother tucked a tendril of C.J.'s hair behind her ear. "You're married now, honey. You don't need me as much anymore."

"I'll always need you," C.J. said loyally, pouring them both a cup of coffee. "But I like thinking about you living near Aunt Betty, having someone to pal around with. Doing new things." They sat down at the kitchen table. "The movers come on Tuesday, right? It looks like we'll be ready by then."

"Honey…I'm so happy for you. Michael is

wonderful.'' A tiny frown appeared above her eyebrows. ''I can see that your marriage isn't like mine was—'' she hesitated ''—but every couple makes their own marriage. I know the two of you are right for each other.''

Guilt made C.J. look away. She wanted to prepare her mother for the inevitable divorce but didn't know how to do it.

''There are a lot of adjustments,'' she said carefully. ''Some are easier than others.''

Her mother laughed and patted her hand. ''Compromise is the key. You're both sensible adults. There's always a compromise.''

Knowing she had deceived her mother didn't get easier with time. ''I don't know, Mom,'' she said, feeling as if she was choking.

''You've been acting so strange.... Are you pregnant?''

A burst of laughter bubbled up from her throat, and C.J. threw up her hands. ''Is that next? Are you going to keep after me about getting pregnant?''

Her mother smiled. ''Neither of us is getting any younger. I expect I'll be mentioning grandchildren off and on.''

''Oh, Mom. I love you. I'm really going to miss you.''

"Hi," Michael called from the doorway. "Are my two favorite girls ready for some pizza?" He strode into the kitchen carrying two hot pizza boxes. After setting them on the table, he looked at the scattered packing cartons. "Looks like you made some progress. After supper, I'll pack the bookcases."

C.J. watched him hug her mother, then lifted her cheek for his kiss. He was practical enough to think of supper, and thoughtful enough to pick up the pizza.

There were so many, many things she liked about him.

It troubled her that they were building a short history together, blending into each other's families. Every other Friday evening, Bill and Susan came to their place for dinner or they went to Bill and Susan's. On Sunday afternoons they stopped by her mother's for coffee and a long visit. They knew each other's friends now and had a busy social life.

Everything would have been so perfect if their marriage had been real. If it didn't end at the bedroom door.

But C.J. didn't dare think about sex, or she would go crazy. Michael had never mentioned that fabulous night in Hawaii, and she was determined to say nothing, either. But she couldn't pretend that it had never happened.

Lifting a hand to her cheek, imagining that her skin still tingled from his hasty kiss, she stared into space, remembering, almost smelling the fragrance of plumeria, almost feeling Michael's lips roaming her body.

The marriage might not be real, but the divorce would be. She gazed at Michael with her heart in her eyes. The divorce was going to hurt like nothing she had ever experienced.

WHEN APRIL'S LAST snowstorm ended, shoots of green poked through the melting drifts. In mid-May, the tulips C.J. had planted last fall unfurled cups of bright red and yellow. She paused to admire the blooms before she squared her shoulders, then entered the town house. When she'd planted the tulips, she hadn't imagined that she would dread seeing them blossom. "I'm home. Something sure smells good. Lasagna?"

"You're late," Michael said irritably, turning from the oven.

As always, she had an intense urge to kiss him when she came home. "Sorry," she said, setting down her flight bag and stretching. "My car wouldn't start."

"I wish you'd let me buy you something reliable. That car is falling apart. You can be so damned stubborn at times."

"By this time next year, I'll have enough saved to buy my own car." Stepping around her flight bag, she picked up the mail and rifled through it. "Here's a letter from Mom." She scanned the pages, then set aside the letter to read later. "She sends her love."

"We need to talk about your car. I don't like to think about you coming in on a late flight, then being alone in a dark parking lot with a car that won't start."

She knew she should feel grateful for his concern, but his continual harping about her car irritated her. "Look, Michael, I don't want you to buy me a car, all right?" She tried not to think about how handsome he looked wearing an apron, his face flushed with heat from the oven. "When this is over, I don't want you to feel like I took advantage of you."

"Pride goeth before a car that won't starteth," he said, staring at her. "It's an old saying."

Forcing a smile, she shuffled through the rest of the mail. Not looking up, she asked in a voice that she hoped was casual, "Did you talk to Bill yet?'' They had agreed that Michael's brother would handle the divorce.

"It was crazy at the firm today. I didn't get to it.''

Relief sagged through her body. ''I guess there's no hurry.''

"I know you're eager to get divorced and get on with your life,'' Michael snapped, bending to the oven to remove a pan of lasagna. ''I'll call Bill tomorrow.''

"It seems to me that you're the one who's eager to buy me a goodbye gift and hit the road.'' C.J. leaned against the countertop. Lately, as the agreed-upon moment for the divorce approached, they'd both been unusually snappish.

He leaned into the fridge to remove the salad, not looking at her. ''People are going to ask why we're getting a divorce. How do you want to answer that question?''

She'd thought about it. Cried over it, if the truth were known. ''We could say we rushed into marriage without much of a courtship.''

"C.J., we've known each other for years. We can't claim we rushed into this. Let's just say we were better as friends than spouses.''

But the qualities that made him her best friend were the same qualities that made him a good husband. And he *was* a good husband, everything she had ever wanted or hoped a husband would be. Except they didn't have a physical relationship. But it was too painful to think about that. Or to remember how it might have been.

"I'll say it just didn't work out," she commented in a low voice. Except it was working out. Everything except the old man-woman thing. But they had honored their decision. Sex wrecked friendships. But not having sex was turning out to be hard on this particular friendship. She thought about it all of the time. Like now, for instance.

"C.J.?" he said suddenly, staring down at the meal he had prepared. "I have to get out of here. Let's go to a movie, okay?"

"Well, good heavens. Hell just froze over. Michael Court made a spontaneous suggestion for an evening out."

He grinned and became the Michael that she knew and loved. "Smart ass. What do you want to see? This will keep, and we'll eat when we get home."

In retrospect, going to a movie wasn't a good idea. They saw a light romantic comedy about a couple falling in love, not a great choice for a couple preparing to file for a divorce.

When they came out of the theater, they were both quiet. And they became quieter when they passed a maternity shop. Both paused to glance at the display window. C.J. didn't know what Michael was thinking, but she was thinking about babies. If their marriage had been real, they might have been planning their family by now. They might have gone home and spent the evening making love, dreaming that a baby would result.

A sigh lifted her chest as they continued walking toward the parking lot. In the almost five months they had lived together, they had talked about everything under the sun except the future. They had no future, at least not together. And talking about a future that didn't include each other seemed awkward and tactless.

Right now, this minute, C.J. wanted to turn to Michael, grab him and beg him not to leave. She wanted to tell him that she'd fallen hopelessly in love with him and beg him to make this a real marriage.

But that wasn't their arrangement. And Michael would be horrified if she admitted she loved him so much it hurt. He was probably counting the days until he could get back to his own apartment and on with his life. If she was his friend, she wouldn't make it hard for him. No begging him to stay. No telling him that things had changed and she loved him. If she really cared about him, if she was a true friend, she'd make the divorce as easy as possible and honor her side of the bargain.

But, oh God, it hurt. She loved him so much. Now she knew why she had never married. Unconsciously, she'd compared every man to Michael and none of them held a candle to him. She had always loved him, but she hadn't let herself admit it.

"I don't want to be home when you move out," she whispered. "Please do it when I'm on a layover."

Later that night they almost collided in the hallway leading to the bathroom. They both said "Sorry," then C.J. embarrassed herself by bursting into tears. They came together in a long embrace, then she ran into her bedroom and slammed the door.

MICHAEL SPOKE TO BILL, their divorce attorney, the next day. He moved back to his small apartment the following Friday. Looking around, he wondered how he had ever thought this was a comfortable place to live. It was too small. Too spare. There was none of C.J.'s clutter to give the place a homey touch.

There was no reason to cook tonight. He could eat out or grab something at the deli.

No reason to watch the clock. C.J. wasn't going to walk through the door.

No reason to pat on some after-shave or check the TV schedule or make plans for the weekend.

He had no idea what to do with himself. He supposed he would work over the weekend. And suddenly he saw himself falling back into the old patterns of solitude and isolation, working evenings and weekends because he had no reason to go home, no one waiting for him.

Angry without really knowing why, he flung himself into a chair and stared at the ceiling. It wasn't supposed to feel like this. Hell, it hadn't been a real marriage, so why did it feel like a real divorce?

The whole thing felt wrong. He didn't feel good about deceiving their families and friends, and he didn't feel good about inheriting his grandfather's money because he hadn't honestly met the stipulation. He'd found a way around it, and he'd used C.J. to do it. He didn't feel good about that, either.

He'd put her life on delay. And she'd refused

to allow him to buy her something, anything, to show his appreciation. It was a bum deal for her.

It felt like a bum deal for him, too, and he didn't understand that. He should have been happy tonight. Instead, he ached inside, missing C.J.

He must have looked at the telephone a hundred times, wondering if she was missing him, too.

"YOU KNOW ME," C.J. said to Cindy Wheeler, speaking in a light voice. "Never finish what I start. I guess that applies to marriage, too."

They were walking through the airport, heading for the gate. Every man she passed looked like Michael, and her heart was bouncing around her chest like a Ping-Pong ball. She wanted one of them to be him.

Cindy looked at her. "I see through you. You're treating this like it's no big deal, like you expected a divorce. But your eyes are still red and swollen from crying. You miss him, don't you?"

Suddenly her throat was tight and hot, and she couldn't answer. But yes. She missed him the way she would have missed an amputated limb.

It had been three weeks now, three long, lonely weeks of utter misery.

"It just didn't work out," she said when she could speak. "We're too different." She told Cindy about their ice sculpture analogy. "He likes solid, lasting things, I like frivolous, silly things. He's tidy, I make clutter. He's scheduled, I'm spontaneous. I start projects, he finishes them. He's orderly, I'm scattered." It helped to list the reasons that a real marriage wouldn't be possible.

But oddly, she enjoyed their differences. She hadn't expected to. But Michael's practicality anchored her. The structure of his life brought order to hers. They complemented each other in ways she hadn't anticipated and couldn't have imagined.

"I'm sorry, I can't talk about this right now," she said to Cindy. "See you the day after tomorrow."

The phone was ringing when she let herself into the silent town house. "Hello?" she said in a listless voice.

"I miss you."

She pressed the receiver tight against her ear, sat down abruptly and waited for her heart to stop racing. "I miss you, too."

"Strange, isn't it?"

"Yeah. Sometimes you drove me crazy picking

up after me, and I know there were times I must have driven you nuts, too.''

"C.J....do you feel mad as hell?''

Surprise lifted her eyebrows. ''How did you know that?''

"Because I'm mad, too. And I don't know why.'' He sighed, and she pictured him pushing his hand through his hair. ''I'm as angry as if this damned divorce were real.''

"Me, too. And I don't understand it. We really aren't suited to each other,'' she said, recalling the things she had told Cindy, all of them true. "We're opposites in almost every way. I don't know why I miss you so much.''

"Me, neither. I don't know how one small woman can create so much clutter in so short a time. And the jigsaw puzzle on the dining room table has been there since before we got married. Are you ever going to finish putting it together?''

She laughed, and then sudden tears sprang into her eyes. ''Oh, Michael. We were idiots to think this would be easy. Telling Mom that we're getting a divorce was one of the hardest things I ever had to do. She cried and I felt lower than a cockroach.''

"Susan cried, too,'' he said in a low voice. "Bill thinks I'm an idiot.''

"I never felt so guilty in my life. Everyone has been so supportive and sympathetic." She gazed past the draperies at the fading sky. "And all the time it was just a fraud." After that, there was nothing more to say. Everything she wanted to say she couldn't. She desperately wanted to tell him, *I love you. Please come home.*

"Well," he said when the silence had stretched into discomfort, "I just wanted to say hello. Check up on an old friend."

It broke her heart that they couldn't think of anything to say to each other. "Michael?" she asked in a whisper. "Is our friendship going to survive this?"

It wasn't his fault that he didn't love her, that he thought of her as just a friend. She had never expected anything else. That had been their agreement. She shouldn't be angry, shouldn't feel let down or so rotten. But she did feel those things.

Everyone had gotten what they wanted. Michael had paid off his office building. Her mother was now in Florida after giving C.J. a wonderful wedding. But C.J. had ended up with a broken heart.

And the worst part was, she didn't want to see Michael again. It would be too painful. So, despite everything they said, despite their best intentions, she'd also lost her best friend.

Tears rolled down her cheeks as she quietly hung up the phone.

WHEN HE SAW A VAPOR TRAIL crossing the sky, he thought of C.J. He doodled her name on the margin of blueprints. Twice a day he reached for the phone to call her and tell her something he'd just thought of. He dreamed of her at night, woke up thinking about her.

He'd never been this miserable.

"Michael, did you hear anything I just said?"

He blinked at his brother. "I don't know. What did you just say?"

"I just said this is the damnedest divorce I ever handled. You keep giving things to C.J., and she keeps giving them back." He gazed down at the papers on his desk. "She's insisting on sticking to the prenuptial agreement. Rightly so, in my opinion. She doesn't want a new car, doesn't want her town house paid off, doesn't want you to set up a trust for her. She just wants a divorce."

That's what killed him inside. C.J. wanted the divorce. Every time the phone rang, he prayed it was her, telling him to come home. But it never was.

"Michael, let's talk a minute." Bill folded his hands on top of the papers. "Why in the hell are you and C.J. getting a divorce?"

"That's what we agreed to."

"My question is, why? There's no anger on either side. You're both bending over backward to be fair, even loving. Did you try counseling? Maybe the difficulties can be worked out."

"She doesn't love me," he said impulsively, then flushed with embarrassment. "She never did."

"That is the stupidest thing I've ever heard you say. Every time she looked at you, it was obvious that she loved you."

Michael stared at him and hope leapt into his heart. No, C.J. was merely acting the role of a new bride. She didn't love him. They were best friends, and that was all.

"And I think you still love her."

"Of course I do," he said without thinking. "I've always loved her." He sat up straight and gripped the arms of his chair.

Good God. He had always loved her. Always.

"You know, I have this sinking suspicion... Michael, surely... Have you told C.J. that you still love her?" Bill stared at him in astonishment, then groaned. "You haven't told her."

Of course not. Admitting to C.J. that he loved her would leave him vulnerable to a painful rejection. And telling her would wreck their friendship. His declaration would always be between them.

Bill shook his head, then glared at the ceiling. "For a smart guy, you can be so dumb. Now, listen to me. For once I'm going to give you some advice. You and C.J. were made for each other. For heaven's sake, tell her that you love her. Tell her that you refuse to file the divorce papers until you two have given your marriage another try."

He loved her. He couldn't get past that thought. He had always loved her. He always would.

What a fool he was. He could sit here and tell his brother that he loved C.J., but he couldn't tell her. Jumping to his feet, he strode toward the door.

"Michael?"

"You're right," he said in a firm, determined voice. "Don't file those papers unless I tell you it's hopeless."

"Where are you going?" Bill asked, grinning.

"Tomorrow's her birthday. I have a lot to do."

"Just don't buy her anything that plugs in."

Michael laughed. "Oddly, we never had a real courtship. I'm going to court her, and I won't give up until..." His words were swallowed by the closing door.

He loved her. And he was going to win her.

C.J. WAS STILL IN BED when the doorbell rang, sipping coffee and staring blankly at the morning news on TV. Cindy Wheeler had already phoned to wish her happy birthday and invite her to spend the day shopping, but she had declined. She didn't feel like celebrating this year.

Somehow she had always expected that her thirtieth birthday would be special. Something wonderful or silly to mark the end of one decade and the beginning of another. In her secret heart, she'd expected to be married and thinking about starting a family. Instead, she was about to divorce the most wonderful man she'd ever known, a man she loved so much that she ached inside.

She decided she would spend the day in bed, feeling sorry for herself and thinking moody thoughts about getting older, about being lonely, about losing Michael.

There was only one person she wanted to see or talk to, and he wouldn't be at her door, so she ignored the persistent ringing of the doorbell.

But it didn't stop. Whoever was on her doorstep started pounding on the door as well as leaning on the bell.

"Damn it." Throwing back the sheets, she pushed her feet into her slippers and stomped downstairs to tell off whoever was being so inconsiderate. Probably one of the neighborhood kids.

"I'm coming!"

She drew a breath, telling herself to calm down. Then she opened the door and her mouth fell open.

"Don't say anything," Michael said quickly. "Just listen for a minute."

Behind him at the curb was a shiny new red Cadillac. Pots of flowers lined the sidewalk leading to her door. The lawn was covered with unwrapped gifts. Crazy gifts, at least for Michael. Boxes of candy, lingerie, perfume-and-powder sets, dolls, Beanie Babies, a Nintendo set, towels. And more. She couldn't take it all in.

"I must be dreaming."

"C.J., I don't want a divorce. Now, I know that isn't what we agreed to," Michael said earnestly. "But I want to be married to you for the rest of my life. I'm going to court you for however long it takes, I'll never give up, and—"

"Michael! What is all this?"

"That's your new car, the impractical one you wanted," he said, his gaze devouring her. "And the rest...well, there's no law that says a man can't give his wife a few birthday presents. C.J., I love you. I know you only love me as a friend, but I'm going to court you until you love me as a man. I'm determined and I'm persistent. I'm patient enough to wait until I wear you down and you let me come home. I want to spend the rest of my life picking up your clutter, finishing your projects, waking up with you beside me."

"You love me?" she whispered, staring at him. Her heart stopped, then soared.

"I've been fooling myself for years. I've always loved you."

And then she saw his pièce de résistance. A huge ice sculpture in the shape of a heart sat melting on her lawn. And she knew he thought ice sculptures were a wildly impractical waste of money. If he would buy her an ice sculpture...

"Whatever differences we have, darling C.J., we can work them out," he said, casting a speculative look at the nightshirt she had bought in Maui. "Please, give me a chance. Tell me you might learn to love me someday, not just as your friend, but as your husband and lover. Please, give me some hope."

"Oh, Michael, you adorable idiot!" She threw herself forward and wrapped her arms around his neck, pressing against him. "I've loved you from the first time I saw you."

"You have?" He looked astonished, then he held her so tightly that she thought he would crush her, and he was trembling. He kissed her, deeply, passionately, not caring that the neighbors had collected on the sidewalk and were watching with large grins.

When their lips parted, C.J. drew back with a shaken whisper. "Wow."

"You love me, too," he whispered.

"And I want to be married to you." Her scalp tingled and her body was on fire. "Michael? I love the gifts, but there's one birthday present that only you can give." She nibbled his lower lip, then looked up with sparkling eyes. "You'll be happy to know it doesn't cost a cent."

He laughed and swept her up into his arms. "If I walk in your door and carry you up to your bedroom, I'm never leaving. Are you sure that's what you want?" he asked in a low, throaty voice, his eyes on her lips.

"More than anything in this world," she whispered.

Before he carried her inside, she noticed the

small appliances piled beside the door, and laughed. "A toaster and a vacuum cleaner?"

"Yours need to be replaced," he said, grinning.

C.J. grabbed his face and kissed him, putting her heart and soul into it. Then he carried her inside and kicked the door shut behind them.

She suspected there would be a lot to discuss in about an hour. Michael would want to map out their future; she would want to let it unfold as it would. Laughing, she buried her face in the crook of his neck and clung to him as he carried her up the staircase, almost running. They had waited so long.

"Michael?" she murmured against his neck. "Let's go to Las Vegas, find an Elvis impersonator and have a real wedding."

He laughed and tossed her onto the bed, then lay down beside her and took her into his arms. "And this time we won't be deceiving anyone."

The only people they had deceived were themselves. But that was over now. And the old man-woman thing was even more fantastic than either of them remembered.

The Elements of Romance

Your astrological love guide for 1999

PART I

Part I

The Elements of Romance

Every sign in the zodiac possesses a style, an
approach to life all its own. And, too, every true
romantic under the stars has her own way of
expressing her heart's desires.

What kind of romantic are you? The answer
is "elemental"—at least according to your
horoscope. That is, the element your astrological sign belongs to can tell you a lot about your
romantic style.

All twelve astrological signs come under one
of four groupings called elements. These are:
fire, earth, air and water. The elements have
been used for thousands of years in various
branches of metaphysical studies, including
tarot and astrology.

Simply put, signs of a like element have certain characteristics in common—one of which is how you approach romance.

What's your ideal courtship scenario? What kind of hero are you attracted to? You can get important clues to these and other issues from knowing your element.

In Part I, we'll examine in detail your romantic style as revealed through your astrological element.

Part II is devoted to a sign-by-sign rundown on the "Heroes of the Zodiac." What does your guy's sign say about him? Look him up and find out.

In Part III, we look ahead through 1999. Turn to your own sign and get an overview of your romantic prospects for the year ahead.

The Impassioned Romantics—Fire

ARIES (March 21–April 19)
LEO (July 23–August 22)
SAGITTARIUS (November 22–December 21)

You're the most dramatic of romantics, and yearn to fall in love in an epic way. Romance must be larger than life for you, something that sweeps you away from the ordinary.

A constant stream of hearts and flowers is impractical, it's true. But you do demand of your beloved a grand romantic gesture from time to time—such as filling the back seat of your car with roses, or whisking you off in a hot-air balloon to sip champagne as you float high above the countryside.

The fire signs possess a positive and dynamic approach to all aspects of life. You have a personality that is warm and exciting, the kind that can light up a dull gathering just by entering the room.

Leo has the most dramatic flair, while Sagittarius and Aries may appear more casual, even offhand, about the whole thing. But you have but to scratch the surface to ignite a true fire romantic.

Fire equates with passion, and you can give Scorpio a run for the money in the sexiest sign contest. Sometimes you do play with fire and fall for the wrong guy. But sex is certainly not all you have in mind, for to be passionate about life is to burn for experience. The fire signs seem to blaze with an unflagging inner zest.

You need a partner with whom you can

throw yourself into common interests and activities. Doing things together is almost as important as sharing feelings and thoughts. You can easily envisage yourself climbing Mount Everest with your beloved, or teaming up to detect and foil a plot by evil diamond smugglers. As well, a cause you can both feel impassioned about, such as saving an endangered species or raising funds for a charity, can provide a close and lasting bond.

Most of all, you believe in the lightning-bolt, love-at-first-sight experience. You really enjoy hearing about other couples who got together in this way—and you feel it can and should happen to you. Instant passion blended with complete understanding is your ideal scenario. You truly believe two people can look into each other's eyes and become a couple the first time they meet.

Should impetuousness lead you to romantic disappointment, you tend to bounce back more quickly than people associated with other elements. You're also likely to remain friends with your exes. For you, life is just too short to hold a grudge when another new and far more exciting romance could await just around the corner.

The Down-to-Earth Romantics–Earth

TAURUS (April 20–May 20)
VIRGO (August 23–September 22)
CAPRICORN (December 22–January 19)

Down-to-earth, salt of the earth—your approach to romance is definitely practical. Even when being swept off your feet, you manage to keep at least one toe on terra firma. No one has more old-fashioned common sense than you do.

Earth signs are uncomfortable with a lot of extravagant wooing. You do appreciate the finer things in life, but your sense of responsibility often interferes with enjoyment. Should your loved one blow a bundle on a night out, you worry about the cost too much to let yourself go.

Taurus is the most cautious and conservative earth sign, with Virgo close behind. Capricorns underwent a major transformation in the early 1990s. Many of you are now more open to the intangible side of life—like romance.

But in general, all earth signs remain sceptical about love at first sight or promises of castles in the air. Your hero must respect your need to ease slowly into a relationship and be willing to work with you to make it succeed. You believe everything, even love, comes only through some effort.

For you, the most important element of romance is building a life together, and that process usually includes building a *home* together. You don't like to rush this phase, either. You like to watch the bricks go up, one by one. You enjoy all the little details involved in growing closer to someone.

The earth signs are very sensual, but not in an overt way. You're uncomfortable with showing too much affection in public. For you, growing intimacy, especially passion, is a very private affair.

You like to think any commitment is forever—and when it isn't, you become more disillusioned than most people. Earth signs also take a long time to get over disappointment. Yet, though you don't like change, you do believe one or both partners can undergo a transformation through love. As an earth romantic, you know love has the power to redeem.

Being an earth sign and a romantic to many people seems a contradiction. For isn't romance itself an intangible, a fantasy? How does that mesh with being practical?

You see no problem here. For you know the only truly happy ending—whether in a fictional or real-life love story—is the one where you both live happily ever after. And that means in the real world, with both feet firmly on the ground.

The Social Romantics–Air

GEMINI (May 21–June 21)
LIBRA (September 23–October 23)
AQUARIUS (January 20–February 18)

The setting is perfect for romance. Your eyes sweep across the ballroom, sparkling with chandeliers and just-poured champagne. Dialogue swirls around you as effervescent as the setting. You finally spot your handsome, dashing hero talking to the ambassador....

If you're an air sign, this scenario speaks to your romantic heart. Your fantasy may not be as extravagant as fancy-dress balls. But if a prospective hero can't blend with your friends or help you explore new social horizons, then you won't cast him in a lead role.

The social mix does change, however, depending on your sign. With Geminis, the crowd leans heavily toward the intellectual elite. Librans fill their guest lists with people from the cultural world. And of course Aquarians, with their love of the unusual, mix nuclear physicists with opera singers—and perhaps a visitor or two from another planet.

Your element may be air, but that doesn't mean you're "airheaded" when it comes to romance. Just the opposite is true; air signs place the intellect and the world of ideas above all other concerns. Bright and stimulating conversation ranks high on your list of attractive qualities in a man.

Alone with your beloved, good communication is more important than any other demonstrations of affection. Let others sigh deeply and gaze soulfully into their beloved's eyes, or shower them with rose petals. You'd rather be with a hero who can articulate his feelings.

Paradoxically, you're often drawn to enigmatic types. This is because your own constantly active mind loves a puzzle. A potential hero who is a bit complicated intrigues you. You always assume that if you apply your intellect, you can figure him out. And if he can match wits with you and even top you now and then, you're likely to stay fascinated for life.

If you're like most air romantics, you're far too restless in youth to settle down too quickly. And as much as you need companionship, your standards are very high. You believe in an ideal mate—which may be hard to come by in imperfect real life.

But when you stop focusing too much on the ideals of romance, you can fashion the kind of relationship other people envy—one with excellent communication, played out against the backdrop of a glittering social life. Some might say the setting and plot can overshadow the inner workings. That's okay with you—you're probably already planning your next ball.

The Go-With-the-Flow Romantics–Water

CANCER (June 22–July 22)
SCORPIO (October 24–November 21)
PISCES (February 19–March 20)

Two people lock eyes across a crowded dance floor. Suddenly nothing else in the universe exists as they draw closer and closer together. They begin to dance, instantly in tune with each other's rhythms. The unspoken understanding is complete, no dialogue is necessary.

If you're a water sign, you just know when it's love. Like the fire signs, you believe in love at first sight. But unlike the lightning bolts they experience, you prefer the gentle and complete merging of two souls. Intuition is everything to you, and you're more likely than other signs to believe in soul mates.

Pisces, especially, believes that people destined to be together just flow into one another. Scorpio adds more intensity and drama to the mix: nothing short of *une grande passion* will do. For Cancer, the process takes a bit more time to evolve, since home and family are strong factors.

While your heart may yearn for a spiritual or mystical bond, your approach to courtship is on the traditional side. You revel in all the customary trappings: candlelight, soft music, dancing cheek to cheek. But everything is secondary, really, to growing emotional closeness.

For this reason, the new ideal of the "nineties man"—one who isn't afraid of his feelings—is in many ways your true hero. It's just not enough for your ideal guy to be strong and stalwart; he must also have a compassionate side. You dream of a romance in which you both fulfill your hearts' desires.

Like the earth signs, you feel marriage is the natural conclusion to any love affair. But for you, it's less about doing what society dictates, and more about the symbolic fulfillment of all your hopes and dreams of true intimacy.

Naturally, the course of true love rarely flows

in a nice, steady stream. In real life there are always some snags, occasional undertows, sometimes raging torrents. But it is this variety that makes romance so exciting. And your ability to navigate whatever comes your way is your strength. You dream of a great romance where you both come together after facing many disappointments—where love conquers all and always, always triumphs in the end.

PART II

Part II

Heroes of the Zodiac

Looking for a new hero to play a role in your love life? Or maybe you were just introduced to someone and wonder if he's the one. Perhaps you'd simply like more insight into your current costar.

A man's astrological sign reveals a lot about his romantic style. Following is a guide to the twelve heroes of the zodiac, Aries through Pisces: what to look for—and what to look out for!

Aries (March 21–April 19)
"The Warrior"

That upright bearing, firm stride and rugged bone structure—the Aries hero often has a military air. With it comes a certain raw power that's incredibly appealing. In fact, he tends to turn feminine heads and give Scorpio a run for the "Sexiest Sign" title. His wooing can be a bit on the primitive side, though. Aries' natural style is along the lines of "see it, want it, drag it back to cave." Be firm and insist he treat you like a lady. When urged toward civilized behavior, he improves rapidly. He'll soon turn into a passionate, ardent and surprisingly steady hero. He'll take a creative approach to keeping the flame of romance burning.

Taurus (April 20–May 20)
"Mr. Smoothie"

Sensible, down-to-earth, cautious—by reputation, this hero is about as romantic as an old overcoat. But Venus, his ruling planet, has taught him well the arts of love. Though his thrifty side may balk at a dozen roses to lay at your feet, he does know how romantic a single perfect bloom can be. He loves good food and wine, and courts in style if not extravagance.

Taurus men are slow to commit, but once they do, it's for the long haul. This is one romantic guy who means what he says. And he believes firmly in the importance of marriage, home and family. Never, never trifle with the bull, though. Once roused, his anger can be terrible.

Gemini (May 21–June 21)
"Floats Like a Butterfly"

This hero belongs to the planet that gave us "mercurial." The adjective is apt: restless and ever-busy, he enters and exits your life on an erratic time schedule. If you're secure enough to put up with this, you'll never be bored. For you've got yourself the most witty, eclectic and urbane of heroes. He can talk to anyone, anytime, about anything. He knows enough humorous stories to brighten any dinner party. He is genuinely kind and compassionate, but dislikes heavy, unpleasant emotions. Keep it on the light side, and negotiate stylishly rather than confronting him. Then your life together can be a delicious romp, full of good times laced with sparkling dialogue.

Cancer (June 22–July 22)
"The Man in the Moon"

This complex hero is ruled by the moon and his emotions. He's dazzlingly cheerful one minute, moody and withdrawn the next. In time you'll catch on to the phase pattern. And he will reciprocate. For this is a man who knows without being told when you need a hug or a shoulder to cry. Once committed, he's sure to want children. He'll also be totally supportive if you have offspring from a previous marriage. He may not have a lot of style and flash, but he is a solid citizen who doesn't take his commitments lightly on any front. A Cancer hero is the most domesticated of men, who often courts you with his gourmet cooking talents.

Leo (July 23–August 22)
"The Leading Man"

This hero has a well-earned reputation for dramatic flair. Once he casts you opposite him, he can be extravagant and courtly in his wooing. Yet he never, never playacts at romance—it's everything to the Lion. He's got a strong sentimental streak, and his gifts may be both expensive and meaningful. Make certain you are suitably appreciative. Just never make the mistake of taking him for granted. Without frequent applause, he'll sulk and growl. His major downfall is the tendency to be possessive, sometimes overbearing. Keep him purring by setting limits at the start and establishing total trust. You'll then have a truly gallant, stylish and tenderly protective hero.

Virgo (August 23–September 22)
"The Sensual Accountant"

At first he seems a poor candidate for a starring role in your romance. The least sentimental of all signs, a Virgo can be analytical to the point of coldness. But behind that carefully tailored, conservative suit lies a quiet romantic. He doesn't go for big displays of affection, especially in public. But he can come up with incredibly thoughtful gestures that warm your heart. This is no flash-in-the-pan guy, either. The Virgo takes his sweet time in his courting and believes in long engagements. Once committed, he can be surprisingly sexy and an inventive lover. He'll be thrilled if you always dress in good taste and occasionally fuss over his health.

Libra (September 23–October 23)
"The Charmer"

This hero has a smile that makes women's knees go weak. That's as true if you're a blushing twenty-something or a stately senior he just helped across the street. He makes instant fans for life of both sexes wherever he goes, and people invariably remember his name. He's equally at home in a box seat at the opera or at a hockey game, and he's on everyone's guest list. If you don't like competition, pass this one by. His little black book tends to be a rather large database. But when you're with him, he makes you feel as if you're the only woman in the world. If you can keep challenging his mind and spirit, the Libra can settle down to become a very devoted partner in life and in love.

Scorpio (October 24–November 21)
"Heathcliff II"

This hero is definitely cast in the Gothic mold: dark, brooding, and on the slightly tortured side. The Scorpio is also overtly sexy, with a hypnotic power that draws you under his spell. This passionate romantic believes in loving with all his soul, and in the redeeming power of love. However, like heroines in stories of old, you may have to go through many trials to gain his trust. This hero doesn't fall easily, but once he does, his devotion is as complete as it gets. At his best, this is the hero who will support your needs and desires in every way that is humanly possible. At his worst, he uses his keen sense of your inner workings to wound. Avoid the bad ones at all costs.

Sagittarius (November 22–December 21)
"The Swashbuckler"

If you long for someone to sweep you up onto a white charger and out of the everyday, a Sagittarian hero is for you. This guy has a great lust for life and a rollicking sense of adventure. And he's always willing to take you along for the ride. His courtships tend to be conducted on white-water rafts or mountain outcroppings. He's honest to a fault—literally. His bluntness can be hurtful, and tends to cramp any more tender romantic style you're trying to establish. But if you want an equal partner for life who will encourage and support your loftiest dreams, a Sagittarian is for you. Don't try to make him settle down too early, though. He's a late bloomer marriagewise.

Capricorn (December 22–January 19)
"The Corporate Climber"

Writers of traditional and contemporary romances tend to keep this sign under observation. In so many ways the male of the species epitomizes the modern hero. Upwardly mobile and successful, his Gucci loafer is firmly placed on the next rung up the corporate ladder. A secret: as assured as he is in the boardroom, he can be ultrareserved, even shy and bumbling, one-on-one. But there is a latent romantic deep within this driven hero, even if getting to the clinch may take persistence. He's slow to ignite, but once you break down the fears and resistance, you'll have a stalwart hero who never, ever forgets your birthday or Valentine's Day.

Aquarius (January 20–February 18)
"The Mad Scientist"

A hero of this sign usually lives up to his reputation for eccentricity, even in romance. He will serve you hamburgers on antique silver, and caviar and peacock tongues on plastic kiddie plates. He's often accused of living in his own world, but it is certainly one of constant surprises. Since he's the most gregarious sign, love him, love his collection of oddball friends. Avoid mushy shows of sentiment with him, and always give this hero lots of space. He'll do the same for you in a way that is wonderfully supportive. Life with an Aquarian is certainly never dull—but rather a constant stream of surprises, lightning bolts and electric connections.

Pisces (February 19–March 20)
"Beautiful Dreamer"

Mystic, poet, visionary—the Pisces hero's eyes seem to be always focused on some distant horizon. They also tend to be dreamily seductive, while his voice is soft and appealing. Before you realize it, you're under his spell, wrapped in a rapturous pink cloud. But one of you must keep a foot on the ground. It had better be you, because that's one talent a Pisces doesn't often possess. But boundless kindness, compassion and empathy are his strong suits. Actually, he's a bit of a chameleon, with the ability to change to suit your expectations. Just never assume he's superficial: this hero has more depth of psyche than any other. He can very well become all men to you.

PART III

Part III

1999—a new year, a new romance?

Now it's time to look up your own sign, and see what 1999 holds in store for you.

If you were born on the cusp of two signs, or around the time they change, some horoscopes might tell you you're one sign, another that you're the following sign. For instance, if your birthday is May 21, this horoscope indicates you are a Gemini, while another might say Taurus. Because the year isn't precisely 365 days long, the calendar date a sign changes varies slightly from year to year. Sometimes the only way to know for sure is to have your chart done by an astrologer.

Your 1999 Romance Outlook
Aries (March 21–April 19)

The old tune about doing it your way rings hollow now. Being in harmony with a special someone hits the top of the charts for you. Despite some early friction, most of the year should go smoothly in relationships. You may settle down with an exciting new hero by winter's end.

Timeline: Your birthday sparkles with romantic opportunity. A love interest begins to shine in a new light. Escape into your favorite romance novel in May; fictional heroes are more satisfying than the real thing. But in June, a company picnic or other work-related event could find you sharing more than a table with someone new. Fall brings a more serious trend. Look for a new or existing relationship to take a more committed turn around October.

Times when love comes easily your way: February 21–March 17, June 6–25, October 4–11
Take the romantic initiative: June 3–14, September 3 and December 6–8

Your 1999 Romance Outlook
Taurus (April 20–May 20)

The key to romantic success is to resist taking any relationship for granted. Treat each one like a garden—tend it a little bit each day, do some spadework when necessary, and prune out the weeds before they become a problem. And if you can open up to new experiences, this could be one of the more exciting and fulfilling years of your life.

Timeline: Early April finds you on the horns of a dilemma: should you follow your heart onto new ground or play it safe? No easy solution appears. Have patience, and look for a breakthrough by May. Summer doldrums are just fine with easygoing you. You're gently flirtatious, especially when away from home. Someone new may find your charms hard to resist around mid-August. The fall is stable, and from November on, you can write your own ticket on the "love boat."

Times when love comes easily your way: January 6–9, March 17, July 24–30, November 24–27
Take the romantic initiative: April 2–8, September 11–12

Your 1999 Romance Outlook
Gemini (May 21–June 21)

Most of the planets are on your side now. But the road to your romantic dreams still feels like a minefield. Power is the explosive issue—how much you have and how wisely you use it. Anything can be negotiated, though, if you're clear about your needs. Do that, and the year ahead holds great romantic promise.

Timeline: New admirers crop up where you least expect them. Most fertile spots through April: office coffeepots or water coolers, community centers and cozy cafés. A more stable rapport begins to take root in June. With a little effort, a fruitful summer romance could bloom. Someone else's romance benefits from your flair for on-the-spot diplomacy in October. Planetary patterns in December are troublesome only if you let a light flirtation take you too far too quickly.

Times when love comes easily your way: February 6–11, May 12–20, November 14
Take the romantic initiative: June 6–12, October 7 and December 6–8

Your 1999 Romance Outlook
Cancer (June 22–July 22)

Value received for value given is very much the issue this year. Too often, you lavish time and loving energy on heroes who just don't deserve the bounty. Stop selling yourself short, and watch your self-esteem steadily rise. With it comes the ability to attract a hero with true nobility of spirit.

Timeline: The eclipse mid-February burns through the mists of confusion surrounding a relationship decision. Clarity of purpose is refreshing. Your working life holds the most romantic promise in April. Shared interests could springboard you into a long-term romance. Batten the romantic hatches in July and weather the storms generated by the eclipse. By mid-August you satisfactorily resolve an old issue over shared space or resources. A quietly gregarious trend kicks in in mid-November. You spend the holidays with a full social calendar and some-one supportive by your side.

Times when love comes easily your way: January 3–9, March 15–20, September 5–15
Take the romantic initiative: February 14–22, June 23–30, November 14–16

Your 1999 Romance Outlook
Leo (July 23–August 22)

Even the kind of Leo who tries to hide her softer side under a bushel feels ready to let the love shine through this year. You may undergo a transformation of some sort, opting for a totally new type of hero. Just make sure you audition him thoroughly before casting him in a leading role.

Timeline: You detect a decided chink in your knight's armor around mid-February. No patchwork solutions will do. Don't gloss over the crack, or it may prove a fatal flaw by April. Most of the spring is lighthearted. May has a reputation as a lusty month, but it's tenderness you're after. From the fifteenth on, dalliance is oh-so-sweet. Fall's trends are easygoing, and you can take everything pretty much as it comes. A romantic spark kindled in December could turn into a very steady flame the other side of 2000.

Times when love comes easily your way: February 21–March 4, August 6–25, November 5-11
Take the romantic initiative: March 6–14, October 5–7 and December 6–8

Your 1999 Romance Outlook
Virgo (August 23–September 22)

Letting go of old attachments is the key to romantic success. If you're married, bury the hatchet once and for all about a long-standing sticking point. No new relationship will benefit from bringing in old baggage, either. Once you jettison the excess, this is the year for a new flowering in romance.

Timeline: Planetary passages augur that you be more reclusive than usual early in the year. Others worry about you. But you know a little quiet revamping of your romantic strategy is necessary. Fresh insights make you more assured in April. You might even make the first move. The time around your birthday prompts you toward self-improvement. Joining a new health or sports club offers romantic opportunities, as well, in mid-October. Whether you're in a new or existing rapport, affection and trust warm the winter months.

Times when love comes easily your way: January 6–14, March 29–April 5, November 4–11 Take the romantic initiative: May 11–14, October 23–27, and December 22–30

Your 1999 Romance Outlook
Libra (September 23–October 23)

This is a banner year for romance. But instead of waiting for the hearts and flowers to be delivered, wave a few flags. Put aside your hesitancy and drop hints in the right quarters. Whether you're in a new or existing love relationship, it flourishes with some flamboyant creative direction. Exploit your imagination to the fullest.

Timeline: A misunderstanding in late January melts like chocolate on a radiator the following month. Life holds many sweet moments after that. Just keep an eye on your tendency to trigger disputes without meaning to between March 18 and early June. A summer romance has too much sizzle for comfort. You're able to turn down the heat to a tolerable level, and by October you should be on surer footing. The darkest days of winter could provide the most lighthearted and romantic moments of the year.

Times when love comes easily your way: April 4–9, June 6–25, November 27–December 1
Take the romantic initiative: June 3–14, October 23–25, and November 12–15

Your 1999 Romance Outlook
Scorpio (October 24–November 21)

It's decision '99 for many Scorpios: should you settle down or continue to play the field? Since you don't make commitments lightly, this won't be an easy decision. Just when you're thinking this is the one, a light flirtation looks appealing. Take your time, and explore all options, if you're eligible.

Timeline: Mixing business with pleasure is tempting early in February, but keep your libido in check. Dalliance with a devastating associate could have repercussions later on. Put a message in a bottle in March. Though the method may be roundabout, you can discreetly let someone know you're interested. A full work schedule over the summer might mean not enough time for romance. Escape into your favorite book then. In October you're prone to long walks, gazing at distant skylines, sighing over lost love. By December, though, you're hot on the trail of someone new.

Times when love comes easily your way: March 6–19, July 16–22, November 17–24
Take the romantic initiative: May 14–19, October 3–6, and October 20–27

Your 1999 Romance Outlook
Sagittarius (November 22–December 21)

Your gambit in a current relationship comes to naught. This fascinatingly savvy hero knows your gamesmanship far, far too well. Is this truly your grand passion? Put this one to the test of time. Only it will tell if you have indeed landed Mr. Right—your true friend for life.

Timeline: As the New Year dawns, heading for distant horizons makes you happiest—with or without your hero. The seeds you planted last year begin to sprout in May. Someone who was not open to your overtures is more receptive then. In contrast, mid-July's eclipse fires the attentions of an ardent admirer. Your response, however, is only lukewarm. Fall brings a holding pattern in any ongoing relationship. Though you may feel as if you're going in circles, enjoy the calm. Mid-November brings some turbulence, but sunny skies over a new romance are forecast for December.

Times when love comes easily your way: January 30–February 2, May 6–12, November 27–December 4
Take the romantic initiative: March 9–18, July 24–27, and November 5–16

Your 1999 Romance Outlook
Capricorn (December 22–January 19)

Your natural seriousness is amplified this year. But resist the urge to devote yourself entirely to work. Keep an opening in your agenda for romance. If you do, you'll find someone new and exciting waiting to fill the slot. A wider social circle is a nice bonus.

Timeline: You need to get physical around Valentine's Day. Just don't let your libido override your common sense. You're quick to rebuff someone supportive late in April. Try to be more open; you could find interesting romantic lead material under an unpromising shell. Mini-vacations close to home suit you just fine this summer. A sun-filled and cozy new rapport could blossom. This fall, the bread you cast on the waters has a way of flowing steadily outward. Be patient. The tide will turn, fulfilling your romantic dreams by winter's end.

Times when love comes easily your way: February 21–March 17, June 6–25, October 4–11
Take the romantic initiative: February 14–19, August 16–17, and November 28–December 6

Your 1999 Romance Outlook
Aquarius (January 20–February 18)

It seems as if nothing less than a soul mate will do this year. You yearn for someone who shares your highest dreams and aspirations. Potential heroes all have an air of mystery about them, though. Make sure you get the whole story before you let anyone star in your real-life plotline.

Timeline: You're tempted to keep an admirer in limbo, but by March you're ready to open the door. Since you're giddy with spring in April anyway, get into the silly season. Someone warm and romantic will find your madness quite divine. Mid-July, confrontations leave a gap in your self-confidence. Let go of any relationship that isn't working, and another far more vibrant and fulfilling one will soon fill the vacuum. After a ho-hum fall, a holiday social whirl leaves you breathless. You may really have something to celebrate by January.

Times when love comes easily your way: January 21–February 1, July 7–21, December 8–15
Take the romantic initiative: May 3–14, October 23 and October 29–November 4

Your 1999 Romance Outlook
Pisces (February 19–March 20)

Old patterns are definitely changing this year. With fewer cares about finances and shared space, romance gets a freer rein. You're ready to let it take flight, filling your life with light and laughter. This increases your chances of achieving the kind of long-term rapport you desire—with someone who's steady but never, never boring.

Timeline: A close relationship takes a complicated turn for no apparent reason in January. Don't let yourself be bulldozed. Wisdom and gentleness are always your strengths. Spring fever raises the heat level in your main relationship in March. It may carry on at a slow simmer through June. Take extra time to work at achieving inner peace over the summer. October provides the romantic high point of the year.

From this elevated vantage point, long-term commitment looks pretty good to you.

Times when love comes easily your way: February 21–March 2, May 6–25, October 25–31 Take the romantic initiative: March 3–14, October 11–20 and December 8–14

A marriage of convenience?

SPOUSE FOR HIRE

This January, don't miss our newest three-story collection about three resourceful women who hire husbands for a limited time. But what happens when these three handsome, charming and impossibly sexy husbands turn out to be too good to let get away? Is it time to renegotiate?

THE COWBOY TAKES A WIFE
by *Joan Johnston*

COMPLIMENTS OF THE GROOM
by *Kasey Michaels*

SUTTER'S WIFE
by *Lee Magner*

Available January 1999
wherever Harlequin and Silhouette books are sold.

HARLEQUIN®
Makes any time special ™

Silhouette®

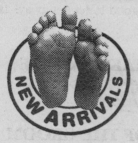

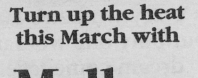

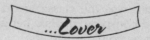
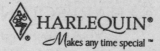

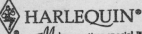